'The first superman story and still by all odds the best'
Damon Knight

'Olaf Stapledon was one of the creative thinkers of our time. His influence on philosophy and science fiction is incalculable'
Greg Bear

'His future scenarios still remain awe-inspiring'
Arthur C. Clarke

'Stapledon is the great classical example . . . the ultimate SF writer'
Brian Aldiss

'The visionary fantasies of Olaf Stapledon are an overflowing fountain of dazzling speculative ideas. In forty years of reading science fiction I've never encountered anything to match the range and fertility of his universe-roving mind'
Robert Silverberg

'Stapledon's literary imagination was almost boundless'
Jorge Luis Borges

Also by Olaf Stapledon

NOVELS

Last and First Men (1930)

Last Men in London (1932)

Odd John (1935)

Star Maker (1937)

Darkness and the Light (1942)

Sirius (1944)

Old Man in a New World (1944)

Death into Life (1946)

The Flames (1947)

A Man Divided (1950)

The Opening of the Eyes (1954)

Nebula Maker (1976)

Four Encounters (1976)

NON-FICTION

A Modern Theory of Ethics (1929)

Waking World (1934)

Philosophy and Living (1939)

New Hope for Britain (1939)

Saints and Revolutionaries (1939)

Beyond the 'ISMS' (1942)

Youth and Tomorrow (1946)

SF MASTERWORKS

Odd John

OLAF STAPLEDON

Text copyright © Olaf Stapledon 1935
Introduction copyright © Adam Roberts 2011
All rights reserved

This edition first published in Great Britain in 2012 by
Gollancz
An imprint of the Orion Publishing Group
Orion House, 5 Upper St Martin's Lane,
London WC2H 9EA
An Hachette UK Company

1 3 5 7 9 10 8 6 4 2

A CIP catalogue record for this book
is available from the British Library

ISBN 978 0 575 07224 4

Typeset at The Spartan Press Ltd,
Lymington, Hants

Printed in Great Britain by
Clays Ltd, St Ives plc

The Orion Publishing Group's policy is to use papers that
are natural, renewable and recyclable products and made
from wood grown in sustainable forests. The logging and
manufacturing processes are expected to conform to the
environmental regulations of the country of origin.

www.orionbooks.co.uk

INTRODUCTION

There have been plenty of stories about supermen but Olaf Stapledon's superman story is unlike any other. It is, we might say, *odd*. Unlike other writers, Stapledon sees the idea that an individual might be born with more-than-human powers of mind and body not in terms of simple power fantasies, either power over regular humanity or the power to *help* regular humanity. For Stapledon, power is much odder than that. Indeed, the oddest thing about his John is not his strange physical appearance, his extraordinary mental powers, his precocity or inventiveness. The oddest thing about this superman novel is that it has remarkably little interest in ordinary mankind at all. Its attention is elsewhere.

That's not entirely true, of course. In the early stages of the novel Stapledon can't resist the opportunity to use his superboy satirically to critique the hypocrisies of the ordinary human society. John's interview with the buffoonish millionaire 'Mr Magnate' is a case in point. It's not that this scene lacks bite, or that it isn't funny; but it's hard to shake the sense that Stapledon's heart isn't really *in* this aspect of his project. The novel isn't fundamentally interested in superhumanity as a lens through which to anatomise our world. Rather, Stapledon is genuinely – spiritually, we might say – fascinated by the concept of superhumanity itself.

It is this that sets the book apart from the clutch of specifically British 'superman' fictions written at the end of the nineteenth and beginning of the twentieth centuries; a body of writings to which Stapledon's novel is indebted and which it is, simultaneously, critiquing. Indeed, Stapledon makes specific reference to one of these novels: J. D. Beresford's *The Hampdenshire Wonder* (1911), a story about a child with superhuman intelligence and his struggle with the various hostilities of conventional humanity's reactionary inertia. Beresford's child, Victor Stott is physically unprepossessing but mentally so far in advance of ordinary humanity that he feels himself to be literally alienated ('he was entirely alone,' we are told, 'among aliens who were unable to comprehend him, who could not flatter him, whose opinions were valueless to him'). *The Hampdenshire Wonder* ends tragically with Stott's untimely death, although the novel is deliberately unclear as to whether this is the result of an accident, or more sinister forces at work. Stapledon, in an uncharacteristically bold piece of intertextuality, name-checks the book in the first chapter of his own novel – 'Mr J. D. Beresford's account of the unhappy Victor Stott' – and *Odd John* maps out a rather similar, although expanded, narrative trajectory. But in fact Beresford's novel was only one of a number of early 20th-century explorations of the theme of the coming of trans-humans.

To mention only a few of the more prominent examples: Joseph Conrad and Ford Madox Ford collaborated on *The Inheritors* (1901) about a group of emotionally chilly *homo superior*, 'the Fourth Dimension', seeking to supplant ordinary humanity. The novel does not spell out the eventual result of the clash between the old and the new, but the reader is left in little doubt that the 'fourth dimension', personified in the figure of an irresistible beautiful and forceful woman, will triumph. George Bernard Shaw's *Back to Methuselah* (these five linked plays were first performed in the UK in 1923) posits the spontaneous coming-into-being of a species of superhuman 'ancients', who first live amongst and eventually (the last play is set in the year 31,920) supplant ordinary humanity. Like Stapledon, Shaw imagines his *homo superior* characters as long-lived, and possessing a fundamentally spiritual connection with the cosmos we ordinary people lack. Indeed, in Shaw's world an ordinary human can die, of 'discouragement', simply by looking into the eye of an 'ancient'. But Shaw's emphasis is on the limitations of his human characters, rather than the limitless possibilities of super-humanity.

The most direct conceptual source for this interest in *homo superior* is Nietzsche's philosophy, and his hymn to the possibilities of superseding mundane humanity, *Also Sprach Zarathustra* (1883–85). Certainly, the first half of the twentieth-century marked the high-water-point of Nietzsche's influence upon European and American culture; material and social ideas of 'progress' bled into metaphysical speculation, and many took the idea of Nietzsche's *Übermensch* literally. Nietzsche's actual idea is not so clumsily literal. The actual being-in-the-world of his superperson can only be gestured towards, not captured in prose – even in the experimental musical-poetic prose Nietzsche dreamt up for his project.

Stapledon writes much more straightforward and prosaically, but his book is just as insistent that its central theme is, in fact, inexpressible. Like the 'superior' music the supernormals enjoy, which sounds merely cacophonous to ordinary ears, the main chords of *Odd John* are – the central character repeatedly insists – simply beyond our mental capacities. One way the novel articulates this is through the metaphor of flight. We (John says) know less of his view of the universe 'than an ostrich knows about the upper air.' In a rather neatly-put phrase, John says that Man 'is about as clever along his own line as the earliest birds were at flight. He's a sort of archiopteryx of the spirit.'

This evolutionary theme is discretely, but unmissably, developed. Like Nietzsche, Stapledon sees the coming of a more advanced *homo* to be natural and inevitable. His John *is* freakish – odd – but not in the sense of being *ontologically* eccentric. Evolution works via mutation and freakishness after all; its currency is, in a precise sense, oddity. More to the point, the novel is centrally and perhaps paradoxically interested in the impossibility of its own representation. *Odd John* can gesture towards what its superman knows and perceives, but by definition that knowledge and perception is beyond our present-day capacity to embody it.

In various ways Stapledon illustrates that his supernormals

live (in appropriately Nietzschean phrase) beyond good and evil. They use conventional morality only in order to fit in with ordinary human society. Otherwise they dispense with it; and they are prepared to do anything they judge reasonable – up to and including mass murder – if they deem it in their own interests. This is as true of sex as it is of violence: chapter 8, largely concerned with John's sexual experimentation, ends with this striking paragraph:

> At last John told me something which it is better not to report. I did, indeed, write a careful account of this most disturbing incident in his career; and I confess that at the time I was so deeply under the spell of his personality that I could not feel his behaviour to have been vile ... Years later, when I innocently showed my manuscript to others of my species, they pointed out that to publish such a matter would be to shock many sensitive readers, and to incur the charge of sheer licentiousness.

'I am,' says the narrator, 'a respectable member of the English middle class, and wish to remain so.' I am too, as it happens; although I have fewer qualms about making explicit what the novel intimates (howsoever unmissably) here – that John has sex with his own mother. He needed 'soothing', we're told; 'delicate and intimate contact with a being whose sensibility and insight were not wholly incomparable with his own'. But he also needed to 'assert his moral independence of *homo sapiens*' by breaking 'what was one of the most cherished of all the taboos of that species.' At this point in the book we might wonder whether 'Odd John' isn't short for 'Oedipal John'.

That incest remains unspeakable when cold-blooded mass murder (for instance) doesn't says something, perhaps, about the relative values of our society. That Stapledon's narrator can't even bring himself to use the i-word says more. And this fore-grounding of the perspective through which John's career is filtered is canny. It is one of the main themes of the work: a narrative that denies its own representational grounds. This is as true of the individual sentences out of which the story is made as it is of its larger philosophical meditations. I'm talking about the sometimes clangingly antiquated idiom of the book (all the 'Stephen, old man, I'm sorry I made you lose your hair'; 'I say, Fido old thing' and 'what stuff!') will interfere with our ability to enter imaginatively into Stapledon's vision. This is a book whose expressive idiom *has* dated, occasionally even comically so. But it seems to me that this is, as it were, factored into the limitations of the frame. It points up precisely the insufficiency of the mode of telling to the tale itself.

This in turn, I think, relates to the ending of the novel. I can discuss this without spoilers because Stapledon spells it out right at the beginning of the first chapter: John founds a colony of supernormals on an uncharted island in the Pacific, but the governments of the world discover it and, afraid of the potential of these young superbeings, or perhaps simply afraid of what they do not understand, destroy it. Nevertheless, this ending is, to use an appropriate word, *odd*. By this stage in their development the supernormals have conquered matter, time and space; they are telepathic, spiritually transcendent geniuses, capable of a whole range of what a later generation would call 'Jedi mind tricks', and able to fuse atoms and generate nuclear power by thought alone. They have already demonstrated themselves perfectly capable of killing any ordinary humans who interfere with their plans, and the book makes it plain that they would have, according to their own supernormal morality, no qualms at perpetrating speciecide upon the whole of humanity. Why, then, do they permit first lone ships and then human flotillas to bother them; and why do they explode their own settlement rather than fight off the invaders? John says something about how resistance 'would bring the whole force of the inferior species against us, and there would be no peace till we had conquered the world.' But impatience seems a strange trait in a near-immortal race of superbeings; one nowhere else exhibited by the characters of the novel. More to the point, there is never any doubt that John and his people would defeat *homo sapiens*, if it came to a fight. Nor do the supernormals ever doubt that their own extinction at the hands of ordinary humankind will follow (since they can see the future, this should not surprise us). The shift from ruthless extermination of humans to a quasi-Gandhi passive resistance even unto death reads very oddly indeed.

But perhaps this is precisely the point. The last weeks of the colony see them hurrying to complete their 'real work', an unspecified 'spiritual' task. The implication, surely, is that the apparent course of the novel is actually a kind of obfuscation, a final cashing-in of the text's inability to provide insight into the lives of the supernormals. According to the mundane narrative they all die, and the novel gives us no reason to suspect that anything else happens. But if we read with enough sensitivity to the way the novel repeatedly separates out what middle-class English words can say about the supernormals and what they actually *do* and *are*, we may glimpse, out of the corner of the mind's eye, a very different conclusion: an ending in which the supernormals do not die, but rather translate themselves beyond the limitations of matter, and the threat of homo sapiens, forever. I prefer that reading. It is more open-ended, more satisfying, but above all it is odder.

Adam Roberts

I
John and the Author

When I told John that I intended to write his biography, he laughed. 'My dear *man*!' he said, 'But of course it was inevitable.' The word 'man' on John's lips was often equivalent to 'fool'.

'Well,' I protested, 'a cat may look at a king.'

He replied, 'Yes, but can it really *see* the king? Can you, puss, really see me?'

This from a queer child to a full-grown man.

John was right. Though I had known him since he was a baby, and was in a sense intimate with him, I knew almost nothing of the inner, the real John. To this day I know little but the amazing facts of his career. I know that he never walked till he was six, that before he was ten he committed several burglaries and killed a policeman, that at eighteen, when he still looked a young boy, he founded his preposterous colony in the South Seas, and that at twenty-three, in appearance but little altered, he outwitted the six warships that six Great Powers had sent to seize him. I know also how John and all his followers died.

Such facts I know; and even at the risk of destruction by one or other of the six Great Powers, I shall tell the world all that I can remember.

Something else I know, which will be very difficult to explain. In a confused way I know why he founded his colony. I know too that although he gave his whole energy to this task, he never seriously expected to succeed. He was convinced that sooner or later the world would find him out and destroy his work. 'Our chance,' he once said, 'is not as much as one in a million.' And then he laughed.

John's laugh was strangely disturbing. It was a low, rapid,

crisp chuckle. It reminded me of that whispered crackling prelude which sometimes precedes a really great crash of thunder. But no thunder followed it, only a moment's silence; and for his hearers an odd tingling of the scalp.

I believe that this inhuman, this ruthless but never malicious laugh of John's contained the key to all that baffles me in his character. Again and again I asked myself *why* he laughed just then, what precisely was he laughing *at*, what did his laughter really mean, was that strange noise really laughter at all, or some emotional reaction incomprehensible to my kind? Why, for instance, did the infant John laugh through his tears when he had upset a kettle and was badly scalded? I was not present at his death, but I feel sure that, when his end came, his last breath spent itself in zestful laughter. Why?

In failing to answer these questions, I fail to understand the essential John. His laughter, I am convinced, sprang from some aspect of his experience entirely beyond my vision. I am therefore, of course as John affirmed, a very incompetent biographer. But if I keep silence, the facts of his unique career will be lost for ever. In spite of my incompetence, I must record all that I can, in the hope that, if these pages fall into the hands of some being of John's own stature, he may imaginatively see through them to the strange but glorious spirit of John himself.

That others of his kind, or approximately of his kind, are now alive, and that yet others will appear, is at least probable. But as John himself discovered, the great majority of these very rare supernormals, whom John sometimes called 'wide-awakes', are either so delicate physically or so unbalanced mentally that they leave no considerable mark on the world. How pathetically one-sided the supernormal development may be is revealed in Mr J. D. Beresford's account of the unhappy Victor Stott. I hope that the following brief record will at least suggest a mind at once more strikingly 'superhuman' and more broadly human.

That the reader may look for something more than an intellectual prodigy I will here at the outset try to give an impression of John's appearance in his twenty-third and last summer.

He was indeed far more like a boy than a man, though in some moods his youthful face would assume a curious experienced and even patriarchal expression. Slender, long limbed, and with that unfinished coltish look characteristic of puberty, he had also a curiously finished grace all his own. Indeed to those who had come to know him he seemed a creature of ever-novel beauty. But strangers were often revolted by his uncouth proportions. They called him spiderish. His body, they complained, was so insignificant, his legs and arms so long and lithe, his head all eye and brow.

Now that I have set down these characters I cannot conceive how they might make for beauty. But in John they did, at least for those of us who could look at him without preconceptions derived from Greek gods, or film stars. With characteristic lack of false modesty, John once said to me, 'My looks are a rough test of people. If they don't begin to see me beautiful when they have had a chance to learn, I know they're dead inside, and dangerous.'

But let me complete the description. Like his fellow-colonists, John mostly went naked. His maleness, thus revealed, was immature in spite of his twenty-three years. His skin, burnt by the Polynesian sun, was of a grey, almost a green, brown, warming to a ruddier tint in the cheeks. His hands were extremely large and sinewy. Somehow they seemed more mature than the rest of his body. 'Spiderish' seemed appropriate in this connection also. His head was certainly large but not out of proportion to his long limbs. Evidently the unique development of his brain depended more on manifold convolutions than on sheer bulk. All the same his was a much larger head than it looked, for its visible bulk was scarcely at all occupied by the hair, which was but a close skull-cap, a mere superficies of negroid but almost white wool. His nose was small but broad, rather Mongolian perhaps. His lips, large but definite, were always active. They expressed a kind of running commentary on his thoughts and feelings. Yet many a time I have seen those lips harden into granitic stubbornness. John's eyes were indeed, according to ordinary standards, much too big for his face, which acquired thus a strangely cat-like or falcon-like expression. This was emphasized by the low and level eyebrows, but often completely abolished by a thoroughly boyish and even mischievous smile. The whites of John's eyes were almost invisible. The pupils were immense. The oddly green irises were as a rule mere filaments. But in tropical sunshine the pupils narrowed to mere pin-pricks. Altogether, his eyes were the most obviously 'queer' part of him. His glance, however, had none of that weirdly compelling power recorded in the case of Victor Stott. Or rather, to feel their magic, one needed to have already learnt something of the formidable spirit that used them.

II
The First Phase

John's father, Thomas Wainwright, had reason to believe that Spaniards and Moroccans had long ago contributed to his making. There was indeed something of the Latin, even perhaps of the Arab, in his nature. Everyone admitted that he had a certain brilliance; but he was odd, and was generally regarded as a failure. A medical practice in a North-country suburb gave little scope for his powers, and many opportunities of rubbing people up the wrong way. Several remarkable cures stood to his credit; but he had no bedside manner, and his patients never accorded him the trust which is so necessary for a doctor's success.

His wife was no less a mongrel than her husband, but one of a very different kind. She was of Swedish extraction. Finns and Lapps were also among her ancestors. Scandinavian in appearance, she was a great sluggish blonde, who even as a matron dazzled the young male eye. It was originally through her attraction that I became the youthful friend of her husband, and later the slave of her more than brilliant son. Some said she was 'just a magnificent female animal', and so dull as to be subnormal. Certainly conversation with her was sometimes almost as one-sided as conversation with a cow. Yet she was no fool. Her house was always in good order, though she seemed to spend no thought upon it. With the same absent-minded skill she managed her rather difficult husband. He called her 'Pax.' 'So peaceful,' he would explain. Curiously her children also adopted this name for her. Their father they called invariably 'Doc'. The two elder, girl and boy, affected to smile at their mother's ignorance of the world; but they counted on her advice. John, the youngest by four years, once said something which suggested that we had all misjudged her. Some one had remarked on her extraordinary dumbness. Out flashed John's disconcerting laugh, and then, 'No one notices the things that interest Pax, and so she just doesn't talk.'

John's birth had put the great maternal animal to a severe strain. She carried her burden for eleven months, till the doctors decided that at all costs she must be relieved. Yet when the baby was at last brought to light, it had the grotesque appearance of a seven-month fetus. Only with great difficulty was it kept alive in an incubator. Not till a year after the forced birth was this artificial womb deemed no longer necessary.

I saw John frequently during his first year, for between me and the father, though he was many years my senior, there had by now grown up a curious intimacy based on common intellectual interests, and perhaps partly on a common admiration for Pax.

I can remember my shock of disgust when I first saw the thing they had called John. It seemed impossible that such an inert and pulpy bit of flesh could ever develop into a human being. It was like some obscene fruit, more vegetable than animal, save for an occasional incongruous spasm of activity.

When John was a year old, however, he looked almost like a normal new-born infant, save that his eyes were shut. At eighteen months he opened them; and it was as though a sleeping city had suddenly leapt into life. Formidable eyes they were for a baby, eyes seen under a magnifying glass, each great pupil like the mouth of a cave, the iris a mere rim, an edging of bright emerald. Strange how two black holes can gleam with life! It was shortly after his eyes had opened that Pax began to call her strange son '*Odd* John'. She gave the words a particular and subtle intonation which, though it scarcely varied, seemed to express sometimes merely affectionate apology for the creature's oddity, but sometimes defiance, and sometimes triumph, and occasionally awe. The adjective stuck to John throughout his life.

Henceforth John was definitely a person and a very wide-awake person, too. Week by week he became more and more active and more and more interested. He was for ever busy with eyes and ears and limbs.

During the next two years John's body developed pre-cariously, but without disaster. There were always difficulties over feeding, but when he had reached the age of three he was a tolerably healthy child, though odd, and in appearance extremely backward. This backwardness distressed Thomas. Pax, however, insisted that most babies grew too fast. 'They don't give their minds a chance to knit themselves properly,' she declared. The unhappy father shook his head.

When John was in his fifth year I used to see him nearly every morning as I passed the Wainwrights' house on my way to the railway station. He would be in his pram in the garden rioting with limbs and voice. The din, I thought, had an odd quality. It differed indescribably from the vocalization of any ordinary baby, as the call of one kind of monkey differs from that of another species. It was a rich and subtle shindy, full of quaint modulations and variations. One could scarcely believe that this was a backward child of four. Both behaviour and appearance suggested an extremely bright six-month infant. He was too wide awake to be backward, too backward to be four. It was not only that those prodigious eyes were so alert and penetrating. Even his clumsy efforts to manipulate his toys seemed purposeful beyond his years. Though he could not manage his fingers at all well, his mind seemed to be already setting them very definite and intelligent tasks. Their failure distressed him.

John was certainly intelligent. We were all now agreed on that point. Yet he showed no sign of crawling, and no sign of talking.

Then suddenly, long before he had attempted to move about in his world, he became articulate. On a certain Tuesday he was merely babbling as usual. On Wednesday he was exceptionally quiet, and seemed for the first time to understand something of his mother's baby-talk. On Thursday morning he startled the family by remarking very slowly but very correctly, 'I – want – milk'. That afternoon he said to a visitor who no longer interested him. 'Go – away. I – do – not – like – you – much.'

These linguistic achievements were obviously of quite a different type from the first remarks of ordinary children.

Friday and Saturday John spent in careful conversation with his delighted relatives. By the following Tuesday, a week after his first attempt, he was a better linguist than his seven-year-old brother, and speech had already begun to lose its novelty for him. It had ceased to be a new art, and had become merely a useful means of communication, to be extended and refined only as new spheres of experience came within his ken and demanded expression.

Now that John could talk, his parents learned one or two surprising facts about him. For instance, he could remember his birth. And immediately after that painful crisis, when he had been severed from his mother, he actually had to *learn* to breathe. Before any breathing reflex awoke, he had been kept alive by artificial respiration, and from this experience he had discovered how to control his lungs. With a prolonged and desperate effort of will he had, so to speak, cranked the engine, until at last it 'fired' and acted spontaneously. His heart also, it appeared, was largely under voluntary control. Certainly early 'cardiac troubles', very alarming to his parents, had in fact been voluntary interferences of a too daring nature. His emotional reflexes also were far more under control than in the rest of us. Thus if, in some anger-provoking situation, he did not *wish* to feel angry, he could easily inhibit the anger reflexes. And if anger seemed desirable he could produce it. He was indeed 'Odd John'.

About nine months after John had learnt to speak, someone gave him a child's abacus. For the rest of that day there was no talking, no hilarity; and meals were dismissed with impatience.

John had suddenly discovered the intricate delights of numbers. Hour after hour he performed all manner of operations on the new toy. Then suddenly he flung it away and lay back staring at the ceiling.

His mother thought he was tired. She spoke to him. He took no notice. She gently shook his arm. No response. 'John!' she cried in some alarm, and shook more violently. 'Shut up, Pax,' he said, 'I'm busy with numbers.'

Then, after a pause, 'Pax, what do you call the numbers after twelve?' She counted up to twenty, then up to thirty. 'You're as stupid as that toy, Pax.' When she asked why, he found he had not words to explain himself; but after be had indicated various operations on the abacus, and she had told him the names of them, he said slowly and triumphantly, 'You're stupid, Pax, dear, because you (and the toy there) "count" in tens and not in twelves. And that's stupid because twelves have "fourths" and "threeths", I mean "thirds", and tens have not.' When she explained that all men counted in tens because when counting began, they used their five fingers, he looked fixedly at her, then laughed his crackling, crowing laugh. Presently he said, 'Then all men are stupid.'

This, I think, was John's first realization of the stupidity of *Homo sapiens*, but not the last.

Thomas was jubilant over John's mathematical shrewdness, and wanted to report his case to the British Psychological Society. But Pax showed an unexpected determination to 'keep it all dark for the present'. 'He shall not be experimented on,' she insisted. 'They'd probably hurt him. And anyhow they'd make a silly fuss.' Thomas and I laughed at her fears, but she won the battle.

John was now nearly five, but still in appearance a mere baby. He could not walk. He could not, or would not, crawl. His legs were still those of an infant. Moreover, his walking was probably seriously delayed by mathematics, for during the next few months he could not be persuaded to give his attention to anything but numbers and the properties of space. He would lie in his pram in the garden by the hour doing 'mental arithmetic' and 'mental geometry', never moving a muscle, never making a sound. This was most unhealthy for a growing child, and he began to ail. Yet nothing would induce him to live a more normal and active life.

Visitors often refused to believe that he was mentally active out there for all those hours. He looked pale and 'absent'. They privately thought he was in a state of coma, and developing as an imbecile. But occasionally he would volunteer a few words which would confound them.

John's attack upon geometry began with an interest in his brother's box of bricks and in a diaper wallpaper. Then came a phase of cutting up cheese and soap into slabs, cubes, cones, and even into spheres and ovoids. At first John was extremely clumsy with a knife, cutting his fingers and greatly distressing his mother. But in a few days he had become amazingly dextrous. As usual, though he was backward in taking up a new activity, once he had set his mind to it, his progress was fantastically rapid. His next stage was to make use of his sister's school-set of geometrical instruments. For a week he was enraptured, covering innumerable sheets.

Then suddenly he refused to take any further interest in visual geometry. He preferred to lie back and meditate. One morning he was troubled by some question which he could not formulate. Pax could make nothing of his efforts, but later his father helped him to extend his vocabulary enough to ask, 'Why are there only three dimensions? When I grow up shall I find more?'

Some weeks later came a much more startling question. 'If you went in a straight line, on and on and on, how far would you have to go to get right back here?'

We laughed, and Pax exclaimed, '*Odd* John!' This was early in 1915. Then Thomas remembered some talk about a 'theory of relativity' that was upsetting all the old ideas of geometry. In time he became so impressed by this odd question of John's, and others like it, that he insisted on bringing a mathematician from the university to talk to the child.

Pax protested, but not even she guessed that the result would be disastrous.

The visitor was at first patronizing, then enthusiastic, then bewildered; then, with obvious relief, patronizing again; then badly flustered. When Pax tactfully persuaded him to go (for the child's sake, of course), he asked if he might come again, with a colleague.

A few days later the two of them turned up and remained in conference with the baby for hours. Thomas was unfortunately going the round of his patients. Pax sat beside John's high chair, silently knitting, and occasionally trying to help her child to express himself. But the conversation was far beyond her depth. During a pause for a cup of tea, one of the visitors said, 'It's the child's imaginative power that is so amazing. He knows none of the jargon and none of the history, but he has *seen* it all already for himself. It's incredible, he seems to visualize what can't be visualized.'

Later in the afternoon, so Pax reported, the visitors began to grow rather agitated, and even angry; and John's irritatingly quiet laugh seemed to make matters worse. When at last she insisted on putting a stop to the discussion, as it was John's bedtime, she noticed that both the guests were definitely 'out of control'. 'There was a wild look about them both,' she said, 'and when I shooed them out of the garden they were still wrangling; and they never said goodbye.'

But it was a shock to learn, a few days later, that two mathematicians on the university staff had been found sitting under a street lamp together at 2 am drawing diagrams on the pavement and disputing about 'the curvature of space'.

Thomas regarded his youngest child simply as an exceptionally striking case of the 'infant prodigy'. His favourite comment was, 'Of course, it will all fizzle out when he gets older.' But Pax would say, 'I wonder.'

John worried mathematics for another month, then suddenly put it all behind him. When father asked him why he had given it up, he said, 'There's not much in number really. Of course, it's marvellously pretty, but when you've done it all – well, that's that. I've *finished* number. I know all there is in that game. I want another. You can't suck the same piece of sugar for ever.'

During the next twelve months John gave his parents no further surprises. It is true he learned to read and write, and took no more than a week to outstrip his brother and sister. But after his mathematical triumphs this was only a modest achievement. The surprising thing was that the will to read should have developed so late. Pax often read aloud to him out of books belonging to the elder children, and apparently he did not see why she should be relieved of this duty.

But there came a time when Anne, his sister, was ill, and his mother was too occupied to read to him. One day he clamoured for her to start a new book, but she would not. 'Well, show *me* how to read before you go,' he demanded. She smiled, and said, 'It's a long job. When Anne's better I'll show you.'

In a few days she began the task, in the orthodox manner. But John had no patience with the orthodox manner. He invented a method of his own. He made Pax read aloud to him and pass her finger along the line as she read, so that he could follow, word by word. Pax could not help laughing at the barbarousness of this method, but with John it worked. He simply remembered the 'look' of every 'noise' that she made, for his power of retention seemed to be infallible. Presently, without stopping her, he began analysing out the sounds of the different letters, and was soon cursing the illogicality of English spelling. By the end of the lesson John could read, though of course his vocabulary was limited. During the following week he devoured all the children's books in the house, and even a few 'grown-up' books. These, of course, meant almost nothing to him, even though the words were mostly familiar. He soon gave them up in disgust. One day he picked up his sister's school geometry, but tossed it aside in five minutes with the remark, 'Baby book!'

Henceforth John was able to read anything that interested him; but he showed no sign of becoming a book-worm. Reading was an occupation fit only for times of inaction, when his over-taxed hands demanded repose. For he had now entered a phase of almost passionate manual constructiveness, and was making all manner of ingenious models out of cardboard, wire, wood, plasticine, and any other material that came to hand. Drawing, also, occupied much of his time.

III
Enfant Terrible

At last, at the age of six, John turned his attention to locomotion. In this art he had hitherto been even more backward than the appearance of his body seemed to warrant. Intellectual and constructive interests had led to the neglect of all else.

But now at last he discovered the need of independent travel, and also the fascination of conquering the new art. As usual, his method of learning was original and his progress rapid. He never crawled. He began by standing upright with his hands on a chair, balancing alternately on each foot. An hour of this exhausted him, and for the first time in his life he seemed utterly disheartened. He who had treated mathematicians as dull-witted children now conceived a new and wistful respect for his ten-year-old brother, the most active member of the family. For a week he persistently and reverently watched Tommy walking, running, 'ragging' with his sister. Every moment was noted by the anxious John. He also assiduously practised balancing, and even took a few steps, holding his mother's hand.

By the end of the week, however, he had a sort of nervous breakdown, and for days afterwards he never set foot to ground. With an evident sense of defeat, he reverted to reading, even to mathematics.

When he was sufficiently recovered to take the floor again, he walked unaided right across the room, and burst into hysterical tears of joy – a most un-John-like proceeding. The art was now conquered. It was only necessary to strengthen his muscles by exercise.

But John was not content with mere walking. He had

conceived a new aim in life; and with characteristic resolution he set himself to achieve it.

At first he was greatly hampered by his undeveloped body. His legs were still almost fetal, so short and curved they were. But under the influence of constant use, and (seemingly) of his indomitable will, they soon began to grow straight and long and strong. At seven he could run like a rabbit and climb like a cat. In general build he now looked about four; but something wiry and muscular about him suggested an urchin of eight or nine. And though his face was infantile in shape, its expression was sometimes almost that of a man of forty. But the huge eyes and close white wool gave him an ageless, almost an inhuman look.

He had now achieved a very striking control of his muscles. There was no more learning of skilled movements. His limbs, nay the individual muscles themselves, did precisely as he willed. This was shown unmistakably when, in the second month after his first attempt to walk, he learned to swim. He stood in the water for a while watching his sister's well-practised strokes, then lifted his feet from the bottom and did likewise.

For many months John's whole energy was given to emulating the other children in various kinds of physical prowess; and in imposing his will upon them. They were at first delighted with his efforts. All except Tommy, who already realized that he was being outclassed by his kid brother. The older children of the street were more generous, because they were at first less affected by John's successes. But increasingly John put them all in the shade.

It was of course John, looking no more than a rather lanky four-year-old, who, when a precious ball had lodged in one of the roof-gutters, climbed a drain-pipe, crawled along the gutter, threw down the ball; and then for the sheer joy clambered up a channel between two slopes of tiles, and sat astraddle on the crest of the roof. Pax was in town, shopping. The neighbours were of course terrified for the child's life. Then John, foreseeing amusement, simulated panic and inability to move. Apparently he had quite lost his head. He clung trembling to the tiles. He whimpered abjectly. Tears trickled down his cheeks. A local building contractor was hurriedly called up on the phone. He sent men and ladders. When the rescuer appeared on the roof, John 'pulled snooks' at him, and scuttled for his drain-pipe, down which he descended like a monkey, before the eyes of an amazed and outraged crowd.

When Thomas learned of this escapade, he was both horrified and delighted. 'The prodigy,' he said, 'has advanced from mathematics to acrobatics.' But Pax said only, 'I wish he wouldn't draw attention to himself.'

John's devouring passion was now personal prowess and dominance. The unfortunate Tommy, formerly a masterful little devil, was eclipsed and sick at heart. But his sister Anne adored the brilliant John, and was his slave. Hers was an arduous life. I can sympathize with her very keenly, for at a much later stage I was to occupy her post.

John was now either the hero or the loathed enemy of every child in the neighbourhood. At first he had no intuition of the effect his acts would have on others, and was regarded by most as a 'beastly cocky little freak'. The trouble was simply that he always *knew* when others did not, and nearly always *could* when others could not. Strangely he showed no sign of arrogance; but also he made no effort to assume false modesty.

One example, which marked the turning-point in his policy towards his fellows, will show his initial weakness in this respect, and his incredible suppleness of mind.

The big schoolboy neighbour, Stephen, was in the next garden struggling with a dismembered and rather complicated lawn-mower. John climbed the fence, and watched for a few minutes in silence. Presently he laughed. Stephen took no notice. Then John bent down, snatched a cog-wheel from the lad's hands, put it in place, assembled the other parts, turned a nut here and a grub-screw there, and the job was finished. Stephen meanwhile stood in sheepish confusion. John moved toward the fence saying, 'Sorry you're no good at that sort of thing, but I'll always help when I'm free.' To his immense surprise, the other flew at him, knocked him down twice, then pitched him over the fence. John, seated on the grass rubbing various parts of his body, must surely have felt at least a spasm of anger, but curiosity triumphed over rage, and he inquired almost amiably, '*Why* did you want to do that?' But Stephen left the garden without answering.

John sat meditating. Then he heard his father's voice indoors, and rushed to find him. 'Hi! Doc!' he cried, 'if there was a patient you couldn't cure, and one day someone else came and cured him, what would you do?' Thomas, busy with other matters, replied carelessly, 'Dunno! Probably knock him down for interfering.' John gasped, 'Now just *why*? Surely that would be very stupid.' His father, still preoccupied, answered, 'I suppose so, but one isn't always sensible. It depends how the other fellow behaved. If he made me feel a fool, I'm sure I'd *want* to knock him down.' John gazed at his father for some time, then said, 'I see!'

'Doc!' he suddenly began again, 'I must get strong, as strong as Stephen. If I read all those books' (glancing at the medical tomes), 'shall I learn how to get frightfully strong?' The father laughed. 'I'm afraid not,' he said.

Two ambitions now dominated John's behaviour for six months, namely to become an invincible fighter, and to understand his fellow human-beings.

The latter was for John the easier task. He set about studying our conduct and our motives, partly by questioning us, partly by observation. He soon discovered two important facts, first that we were often suprisingly ignorant of our own motives, and second that in many respects he differed from the rest of us. In later years he himself told me that this was the time when he first began to realize his uniqueness.

Need I say that within a fortnight, John was apparently a changed character? He had assumed with perfect accuracy that veneer of modesty and generosity which is so characteristic of the English.

In spite of his youth and his even more youthful appearance John now became the unwilling and unassuming leader in many an escapade. The cry was always, 'John will know what to do,' or 'Fetch that little devil John, he's a marvel at this kind of job.'

In the desultory warfare which was carried on with the children of the Council School (they passed the end of the street four times a day), it was John who planned ambushes; and John who could turn defeat into victory by the miraculous fury of an unexpected onslaught. He was indeed an infant Jove, equipped with thunderbolts instead of fists.

These battles were partly a repercussion of a greater war in Europe, but also, I believe, they were deliberately fostered by John for his own ends. They gave him opportunities both for physical prowess and for a kind of unacknowledged leadership.

No wonder the children of the neighbourhood told one another, 'John's a great little sport now,' while their mothers, impressed more by his manners than his military genius, said to one another, 'John's a dear these days. He's lost all his horrid freakishness and conceit.'

Even Stephen was praiseful. He told his mother, 'That kid's all right really. The hiding did him good. He has apologized about the mower, and hoped he hadn't jiggered it up.'

But fate had a surprise in store for Stephen.

In spite of his father's discouragement, John had been spending odd moments among the medical and physiological books. The anatomical drawings interested him greatly, and to understand them properly, he had to read. His vocabulary was of course very inadequate, so he proceeded in the manner of Victor Stott, and read through from cover to cover, first a large English dictionary, then a dictionary of physiological terms. Very soon he became so fluent that he had only to run his eye rapidly down the middle of a printed page to be able to understand it and retain it indefinitely.

But John was not content with theory. One day, to Pax's horror, he was found cutting up a dead rat on the dining-room floor, having thoughtfully spread a newspaper to protect the carpet. Henceforth his anatomical studies, both practical and theoretical, were supervised by Doc. For a few months John was enthralled. He showed great skill in dissection and microscopy. He catechized his father at every opportunity, and often exposed the confusion of his answers; till at last Pax, remembering the mathematicians, insisted that the tired doctor must have respite. Henceforth John studied unaided.

Then suddenly he dropped biology as he had dropped mathematics. Pax asked, 'Have you finished with "life" as you finished with "number?"' 'No,' replied John, 'but life doesn't hang together like number. It won't make a pattern. There's something wrong with all those books. Of course, I often see they're stupid, but there must be something deeper wrong too, which I can't see.'

About this time, by the way, John was actually sent to school, but his career lasted only three weeks. 'His influence is too disturbing,' said the head mistress, 'and he is quite unteachable. I fear the child, though apt in some limited directions, is really subnormal, and needs special treatment.' Henceforth, to satisfy the law, Pax herself pretended to teach him. To please her, he glanced at the school books, and could repeat them at will. As for understanding them, those that interested him he understood as well as the authors; those that bored him he ignored. Over these he could show the stupidity of a moron.

When he had finished with biology, John gave up all intellectual pursuits and concentrated on his body. That autumn he read nothing but adventure stories and several works on ju-jitsu. Much of his time he spent in practising this art, and in gymnastic excercises of his own invention. Also he dieted himself extremely carefully upon principles of his own. John's digestive organs had been his one weak spot. They seemed to remain infantile longer even than the rest of his body. Up to his sixth year they were unable to cope with anything but specially prepared milk, and fruit juice. The food shortage caused by the war had added to the difficulty of nourishing John, and he was always liable to minor digestive troubles. But now he took matters into his own hands, and worked out an intricate but very scanty diet, consisting of fruit, cheese, malted milk, and whole-meal bread, carefully spaced with rest and exercise. We laughed at him; all but Pax, who saw to it that his demands should be fulfilled.

Whether through diet, or gymnastics, or sheer strength of will, he certainly became exceptionally strong for his weight and age.

One by one the boys of the neighbourhood found themselves drawn into a quarrel with John. One by one they were defeated. Of course it was not strength but agility and cunning that made him fit to cope with opponents much bigger than himself. 'If that kid once gets hold of you the way he wants, you're done,' it used to be said, 'and you can't hit him, he's too quick.'

The strange thing was that in every quarrel it seemed to the public that not John but the other was the aggressor.

The climax was the case of Stephen, now captain of his school's First Fifteen, and a thoroughly good friend to John.

One day when I was talking to Thomas in his study we heard an unusual scuffling in the garden. Looking out, we saw Stephen rushing vainly at the elusive John; who, as he leapt aside, landed his baby fist time after time with dire effect on Stephen's face. It was a face almost unrecognizable with rage and perplexity, shockingly unlike the kindly Stephen. Both combatants were plastered with blood, apparently from Stephen's nose.

John too was a changed being. His lips were drawn back in an inhuman blend of snarl and smile. One eye was half closed from Stephen's only successful blow, the other cavernous like the eye of a mask. For when John was enraged, the iris drew almost entirely out of sight.

The conflict was so unprecedented and so fantastic that for some moments Thomas and I were paralysed. At last Stephen managed to seize the diabolic child; or was allowed to seize him. We dashed downstairs to the rescue. But when we reached the garden, Stephen was lying on his stomach writhing and gasping, with his arms pinned behind him in the grip of John's tarantula hands.

The appearance of John at that moment gave me a startling impression of something fiendish. Crouched and clutching, he seemed indeed a spider preparing to suck the life out of the tortured boy beneath him. The sight, I remember, actually made me feel sick. We stood bewildered by this unexpected turn of events. John looked around, and his eye met mine. Never have I seen so arrogant, so hideous an expression of the lust of power as on that childish face.

For some seconds we gazed at one another. Evidently my look expressed the horror that I felt, for his mood rapidly changed. Rage visibly faded out and gave place first to curiosity then to abstraction. Suddenly John laughed that enigmatic laugh of his. There was no ring of triumph in it, rather a note of self-mockery, and perhaps of awe.

He released his victim, rose and said, 'Get up, Stephen, old man. I'm sorry I made you lose your hair.' But Stephen had fainted.

We never discovered what it was all about. When we questioned John, he said, 'It's all over. Let's forget about it. Poor old Stephen! But no, *I* won't forget.'

When we questioned Stephen a few days later, he said, 'I can't bear to think of it. It was my fault, really. I see that now. Somehow I went mad, when he was intending to be specially decent, too. But to be licked by a kid like that! But he's not a kid, he's lightning.'

Now I do not pretend to be able to understand John, but I cannot help having one or two theories about him. In the present case my theory is this. He was at this time plainly going through a phase of concentrated self-assertion. I do not believe, however, that he had been nursing a spirit of revenge ever since the affair of the mower. I believe he had determined in cold blood to try his strength, or rather his skill, against the most formidable of his acquaintances; and that with this end in view he had deliberately and subtly goaded the wretched Stephen into fury. John's own I suspect, was entirely artificial. He could fight better in a sort of cold fury, so he produced one. As I see it, the great test had to be no friendly bout, but a real wild-beast, desperate encounter. Well, John got what he wanted. And having got it, he saw in a flash and once for all, right through it and beyond it. So at least I believe.

IV
John and his Elders

Though the fight with Stephen was, I believe one of the chief landmarks in John's life, outwardly things went on much as before; save that he gave up fighting, and spent a good deal more time by himself.

Between him and Stephen, friendship was restored, but it was henceforth an uncomfortable friendship. Each seemed anxious to be amicable, but neither felt at ease with the other. Stephen's nerve, I think, had been seriously shaken. It was not that he feared another licking, but that his self-respect had suffered. I took an opportunity to suggest that his defeat had been no disgrace, since John was clearly no ordinary child. Stephen jumped at this consolation. With a hysterical jerk in his voice he said, 'I felt – I can't say what I felt – like a dog biting its master and being punished. I felt – sort of guilty, wicked.'

John, I think, was now beginning to realize more clearly the gulf that separated him from the rest of us. At the same time, he was probably feeling a keen need for companionship, but companionship of a calibre beyond that of normal human beings. He continued to play with his old companions, and was indeed still the moving spirit in most of their activities; but always he played with a certain aloofness, as it were with his tongue in his cheek. Though in appearance he was by far the smallest and most infantile of the whole gang, he reminded me sometimes of a little old man with snowy hair condescending to play with young gorillas. Often he would break away in the middle of some wild game and drift into the garden to lie dreaming on the lawn. Or he would hang around his mother and discuss life with her, while she did her house-work, tidied the garden, or (a common occupation with Pax) just waited for the next thing to happen.

In some ways John with his mother suggested a human foundling with a wolf foster-mother; or, better, a cow foster-mother. He obviously gave her complete trust and affection, and even a deep though perplexed reverence; but he was troubled when she could not follow his thought or understand his innumerable questions about the universe.

The foster-mother image is not perfect. In one respect, indeed, it is entirely false. For though intellectually Pax was by far his inferior, there was evidently another field in which she was at this time his equal, perhaps even his superior. Both mother and son had a peculiar knack of appreciating experience, a peculiar relish which was at bottom, I believe, simply a very special and subtle sense of humour. Often have I seen a covert glance of understanding and amusement pass between them when the rest of us found nothing to tickle us. I guessed that this veiled merriment was in some way connected with John's awakening interest in persons and his rapidly developing insight into his own motives. But what it was in our behaviour that these two found so piquant, I could never discover.

With his father John's relation was very different. He made good use of the doctor's active mind, but between them there was no spontaneous sympathy, and little community of taste save intellectual interest. I have often seen on John's face while he was listening to his father a fleeting contortion of ridicule, even disgust. This happened especially at times when Thomas believed himself to be giving the boy some profound comment on human nature or the universe. Needless to say it was not only Thomas, but myself also and many another that roused in John this ridicule or revulsion. But Thomas was the chief offender, perhaps because he was the most brilliant, and the most impressive example of the mental limitations of his species. I suspect that John often deliberately incited his father to betray himself in this manner. It was as though the boy had said to himself, 'I have somehow to understand these fantastic beings who occupy the planet. Here is a fine specimen. I must experiment on him.'

At this point I had better say that I myself was becoming increasingly intrigued by the fantastic being, John. I was also unwittingly coming under his influence. Looking back on this period, I can see that he had already marked me down for future use, and was undertaking the first steps of my capture. His chief method was the cool assumption that though I was a middle-aged man, I was his slave; that however much I might laugh at him and scold him, I secretly recognized him as a superior being, and was at heart his faithful hound. For the present I might amuse myself playing at an independent life (I was at this time a rather half-hearted free-lance journalist), but sooner or later I must come to heel.

When John was nearly eight and a half in actual years, he was as a rule taken for a very peculiar child of five or six. He still played childish games, and was accepted by other children as a child, though a bit of a freak. Yet he could take part in any adult conversation. Of course, he was always either far too brilliant or far too ignorant of life to play his part in anything like a normal manner; but he was never simply inferior. Even his most naïve remarks were apt to have a startling significance.

But John's naïvety was rapidly disappearing. He was now reading an immense amount at an incredible rate. No book, on any subject which did not lie outside his experience, took him more than a couple of hours to master, however tough its matter. Most he could assimilate thoroughly in a quarter of an hour. But the majority of books he glanced at only for a few moments, then flung aside as worthless.

Now and then, in the course of his reading, he would demand to be taken (by his father or mother or myself) to watch some process of manufacture, or to go down a mine, or see over a ship, or visit some place of historic interest, or to observe experiments in some laboratory. Great efforts were made to fulfill these demands, but in many cases we had not the necessary influence. Many projected trips, moreover, were prevented by Pax's dread of unnecessary publicity for the boy. Whenever we did under-take an expedition, we had to pretend to the authorities that John's presence was accidental, and his interest childish and unintelligent.

John was by no means dependent on his elders for seeing the world. He had developed a habit of entering into conversation with all kinds of persons, 'to find out what they were doing and what they thought about things.' Any one who was tactfully accosted in street or train or country road by this small boy with huge eyes, hair like lamb's wool, and adult speech was likely to find himself led on to say much more than he intended. By such novel research John learned, I am convinced, more about human nature and our modern social problems in a month or two than most of us learn in a lifetime.

I was privileged to witness one of these interviews. On this occasion the subject was the proprietor of a big general store in the neighbouring industrial city. Mr Magnate (it is safer not to reveal his name) was to be accosted while he was travelling to business by the 9:30 train. John consented to my presence, but only on condition that I should pretend to be a stranger.

We let the quarry pass through the turnstile and settle himself in his first-class compartment. Then we went to the booking office, where I rather self-consciously demanded 'a *first* single and a half'. Independently we strayed into Mr Magnate's carriage. When I arrived, John was already settled in the corner opposite to the great man, who occasionally glanced from his paper at the queer child with a cliff for brow and caves for eyes. Soon after I had taken my post, in the corner diagonally opposite to John, two other business men entered, and settled themselves to read their papers.

John was apparently deep in *Comic Cuts*, or some such periodical. Though this had been bought merely to serve as stage property, I believe he was quite capable of enjoying it; for at this time, in spite of his wonderful gifts, he was still at heart 'the little vulgar boy'. In the conversation which followed he was obviously to some extent playing up to the business man's idea of a precocious yet naïve child. But also he *was* a naïve child, backward as well as diabolically intelligent. I myself, though I knew him well, could not decide how much of his talk on this occasion was sincere, and how much mere acting.

When the train had started, John began to watch his prey so intently that Mr Magnate took cover behind a wall of newspaper. Presently John's curiously precise treble gathered all eyes upon him. 'Mr Magnate,' he said, 'may I talk to you?' The newspaper was lowered, and its owner endeavoured to look neither awkward nor condescending.

'Certainly, boy, go ahead. What's your name?'

'Oh, my name's John. I'm a queer child, but that doesn't matter. It's you we're going to talk about.'

We all laughed. Mr Magnate shifted in his seat, but continued to look his part.

'Well,' he said, 'you certainly are a queer child.' He glanced at his adult fellow travellers for confirmation. We duly smiled.

'Yes,' replied John, 'but you see from my point of view you are a queer man.' Mr Magnate hung for a moment between amusement and annoyance; but since we had all laughed, except John, he chose to be tickled and benevolent.

'Surely,' he said, 'there's nothing remarkable about me. I'm just a business man. Why do you think I'm queer?'

'Well,' said John, '*I'm* thought queer because I have more brains than most children. Some say I have more brains than I *ought* to have. *You're* queer because you have more *money* than most people; and (some say) more than you ought to have.'

Once more we laughed, rather anxiously.

John continued: 'I haven't found out yet what to do with my brains, and I'm wondering if you have found out what to do with your money.'

'My dear boy, you may not believe me, but the fact is I have no real choice. Needs of all sorts keep cropping up, and I have to fork out.'

'I see,' said John; 'but then you can't fork out for *all* the possible needs. You must have some sort of big plan or aim to help you to choose.'

'Well now, how shall I put it? I'm James Magnate, with a wife and family and a rather complicated business and a whole lot of obligations rising out of all that. All the money I control, or nearly all, goes in keeping all those balls rolling, so to speak.'

'I see,' said John again. ' "My station and its duties," as Hegel said, and no need to worry about the sense of it all.'

Like a dog encountering an unfamiliar and rather formidable

smell, Mr Magnate sniffed this remark, bristled, and vaguely growled.

'Worry!' he snorted. 'There's plenty of that; but it's practical day-to-day worry about how to get goods cheap enough to sell them at a profit instead of a loss. If I started worrying about "the sense of it all" the business would soon go to pieces. No time for that. I find myself with a pretty big job that the country needs doing, and I just do it.'

There was a pause, then John remarked, 'How splendid it must be to have a pretty big job that needs doing, and to do it well! *Do* you do it well, sir? And does it *really* need doing? But of course you do, and it must; else the country wouldn't pay you for it.'

Mr Magnate looked anxiously at all his fellow travellers in turn, wondering whether his leg was being pulled. He was reassured, however, by John's innocent and respectful gaze. The boy's next remark was rather disconcerting. 'It must be so *snug* to feel both safe and important.'

'Well, I don't know about that,' the great man replied. 'But I give the public what it wants, and as cheaply as I can, and I get enough out of it to keep my family in reasonable comfort.'

'Is that what you make money for, to keep your family in comfort?'

'That and other things. I get rid of my money in all sorts of ways. If you must know, quite a lot goes to the political party that I think can govern the country best. Some goes to hospitals and other charities in our great city. But most goes into the business itself to make it bigger and better.'

'Wait a minute,' said John. 'You've raised a lot of interesting points. I mustn't lose any of them. First, about comfort. You live in that big half-timbered house on the hill, don't you?'

'Yes. It's a copy of an Elizabethan mansion. I could have done without it, but my wife had her heart set on it. And putting it up was a great thing for the local building trade.'

'And you have a Rolls, and a Wolseley?'

'Yes,' said the Magnate, adding with magnanimity, 'Come up

the hill on Saturday and I'll give you a run in the Rolls. When she's doing eighty it feels like thirty.'

John's eyelids sank and rose again, a movement which I knew as an expression of amused contempt. But why was he contemptuous? He was a bit of a speedhog himself. Never, for instance, was he satisfied with *my* cautious driving. Was it that he saw in this remark a cowardly attempt to side-track the conversation? After the interview I learned that he had *already* made several trips in the Magnate car, having suborned the chauffeur. He had even learned to drive it, with cushions behind him, so as to help his short legs to reach the pedals.

'Oh, thank you, I should love to go in your Rolls,' he said, looking gratefully into the benevolent grey eyes of the rich man. 'Of course, you couldn't work properly unless you had reasonable comfort. And that means a big house and two cars, and furs and jewels for your wife, and first-class railway fares, and swank schools for your children.' He paused, while Mr Magnate looked suspiciously at him. Then he added, 'But you won't be *really* comfortable till you've got that knighthood. Why doesn't it come? You've paid enough already, haven't you?'

One of our fellow passengers sniggered. Mr Magnate coloured, gasped, muttered, 'Offensive little brat!' and retired behind his paper.

'Oh, sir, I'm *sorry*,' said John, 'I thought it was all quite respectable. Surely it's just like Poppy Day. Pay your money, and you get your badge, and everyone knows you have done your bit. And that's true comfort, to know that everyone knows you're all right.'

The paper dropped again, and its owner said, with mild firmness, 'Look here, young man! You mustn't believe everything you're told, specially when it's libellous. I know you don't mean harm yourself, but – be more critical of what you hear.'

'I'm frightfully sorry,' said John, looking pained and abashed. 'It's so hard to know what one may say and what not.'

'Yes, of course,' said Magnate amiably. 'Perhaps I had better explain things a bit. Anyone who finds himself in a position like mine, if he's worth his salt, has to make the best possible use of his opportunities for serving the Empire. Now he can do this partly by running his business well, partly by personal influence. And if he is to have influence he must not only be, but also appear, a man of weight. He must spend a good deal on keeping up a certain style in his way of life. The public does attend more to a man who lives a bit expensively than to a man who doesn't. Often it would be more comfortable not to live expensively. Just as it would be more comfortable for a judge in court on a hot day to do without his robe and wig. But he mustn't. He must sacrifice comfort to dignity. At Christmas I bought my wife a rather good diamond necklace (South African – the money stayed in the Empire). Whenever we go to an important function, say a dinner at the Town Hall, she's got to wear it. She doesn't always want to. Says it's heavy or hard, or something. But I say, "My dear, it's a sign that you count. It's a badge of office. Better wear it." And about the knighthood. If anyone says I want to buy one, it's just a mean lie. I give what I can to my party because I know quite well, with my experience, that it's the party of common sense and loyalty. No other party cares seriously for British prosperity and power. No one cares about our great Empire and its mission to lead the world. Well, clearly I *must* support that party in any way open to me. If they saw fit to give me a knighthood, I'd be proud. I'm not one of those prigs who turn up their noses at it. I'd be glad, partly because it would mean that the people who really count were sure I was really serving the Empire, partly because the knighthood would give me more weight to go on serving the Empire with.'

Mr Magnate glanced at his fellow passengers. We all nodded approval. 'Thank you, sir,' said John, with solemn, respectful eyes. 'And it all depends on money, doesn't it? If *I'm* going to do anything big, I must get money, somehow. I have a friend who keeps saying, "Money's power." He has a wife who's always tired and cross, and five children, ugly dull things. He's out of a job. Had to sell his push-bike the other day. He says it's not fair that *he* should be where he is and – *you* where you are. But it's all his own fault really. If he had been as wide awake as you, he'd be as rich as you. Your being rich doesn't make anyone else poor, does it? If all the slum people were as wide awake as you, they'd all have big houses and Rollses and diamonds. They'd all be some use to the Empire, instead of being just a nuisance.'

The man opposite me tittered. Mr Magnate looked at him with the sidelong glance of a shy horse, then pulled himself together and laughed.

'My lad,' he said, 'you're too young to understand these things. I don't think we shall do much good by talking any more about them.'

'I'm sorry,' John replied, seemingly crushed. 'I thought I did understand.' Then after a pause he continued: 'Do you mind if we go on just a *little* bit longer? I want to ask you something else.'

'Oh, very well, what is it?'

'What do you think about?'

'What do I think about? Good heavens, boy! All sorts of things. My business, my home, my wife and children, and – about the state of the country.'

'The state of the country? What about it?'

'Well,' said Mr Magnate, 'that's much too long a story. I think about how England is to recover her foreign trade – so that more money may come into the country, and people may live happier, fuller lives. I think about how we can strengthen the hands of the Government against the foolish people who want to stir up trouble, and those who talk wildly against the Empire. I think—'

Here John interrupted. 'What makes life full and happy?'

'You *are* a box of questions! I should say that for happiness people need plenty of work to keep them out of mischief, and some amusement to keep them fresh.'

'And, of course,' John interposed, 'enough money to *buy* their amusements with.'

'Yes,' said Mr Magnate. 'But not too much. Most of them would only waste it or damage themselves with it. And if they had a lot, they wouldn't work to get more.'

'But you have a lot, and you work.'

'Yes, but I don't work for money exactly. I work because my business is a fascinating game, and because it is necessary to the country. I regard myself as a sort of public servant.'

'But,' said John, 'aren't *they* public servants too? Isn't their work necessary too?'

'Yes, boy. But they don't as a rule look at it that way. They won't work unless they're driven.'

'Oh, I see!' John said. They're a different sort from you. It must be wonderful to be you. I wonder whether I shall turn out like you or like them.'

'Oh, I'm not really different,' said Mr Magnate generously. 'Or if I am, it's just circumstances that have made me so. As for you, young man, I expect you'll go a long way.'

'I want to, terribly,' said John. 'But I don't know *which* way yet. Evidently whatever I do I must have money. But tell me, why do you *bother* about the country, and about other people?'

'I suppose,' said Mr Magnate, laughing, 'I bother about other people because when I see them unhappy I feel unhappy myself. And also,' he added more solemnly, 'because the Bible tells us to love our neighbours. And I suppose I bother about the country partly because I must have something big to be interested in, something bigger than myself.'

'But you *are* big, yourself,' said John, with hero-worship in his eyes, and not a twinkle.

Mr Magnate said hastily, 'No, no, only a humble instrument in the service of a very big thing.'

'What thing do you mean?' asked John.

'Our great Empire, of course, boy.'

We were arriving at our destination. Mr Magnate rose and took his hat from the rack. 'Well, young man,' he said, 'we have had an interesting talk. Come along on Saturday afternoon about 2.30, and we'll get the chauffeur to give you a quarter of an hour's spin in the Rolls.'

'Thank you, sir!' said John. 'And may I see Mrs Magnate's necklace? I love jewels.'

'Certainly you shall,' Mr Magnate answered.

When I had met John again outside the station, his only comment on the journey was his characteristic laugh.

V
Thought and Action

During the six months which followed this incident, John became increasingly independent of his elders. The parents knew that he was well able to look after himself, so they left him almost entirely to his own devices. They seldom questioned him about his doings, for anything like prying was repugnant to them both; and there seemed to be no mystery about John's movements. He was continuing his study of man and man's world. Sometimes he would volunteer an account of some incident in his day's adventure; sometimes he would draw upon his store of data to illustrate a point in discussion.

Though his tastes remained in some respect puerile, it was clear from his conversation that in other respects he was very rapidly developing. He would still spend days at a stretch in making mechanical toys, such as electric boats. His electric railway system spread its ramifications all over the garden in a maze of lines, tunnels, viaducts, glass-roofed stations. He won many a competition in flying home-made model aeroplanes. In all these activities he seemed at heart a typical schoolboy, though abnormally skilful and original. But the actual time spent in this way was really not great. The only boyish occupation which seemed to fill a large proportion of his time was sailing. He had made himself a minute but seaworthy canoe, fitted both with sail and an old motor-bicycle engine. In this he spent many hours exploring the estuary and the sea-coast, and studying the sea-birds, for which he had a surprising passion. This interest, which at times seemed almost obsessive, he explained apologetically by saying, 'They do their simple jobs with so much more *style* than man shows in his complicated job. Watch a gannet in flight, or a curlew probing the mud for food. Man, I suppose, is about as clever along his own line as the earliest birds were at flight. He's a sort of archiopteryx of the spirit.'

Even the most childish activities which sometimes gripped

John were apt to be illuminated in this manner by the more mature side of his nature. His delight in *Comic Cuts*, for instance, was half spontaneous, half a relish of his own silliness in liking the stuff.

At no time of his life did John outgrow his childhood interests. Even in his last phase he was always capable of sheer schoolboy mischief and make-believe. But already this side of his nature was being subordinated to the mature side. We knew, for instance, that he was already forming opinions about the proper aims of the individual, about social policy, about international affairs. We knew also that he was reading a great deal of physics, biology, psychology, astronomy; and that philosophical problems were now seriously occupying him. His reaction to philosophy was curiously unlike that of the normal philosophically minded adult human being. When one of the great classical philosophical puzzles attracted his attention for the first time, he plunged into the literature of the subject, read solidly for a week, and then gave up philosophy entirely till the next puzzle occurred to him.

After several of these raids upon the territory of philosophy he undertook a serious campaign. For nearly three months philosophy appeared to be his main intellectual interest. It was summer time, and he liked to study out of doors. Every morning he would set off on his push-bike with a box of books and food strapped on the carrier. Leaving his bicycle at the top of the clay cliffs which formed the coastline of the estuary, he would climb down to the shore, and settle himself for the day. Having undressed and put on his scanty 'bathers,' he would lie in the full sunshine reading, or thinking. Sometimes he broke off to bathe or wander about the mud flats watching the birds. Shelter from rain was provided by two rusty pieces of corrugated iron sheeting laid across two low walls, which he built of stones from a ruined lime-kiln near at hand. Sometimes, when the tide was up, he went by the sea route in his canoe. On calm days he might be seen a mile or two from the coast, drifting and reading.

I once asked John how his philosophical researches were progressing. His answer is worth recording. 'Philosophy,' he said, 'is really very helpful to the growing mind, but it's terribly disappointing too. At first I thought I'd found the mature human intelligence at work at last. Reading Plato, and Spinoza, and Kant, and some of the modern realists too, I almost felt I had come across people of my own kind. I walked in step with them. I played their game with a sense that it called out powers that I had never exercised before. Sometimes I couldn't follow them. I seemed to miss some vital move. The exhilaration of puzzling over these critical points, and feeling one had met a real master mind at last! But as I went on from philosopher to philosopher and browsed around all over the place, I began to realize the shocking truth that these critical points were not what I thought they were, but just outrageous howlers. It had seemed incredible that these obviously well-developed minds could make simple mistakes; and so I had respectfully dismissed the possibility, and looked for some profound truth. But oh my God, I was wrong! Howler after howler! Sometimes a philosopher's opponents spot his howlers, and are frightfully set up with their own cleverness. But most of them never get spotted at all, so far as I can discover. Philosophy is an amazing tissue of really fine thinking and incredible, puerile mistakes. It's like one of those rubber "bones" they give dogs to chew, damned good for the mind's teeth, but as food – no bloody good at all.'

I ventured to suggest that perhaps he was not really in a position to judge the philosophers. 'After all,' I said, 'you're ridiculously young to tackle philosophy. There are spheres of experience that you have not touched yet.'

'Of course there are,' he said. 'But – well, for instance, I have little sexual experience, yet. But even now I can see that a man is blathering if he says that sex (properly defined) is the real motive behind all agricultural activities. Take another case, I have no religious experience, yet. Maybe I *shall* have it, some day. Maybe there's really no such thing. But I can see quite well that religious experience (properly defined) is no evidence that the sun goes round the earth, and no evidence that the universe has a purpose, such as the fulfilment of personality. The howlers of philosophers are mostly less obvious than these, but of the same kind.'

At the time of which I am speaking, when John was nearly nine, I had no idea that he was leading a double life, and that the hidden part of it was melodramatic. On one single occasion my suspicion was roused for a few moments, but the possibility that flashed upon me was too fantastic and horrible to be seriously entertained.

One morning I happened to go round to the Wainwrights to borrow one of Thomas's medical books. It must have been about 11.30. John, who had recently developed the habit of reading late at night and rising late in the morning, was being turned out of bed by his indignant mother. 'Come and get your breakfast before you dress,' she said. 'I'll keep it no longer.'

Pax offered me 'morning tea,' so we both sat down at the breakfast table. Presently a blinking and scowling John appeared, wearing a dressing-gown over his pyjamas. Pax and I talked about one thing and another. In the course of conversation she said, 'Matilda has come with a really lurid story today.' (Matilda was the washerwoman.) 'She's as pleased as Punch about it. She says a policeman was found murdered in Mr Magnate's garden this morning, stabbed, she says.' John said nothing, and went on with his breakfast. We continued talking for a while, and then the thing happened that startled me. John reached across the table for the butter, exposing part of his arm beyond the end of the dressing-gown sleeve. On the inner side of the wrist was a rather nasty-looking scrape with a certain amount of dirt still in it. I felt pretty sure that there had been no scrape there when I saw him on the previous evening. Nothing very remarkable in that, but what disturbed me was this: John himself saw that scrape, and then glanced quickly at me. For a fraction of a second his eyes held mine; then he took up the butter-dish. In that moment I seemed to see John, in the middle of the night, scraping his arm as he climbed up the drainpipe to his bedroom. And it seemed to me that he was returning from Mr Magnate's. I pulled myself together at once, reminding myself that what I had seen was a very ordinary abrasion, that

John was far too deeply engrossed in his intellectual adventures to indulge in nocturnal pranks, and anyhow far too sensible to risk a murder charge. But that sudden look?

The murder gave the suburb matter for gossip for many weeks. There had recently been a number of extremely clever burglaries in the neighbourhood, and the police were making vigorous efforts to discover the culprit. The murdered man had been found lying on his back in a flower-bed with a neat knife-wound in his chest. He must have died 'instantaneously', for his heart was pierced. A diamond necklace and other valuable pieces of jewellery had disappeared from the house. Slight marks on a window-sill and a drain-pipe suggested that the burglar had climbed in and out by an upper storey. If so, he must have ascended the drainpipe and then accomplished an almost impossible hand-traverse, or rather finger-tip-traverse, up and along one of the ornamental timbers of the pseudo-Eliza-bethan house.

Sundry arrests were made, but the perpetrator of the crime was never detected. The epidemic of burglaries, however, ceased, and in time the whole matter was forgotten.

At this point it seems well to draw upon information given me by John himself at a much later stage, in fact during the last year of his life, when the colony had been successfully founded, and had not yet been discovered by the 'civilized' world. I was already contemplating writing his biography, and had formed a habit of jotting down notes of any striking incident or con-versation as soon as possible after the event. I can, therefore, give the account of the murder approximately in John's own words.

'I was in a bad mess, mentally, in those days,' said John. 'I knew I was different from all other human beings whom I had ever met, but I didn't realize *how* different. I didn't know what I was going to do with my life, but I knew I should soon find something pretty big and desperate to do, and that I must make myself ready for it. Also, remember, I was a child; and I had a child's taste for the melodramatic, combined with an adult's cunning and resolution.

'I can't possibly make you really understand the horrible muddle I was in, because after all your mind doesn't work along the same lines as mine. But think of it this way, if you like. I found myself in a thoroughly bewildering world. The people in it had built up a huge system of thought and knowledge, and I could see quite well that it was shot through and through with error. From my point of view, although so far as it went it was sound enough for practical purposes, as a description of the world it was simply crazy. But what the right description was I could not discover. I was too young. I had insufficient data. Huge fields of experience were still beyond me. So there I was, like someone in the dark in a strange room, just feeling about among unknown objects. And all the while I had a frantic itch to be getting on with my work, if only I could find out what it was.

'Add to all this that as I grew older I grew more and more lonely, because fewer and fewer people were able to meet me half-way. There was Pax. She really could help, bless her, because she really did see things from my angle – sometimes. And even when she didn't she had the sense to guess I was seeing something actual, and not merely fantasies. But at bottom she definitely belonged with the rest of you, not with me. Then there was you, much blinder than Pax, but more sympathetic with the active side of me.'

Here I interposed half seriously, half mischievously, 'At least a trusty hound.' John laughed, and I added, 'And sometimes rising to an understanding beyond my canine capacity, through sheer devotion.' He looked at me and smiled, but did not, as I had hoped he would, assent.

'Well,' he continued, 'I was most damnably lonely. I was living in a world of phantoms, or animated masks. No one seemed really alive. I had a queer notion that if I pricked any of you, there would be no bleeding, but only a gush of wind. And I couldn't make out *why* you were like that, what it was that I missed in you. The trouble really was that I didn't clearly know what it was in *myself* that made me different from you.

'Two clear points emerged from my perplexity. First and simplest, I must make myself independent, I must acquire

35

power. In the crazy world in which I found myself, this meant getting hold of much money. Second I must make haste to sample all sorts of experience, and I must accurately experience my own reactions to all sorts of experience.

'It seemed to me, in my childishness, that I should at any rate *begin* to fulfil both these needs by bringing off a few burglaries. I should get money, and I should get experience, and I should watch my reactions very carefully. Conscience did not prick me at all. I felt that Mr Magnate and his like were fair game.

'I first set about studying the technique, partly by reading, partly by discussing the subject with my friend the policeman whom I was afterwards forced to kill. I also undertook a number of experimental and innocuous burglaries on our neighbours. House after house I entered by night, and after locating but not removing the small treasures which they contained, I retired home to bed, well satisfied with my progress.

'At last I felt ready for serious work. In my first house I took only some old-fashioned jewellery, which, I surmised, would not be missed for some time. Then I began taking modern jewellery, cash, silver plate. I found extraordinarily little difficulty in acquiring the stuff. Getting rid of it was much more ticklish work. I managed to make an arrangement with the purser of a foreign-going vessel. He turned up at his home in our suburb every few weeks and bought my swag. I have no doubt that when he parted with it, in foreign ports be got ten times what he gave me for it. Looking back, I realize how lucky I was that the export side of my venture never brought me to disaster. My purser might so easily have been spotted by the police. Of course, I was still far too ignorant of society to realize the danger. Bright as I was, I had not the data.

'Well, things went swimmingly for some months. I entered dozens of houses and collected several hundred pounds from my purser. But naturally the suburb had got thoroughly excited by this epidemic of house-breaking. Indeed, I had been forced to extend my operations to other districts so as to dissipate the attention of the police. It was clear that if I went on indefinitely I should be caught. But I had been badly bitten by the game. It gave me a sense of independence and power, especially independence, independence of your crazy world.

'I promised myself three more ventures. The first, and the only one to be accomplished, was the Magnate burglary. I went over the ground pretty carefully, and I ascertained the movements of the police pretty thoroughly too. On the actual night all went according to plan until, with my pockets bulging with Mrs Magnate's pearls and diamonds (in her full regalia she must have looked like Queen Elizabeth), I started back along that finger-traverse. Suddenly a torch flashed on me from below, and a quiet cheery voice said, "Got you this time, my lad." I said nothing, for I recognized the voice, and did not wish mine to be recognized in turn. The constable was my own particular pal, Smithson, who had unwittingly taught me so much.

'I hung motionless by my finger-tips, thinking hard, and keeping my face to the wall. But it was useless to conceal my identity, for he said, "Buck up, John, boy, come along down or you'll drop and break your leg. You're a sport, but you're beat this time."

'I must have hung motionless for three seconds at most, but in that time I saw myself and my world as never before. An idea toward which I had been long but doubtfully groping suddenly displayed itself to me with complete clarity and certainty. I had already, some time before, come to think of myself as definitely of a different biological species from *Homo sapiens*, the species of that amiable bloodhound behind the torch. But at last I realized for the first time that this difference carried with it what I should now describe as a far-reaching spiritual difference, that my purpose in life, and my attitude to life, were to be different from anything which the normal species could conceive, that I stood, as it were, on the threshold of a world far beyond the reach of those sixteen hundred million crude animals that at present ruled the planet. The discovery made me feel, almost for the first time in my life, fear, dread. I saw, too, that this burglary game was not worth the candle, that I had been behaving very much like a creature of the inferior species, risking my future and much more than *my* personal success for a cheap kind of

37

self-expression. If that amiable bloodhound got me, I should lose my independence. I should be henceforth known, marked, and in the grip of the law. That simply must not be. All these childish escapades had been a blind, fumbling preparation for a life-work which at last stood out more or less clearly before me. It was my task, unique being that I was, to "advance the spirit" on this planet. That was the phrase which flashed into my mind. And though at that early stage I had only a very dim idea about "spirit" and its "advance", I saw quite clearly that I must set about the more practical side of my task either by taking charge of the common species and teaching it to bring out the best in itself, or, if that proved impossible, by founding a finer human type of my own.

'Such were the thoughts that flashed on me in the first couple of seconds as I hung by my finger-tips in the blaze of poor Smithson's torch. If ever you do write that threatened biography, you'll find it quite impossible to persuade your readers that I, a child of nine, could have had such thoughts in such circumstances. Also, of course, you won't be able to give anything of the actual character of my new attitude, because it involved a kind of experience beyond your grasp.

'During the next two seconds or so I was desperately considering if there was any way to avoid killing the faithful creature. My fingers were giving out. With their last strength I reached the drain-pipe, and began to descend. Half-way I stopped, "How's Mrs Smithson?" I said. "Bad," he answered. "Look sharp, I want to get home." That made matters worse. How *could* I do it? Well, it just *had* to be done, there was no way out of it. I thought of killing myself, and getting out of the whole mess that way. But I couldn't do that. It would be sheer betrayal of the thing I must live for. I thought of just accepting Smithson and the law; but no, that, I knew, was betrayal also. The killing just had to be. It was my own childishness that had got me into this scrape, but now – the killing just had to be. All the same, I hated the job. I had not yet reached the stage of liking *whatever* had to be done. I felt over again, and far more distressingly, the violent repulsion which had surprised me years earlier, when I had to kill a mouse. It was that one I had tamed, you remember, and the maids wouldn't stand it running about the house.

'Well, Smithson had to die. He was standing at the foot of the pipe. I pretended to slip, and fell on him, overbalancing him by kicking off from the wall. We both went down with a crash. With my left hand I seized the torch, and with my right I whipped out my little scout's knife. The position of the human heart was not unknown to me. I plunged the knife home, leaning on it with all my weight. Smithson flung me off with one frantic spasm, then lay still.

'The scrimmage had made a considerable noise, and I heard a bed creak in the house. For a moment I looked at Smithson's open eyes and open mouth. I pulled out the knife, and then there was a spurt of blood.'

John's account of this strange incident showed me how little I had known of his real character at that time.

'You must have felt pretty bad on the way home,' I said.

'As a matter of fact,' he answered, 'I didn't. The bad feeling ended when I made my decision. And I didn't go straight home. I went to Smithson's house, intending to kill his wife. I knew she was down with cancer and in for a lot of pain, and would be broken-hearted over her husband's death; so I decided to take one more risk and put her out of her misery. But when I got there, by secret ways of my own, I found the house lit up and awake. She was evidently having a bad night. So I had to leave her, poor wretch. Even that didn't really upset me. You may say I was saved by the insensitivity of childhood. Perhaps to some extent; though I had a pretty vivid notion of what Pax would suffer if she lost her husband. What really saved me was a kind of fatalism. What must be, must be. I felt no remorse for my own past folly. The "I" that had committed that folly was incapable of realizing how foolish it was being. The new "I", that had suddenly awakened, realized very clearly, and was anxious to make amends so far as possible; but of remorse or shame it felt nothing.'

To this confession I could make only one reply, 'Odd John!'

I then asked John if he was preyed on by the dread of being

caught. 'No,' he said. 'I had done all I could. If they caught me, they caught me. But I had done the job as efficiently as it is ever done. I had worn rubber gloves, and left a few false fingerprints, made by an ingenious little instrument of my own. My only serious anxiety was over my purser. I sold him the swag in small instalments over a period of several months.'

VI
Many Inventions

Although I did not at the time know that John was responsible for the murder, I noticed that a change came over him. He became less communicative, in a way more aloof from his friends, both juvenile and adult, and at the same time more considerate and even gentle. I say 'in a way' more aloof, because, though less ready to talk about himself, and more prone to solitariness, he had also his sociable times. He could indeed be a most sympathetic companion, the sort in whom one was tempted to confide all manner of secret hopes and fears that were scarcely admitted by oneself. One day, for instance, I found myself discovering, under the influence of John's presence and my own effort to explain myself, that I had already become very strongly attracted to a certain Pax-like young woman, and further that I had been kept from recognizing this feeling through an obscure sense of loyalty to John. The discovery of the strength of my feeling for John was more of a shock than the discovery of my feeling for the girl. I knew that I was deeply interested in John, but till that day I had no idea how subtle and far-reaching were the tentacles with which the strange child had penetrated me.

My reaction was a violent and rather panicky rebellion. I flaunted before John the new-found normal sexual attraction which he himself had pointed out to me, and I ridiculed the notion that I was psychologically his captive. He replied, 'Well, be careful. Don't spoil your life for me.' It was strange to be talking like this to a child of less than ten years old. It was distressing to feel that he knew more about me than I knew about myself. For in spite of my denial, I knew that he was right.

Looking back, I recognize that John's interest in my case was partly due to curiosity about a relationship which he himself could not yet experience, partly to straightforward affection for a well-known companion, partly to the need to understand as fully as possible one whom he intended to use for his own ends. For it is clear that he did intend to use me, that he did not for a moment intend me to free myself. He wanted my affair with the Pax-like girl to go forward and complete itself not only because, as my friend, he espoused my need, but also because, if I were to give it up for his sake, I should become a vindictive rather than a willing slave. He preferred, I imagine, to be served by a free and roving hound rather than by a chained and hungry wolf.

His feeling for individuals of the species which, as a species, he heartily despised, was a strange blend of contempt and respect, detachment and affection. He despised us for our stupidity and fecklessness; he respected us for our occasional efforts to surmount our natural disabilities. Though he used us for his own ends with calm aloofness, he could also, when fate or our own folly brought us into trouble, serve us with surprising humility and devotion.

His growing capacity for personal relationships with members of the inferior species was shown most quaintly in his extraordinary friendship with a little girl of six. Judy's home was close to John's, and she had come to regard John as her private property. He played uproarious games with her, helped her to climb trees, and taught her to swim and roller-skate. He told her wildly imaginative stories. He patiently explained to her the sorry jokes of *Comic Cuts*. He drew pictures of battle and murder, shipwreck and volcanic eruption for Judy's sole delight. He mended her toys. He chaffed her for her stupidity or praised her for her intelligence as occasion demanded. If anyone was less than kind to her, John rushed to her defence. In all communal games it was taken for granted that John and Judy must be on the same side. In return for this devotion she mauled him, laughed at him, scolded him, called him 'stoopid Don', showed no respect at all for his marvellous powers, and presented him with all the most cherished results of her enterprise in the 'hand-work' class at school.

I once challenged John, 'Why are you so fond of Judy?' He answered promptly, imitating her unusually backward baby speech, 'Doody *made* for be'n' fon' of. Can't not be fon' of Doody.' Then after a pause he said, 'I'm fond of Judy as I'm fond of sea-birds. She does only simple things, but she does them all with style. She be's Judy as thoroughly and perfectly as a gannet be's a gannet. If she could grow up to do the grown-up things as well as she does the baby things, she'd be glorious. But she won't. When it comes to doing the more difficult things, I suppose she'll mess up her style like – like the rest of you. It's a pity. But meanwhile she's – Judy.'

'What about yourself?' I said. 'Do you expect to grow up without losing your style?'

'I've not *found* my style yet,' he answered. 'I'm groping. I've messed things pretty badly already. But when I *do* find it – well, we shall see. Of course,' he added surprisingly, 'God may find grown-ups as delightful to watch as I find Judy; because, I suppose, he doesn't want them to have a finer style than they actually have. Sometimes I can feel that way about them myself. I can feel their bad style is part of what they are, and strangely fascinating to watch. But I have an idea God expects something different from me. Or, leaving out the God myth, *I* expect something different from me.'

A few weeks after the murder, John developed a surprising interest in a very homely sphere, namely the management of a house. He would spend an hour at a time in following Martha the maid about the house on her morning's work, or in watching the culinary operations. For her entertainment he kept up a stream of small talk compounded of scandal, broad humour, and chaff about her 'gentlemen friends'. The same minute observation, but a very different kind of talk was devoted to Pax when she was in the pantry or the larder, or when she was 'tidying' a room or mending clothes. Sometimes he would break off his tittle-tattle to say, 'Why not do it this way?' Martha's response to such suggestions varied from haughty contempt to grudging acceptance, according to her mood. Pax invariably gave serious attention to the new idea, though sometimes she would begin by protesting, 'But my way works well enough; why bother?' In the end, however, she nearly always adopted John's improvement, with an odd little smile which might equally well have meant maternal pride or indulgence.

Little by little John introduced a number of small labour-saving devices into the house, shifting a hook or a shelf to suit the natural reach of the adult arm, altering the balance of the coalscuttle, reorganizing the larder and the bathroom. He tried to introduce his methods into the surgery, suggesting new ways of cleaning test-tubes, sterilizing instruments and storing drugs; but after a few attempts he gave up this line of activity, since, as he put it, 'Doc likes to muddle along in his own way.'

After two or three weeks John's interest in household economy seemed to fade, save for occasional revivals in relation to some particular problem. He now spent most of his time away from home, ostensibly reading on the shore. But as the autumn advanced, and we began to inquire how he managed to keep himself warm, he apparently developed a passion for long walks by himself. He also spent much time in excursions into the neighbouring city. 'I'm going to town for the day to see some fellows I'm interested in,' he would tell us; and in the evening he would return tired and absorbed.

It was toward the end of the winter that John, now about ten and a half, took me into his confidence with regard to the amazing commercial operations which had been occupying him during the previous six months. One filthy Sunday morning, when the windows were plastered with sleet, he suggested a walk. I indignantly refused. 'Come on,' he insisted. 'It's going to be amusing for you. I want to show you my workshop.' He slowly winked first one huge eye and then the other.

By the time we had reached the shore my inadequate mack-intosh was letting water through on my shoulders, and I was

43

cursing John, and myself too. We tramped along the soaked sands till we reached a spot where the steep clay cliffs gave place to a slope, scarcely less steep, but covered with thorn bushes. John went down on his knees and led the way, crawling on all-fours up a track between the bushes. I was expected to follow. I found it almost impossible to force my larger bulk where John had passed with ease. When I had gone a few yards I was jammed, thorns impaling me on every side. Laughing at my predicament and my curses, John turned and cut me adrift with his knife, the same, doubtless, as had killed the constable. After another ten yards the track brought us into a small clearing on the steep slope. Standing erect at last, I grumbled, 'Is *this* what you call your workshop?' John laughed, and said, 'Lift that.' He was pointing to a rusty sheet of corrugated iron, which lay derelict on the hillside. One end of it was buried under a mass of rubbish. The exposed part was about three feet square. I tugged its free end up a couple of inches, cut my fingers on the rusty jagged edge, and let go with a curse. 'Can't be bothered,' I said. 'Do your own dirty work, if you can.' 'Of course you can't be bothered,' he replied, 'nor would anyone else who found it.' He then worked his hand under the free corners of the sheet, and disentangled some rusty wire. The sheet was now lifted, and opened like a trap door in the hillside. It revealed a black hole between three big stones. John crawled inside, and bade me follow; but before I could wedge my way through he had to move one of the stones. I found myself in a low cave, illuminated by John's flash-light. So *this* was the workshop! It had evidently been cut out of the clay slope and lined with cement. The ceiling was covered with rough planks, and shored up here and there with wooden posts.

John now lit an acetylene lamp, which was let into the outer wall. Shutting its glass face, he remarked, 'its air comes in by a pipe from outside, and its fumes go out by another. There's an independent ventilation system for the room.' Pointing to a dozen round holes in the wall, 'Drain-pipes,' he said. Such pipes were a common sight on the coast, for they were used for draining the fields; and the ever-crumbling cliff often exposed them.

For a few minutes I crouched in silence, surveying the little den. John watched me, with a grin of boyish satisfaction. There was a bench, a small lathe, a blow-lamp, and quantities of tools. On the back wall was a tier of shelves covered with a jumble of articles. John took one of these and handed it to me, saying, 'This is one of my earlier gadgets, the world's perfect wool-winder. No curates need henceforth apply. The Church's undoing! Put the skein on those prongs, and an end of wool in that slot, then waggle the lever, so, and you get a ball of wool as sleek as the curate's head. All made of aluminum sheeting, and a few aluminum knitting needles.'

'Damned ingenious,' I said, 'but what good is it to you?'

'Why, you fool! I'm going to patent it and sell the patent.'

Producing a deep leather pouch, he said, 'This is a detachable and untearable trouser-pocket for boys; and men, if they'll have the sense to use it. The pocket itself clips on to this L-shaped strip, so; and *all* your trousers have strips like this, firmly sewn into the lining. You have *one* pair of pockets for *all* your trousers, so there's no bother about emptying pockets when you change your clothes. And no more holes for Mummy to mend. And no more losing your treasures. Your pocket clips tight shut, so.'

Even my interest in John's amazing enterprise (so childish and so brilliant, I told myself) could not prevent me from feeling wet and chilled. Taking off my dripping mackintosh, I said, 'Don't you get horribly cold working in this hole in the winter?'

'I heat the place with this,' he said, turning to a little oil-stove with a flue leading round the room and through the wall. He proceeded to light it, and put a kettle on the top, saying, 'Let's have some coffee.'

He then gave me a 'gadget for sweeping out corners'. On the end of a long tubular handle was a brush like a big blunt cork-screw. This could be made to rotate by merely pressing it into the awkward corner. The rotatory motion was obtained by a device reminiscent of a 'propelling' pencil, for the actual shaft

45

of the brush was keyed into a spiral groove within the hollow handle.

'It's possible the thing I'm on now will bring more money than anything else, but it's damned hard to make even an inch or two of it by hand.' The article which John now showed me was destined to become one of the most popular and serviceable of modern devices connected with clothing. Throughout Europe and America it has spawned its myriads of offspring. Nearly all the most ingenious and lucrative of John's inventions have had such outstanding success that almost every reader must be familiar with every one of them. I could mention a score of them; but for private reasons, connected with John's family, I must refrain from doing so. I will only say that, save for one universally adopted improvement in road-traffic appliances, he worked entirely in the field of household and personal labour-saving devices. The outstanding fact about John's career as an inventor was his knack of producing not merely occasional successes but a steady flow of 'best sellers'. Consequently to describe only a few minor achievements and interesting failures must give a very false impression of his genius. The reader must supplement this meagre report by means of his own imagination. Let him, in the act of using any of the more cunning and efficient little instruments of modern comfort, remind himself that this may well be one of the many 'gadgets' which were conceived by the urchin-superman in his subterranean lair.

For some time John continued to show me his inventions. I may mention a parsley cutter, a potato-peeler, a number of devices for using old razor-blades as penknife, scissors, and so on. Others, to repeat, were destined never to be taken up, or never to become popular. Of these perhaps the most noteworthy was a startlingly efficient dodge for saving time and trouble in the watercloset. John himself had doubts about some, including the detachable pocket. 'The trouble is,' he said, 'that however good my inventions are, *Homo sapiens* may be too prejudiced to use them. I expect he'll stick to his bloody pockets.'

The kettle was boiling, so he made the coffee and produced a noble cake, made by Pax.

While we were drinking and munching I asked him how he got all his plant. 'It's all paid for,' he said. 'I came in for a bit of money. I'll tell you about that some day. But I want *much* more money, and I'll get it too.'

'You were lucky to find this cave,' I said. He laughed. 'Find it, you chump! I made it. Dug it out with pick and spade and my own lily-white hands.' (At this point he reached out a grubby and sinewy bunch of tentacles for a biscuit.) 'It was the hell of a grind, but it hardened my muscles.'

'And how did you transport the stuff, that lathe, for instance?' 'By sea, of course.' 'Not in the canoe!' I protested. 'Had it all sent to X,' he said, naming a little port on the other side of the estuary. 'There's a bloke over there who acts as my agent in little matters like that. He's safe, because I know things about him that he doesn't want the police to know. Well, he dumped the cases of parts on the shore over there one night while I pinched one of the Sailing Club's cutters and took her over to fetch the stuff. It had to be done at spring tide, and of course the weather was all wrong. When I got the stuff over I nearly died lugging it up here from the shore, though it was all in small pieces. And I only just managed to get the cutter back to her moorings before dawn. Thank God that's all over. Have another cup, won't you?'

Toasting ourselves over the oil-stove, we now discussed the part which John intended me to play in his preposterous adventure. I was at first inclined to scoff at the whole project, but what with his diabolical persuasiveness and the fact that he had already achieved so much, I found myself agreeing to carry out my share of the plan. 'You see,' he said, 'all this stuff must be patented and the patents sold to manufacturers. It's quite useless for a kid like me to interview patents agents and business men. That's where you come in. You're going to launch all these things, sometimes under your own name, sometimes under sham names. I don't want people to know they all come from one little brain.'

'But, John,' I said, 'I should get stung every time. I know nothing about the job.'

'That's all right,' he answered. 'I'll tell you exactly what to

47

do in each case. And if you do make a few mistakes, it doesn't matter.'

One odd feature of the relationship which he had planned for us was that, though we expected to deal with large sums of money, there was not to be any regularized business arrangement between us, no formal agreement about profit-sharing and liabilities. I suggested a written contract, but he dismissed the idea with contempt. 'My dear man,' he said, 'how could I enforce a contract against you without coming out of hiding, which I must not do on any account? Besides, I know perfectly well that so long as you keep in physical and mental health you're entirely reliable. And you ought to know the same of me. This is to be a friendly show. You can take as much as you like of the dibs, when they begin to come in. I'll bet my boots you won't want to take half as much as your services are worth. Of course, if you start taking that girl of yours to the Riviera by air every weekend, we'll have to begin regularizing things. But you won't.'

I asked him about a banking account. 'Oh,' he said, 'I've had one running for some time at a London branch of the— Bank. But the payments will have to be made to you at your bank mostly, so as to keep me dark. These gadgets are to go out as yours, not mine, and as the inventions of lots of imaginary people. You're their agent.'

'But,' I protested, 'don't you see you're giving me absolute power to swindle you out of the whole proceeds? Suppose I just use you? Suppose the taste of power goes to my head, and I collar everything? I'm only *Homo sapiens*, not *Homo superior*.' And for once I privately felt that John was perhaps not so superior after all.

John laughed delightedly at the title, but said, 'My *dear* thing, you just won't. No, no, I refuse to have any business arrangements. That would be too "sapient" altogether. We should never be able to trust one another. Probably I'd cheat you all round, just for fun.'

'Oh, well,' I sighed, 'you'll keep accounts and see how the money goes.'

'Keep accounts, man! What in hell do I want with accounts? I keep 'em in my head, but never look at 'em.'

VII
Financial Ventures

Henceforth my own work was seriously interfered with by my increasing duties in connection with John's commercial enterprise. I spent a great deal of my time travelling about the country, visiting patent agents and manufacturers. Quite often John accompanied me. He had always to be introduced as 'a young friend of mine who would so like to see the inside of a factory'. In this way he picked up a lot of knowledge of the powers and limitations of different kinds of machines, and was thus helped to produce easily manufacturable designs.

It was on these expeditions that I first came to realize that even John had his disability, his one blind spot, I called it. I approached these industrial gentlemen with painful consciousness that they could do what they liked with me. Generally I was kept from disaster by the advice of the patent agents, who, being primarily scientists, were on our side not only professionally but by sympathy. But quite often the manufacturer managed to get at me direct. On several of these occasions I was pretty badly stung. Nevertheless, I learned in time to be more able to hold my own with the commercial mind. John, on the other hand, seemed incapable of believing that these people were actually less interested in producing ingenious articles than in getting the better of us, and of every one else. Of course, he knew intellectually that it was so. He was as contemptuous of the morality as of the intelligence of *Homo sapiens*. But he could not 'feel it in his bones' that men could really 'be such *fools* as to care so much about sheer money-making as a game of skill.' Like any other boy, he could well appreciate the thrill of beating a rival in personal combat, and the thrill of triumph in practical invention.

But the battle of industrial competition made no appeal whatever to him, and it took him many months of bitter experience to realize how much it meant to most men. Though he was himself in the thick of a great commercial adventure, he never felt the fascination of business undertakings as such. Though he could enter zestfully into most of man's instinctive and primitive passions, the more artificial manifestations of those passions, and in particular the lust of economic individualism, found no spontaneous echo in him. In time, of course, he learned to expect men to manifest such passions, and he acquired the technique of dealing with them. But he regarded the whole commercial world with a contempt which suggested now the child, and now the philosopher. He was at once below it and above it.

Thus it was that in the first phase of John's commercial life it fell to me to play the part of hard-headed business man. Unfortunately, as was said, I myself was extremely ill-equipped for the task, and at the outset we parted with several good inventions for a price which we subsequently discovered to be ludicrously inadequate.

But in spite of early disasters we were in the long run amazingly successful. We launched scores of ingenious contrivances which have since become universally recognized as necessary adjuncts of modern life. The public remarked on the spate of minor inventions which (it was said) showed the resilience of human capacity a few years after the war.

Meanwhile our bank balance increased by leaps and bounds, while our expenses remained minute. When I suggested setting up a decent workshop in my name in a convenient place, John would not hear of it. He produced a number of poor arguments against the plan, and I concluded that he was determined to cling to his lair for no reason but boyish love of sensationalism. But presently he divulged his real reason, and it horrified me. 'No,' he said, 'we mustn't spend yet. We must speculate. That bank balance must be multiplied by a hundred, and then by a thousand.'

I protested that I knew nothing about finance, and that we might easily lose all we had. He assured me that he had been studying finance, and that he already had a few neat little plans in mind. 'John,' I said, 'you simply mustn't do it. That's the sort of field where sheer intelligence is not enough. You want half a lifetime's special knowledge of the stock market. And anyhow it's nearly all luck.'

It was no use talking. After all, he had good reason to trust his own judgment rather than mine. And he gave evidence that he had gone into the subject thoroughly, both by reading the financial journals and by ingratiating himself with local stock-brokers on the morning and evening trains to town. He had by now passed far beyond the naïve child that had interviewed Mr Magnate, and he was, as ever, an adept at making people talk about their own work.

'It's now or never,' he said. 'We're entering a boom, inevitable after the war; but in a few years we shall be in the midst of a slump that people will wonder if civilization is going smash. You'll see.'

I laughed at his assurance, and was treated to a lecture on economics and the state of Western society, the sort of thing that in eight or ten years was to be generally accepted among the more advanced students of social problems. At the end of this discourse John said, 'We'll put half our capital into British light industry – motors, electricity and so on, because that sort of thing is bound to go ahead, comparatively. The rest we'll use for speculation.'

'We'll lose the whole lot, I expect,' I grumbled. Then I tried a new line of attack. 'Anyhow isn't all this money-making a bit too trivial for *Homo superior*? I believe you're bitten by the speculation bug after all. I mean, what is the object of it all?'

'It's all right, Fido, old thing,' he answered. (It was about this time that he began to use this nickname for me. When I protested, he assured me that it was meant to be Oaidw, which name, he said, was connected with the Greek for 'brilliant'. 'It's all right. I'm quite sane still. I don't care a damn about finance for its own sake, but in the world of *Hom. sap.* it's the quickest way to get power, which means money. And I must have money, big money. Now don't snort! We've made a good little start, but it's *only* a start.'

'What about "advancing the spirit," as you called it?'

'That's the goal, all right; but you seem to forget I'm only a child, and very backward too, in all that really matters. I must do the things I *can* do before the things I can't *yet* do. And what I can do is to prepare – by getting (*a*) experience, (*b*) independence. See?' Evidently the thing had to be. But it was with grave misgiving that I agreed to act as John's financial agent; and when he insisted on indulging in various wild speculations against my advice, I began to tell myself that I had been a fool to treat him as anything but a brilliant child.

John's financial operations did not spontaneously hold his attention as his practical inventions had done. And by now both kinds of activity were being subordinated increasingly to the study of human society and the absorbing personal contacts which came to him with adolescence. There was a certain absent-mindedness and dilatoriness about his buying and selling of stock, very exasperating to me, his agent. For though most of our common fortune was in my name, I could never bring myself to act without his consent.

During the first six months of our speculative ventures we lost far more than we gained. John at last woke up to the fact that if we went on this way we should lose everything. After hearing of a particularly devastating disaster he indulged in a memorable outburst. 'Blast!' he said. 'It means I must take this damned dull game much more seriously. And there's so much else to be done just now, far more important in the long run. I see it may be as difficult for me to beat *Hom. sap.* at this game as it is for *Hom. sap.* to beat apes at acrobatics. The human body is not equipped for the jungle, and my mind may not be equipped for the jungle of individualistic finance. But I'll get round it somehow, just as *Hom. sap.* got round acrobatics.'

It was characteristic of John that when he had made a serious mistake through lack of experience he never tried to conceal the fact. On this occasion he recounted with complete detachment, neither blaming nor excusing himself, how he, the intellectual superior of all men, had been tricked by a common swindler. One of his financial acquaintances had evidently guessed that the boy's interest in speculation had ulterior sources, in fact that some adult with money to invest was using him as a spy. This individual proceeded to treat John extremely well, and to 'prattle to him about his ventures,' anxiously pledging him to secrecy. In this way *Homo superior* was completely diddled by *Homo sapiens*. John insisted that I should put large sums of money into concerns which his friend had advocated. At first I refused; but John was blandly confident in his alleged 'inside information that it's an absolute scoop,' and finally I consented. I need not recount the history of these disastrous speculations. Suffice it that we lost everything that we had risked, and that John's friend disappeared.

For some time after this disaster we refrained from speculation. John spent a good deal of his time away from home and away from his workshop also. When I asked what he had been up to, he usually said, 'studying finance', but refused any further information. During this period his health began to deteriorate. His digestion, always his weakest spot, gave him some trouble, and he complained of headaches. Evidently he was leading a rather unwholesome life.

He began to spend many of his nights away from home. His father had relatives in London, and increasingly often John was allowed to visit them. But the relatives did not for long tolerate his independence. (He disappeared every morning and returned late at night or not till the next day, and refused to give an account of his actions.) Consequently these visits had to cease. But John, meanwhile, had learnt that, in summer, he could live the life of a stray cat in the Metropolis, in spite of the police. To his parents he said that he knew 'a man who had a flat who would let him sleep there any night'. Actually, as I learned much later, he used to sleep in parks and under bridges.

I learned also how he had occupied himself. By a series of tricks of the 'gate-crashing' type he had managed to make contacts with several big financiers in London, and had set about captivating and amusing them, and unobtrusively picking their brains, before they sent him by car with a covering note to his indignant relatives, or paid his railway fare home to the North, and sent the letter by post.

Here is a specimen, one of many such documents which caused much perturbation to Doc and Pax.

DEAR SIR,

Your small son's bicycle tour came to an untimely end yesterday evening owing to a collision with my car near Guildford. He fully admits that the fault was his own. He is unhurt, but the bicycle is past repair. As it was late, I took him to my home for the night. I congratulate you on having a very remarkable boy whose precocious passion for finance was extremely entertaining to my party. My chauffeur will put him on the 10.26 at Euston this morning. I am telegraphing you to that effect.

Yours faithfully,
(Signed by a personage whose name
I had better not divulge.)

John's parents, and I also, knew that he was on a bicycling tour, but we supposed him to have gone into North Wales. The fact that he had been so soon encountered in Surrey proved that he must have taken his bicycle by train. Needless to say, John did not turn up by the 10.26 from Euston. He gave the chauffeur the slip, poor man, by jumping out of the car in a traffic jam. That night he spent as the guest of another financier. If I remember rightly, he arrived in the late afternoon at the front door with a story that he and his mother were staying somewhere near, and that he had lost his way and forgotten the address. As police inquiries failed to discover his mother in the neighbourhood, he was kept for the night, and then for the following night, in fact for the Saturday and Sunday. I have no doubt that he made good use of the time. On Monday morning, when the great man had gone to business, he disappeared.

After some months spent partly on such adventures, partly on close study of the literature of finance and political economy and social changes, John felt himself ready to take action once more. He knew that I was likely to be sceptical of his plans, so he operated with money standing in his own name, and told me nothing until, six months later, he was able to show me the results in the shape of a considerable sum standing to his credit.

As time passed it became clear that he had mastered financial speculation as effectively as he had mastered mathematics. I have no knowledge of the principles on which he went to work, for henceforth I played no part in his business deals, save occasionally as his agent when a personal interview was to be undertaken. I remember his saying once when we were reviewing our position, 'After all there's not much in this speculation game, once you know your facts and get the hang of the way money trickles about the world. Of course there's a frightful lot of mere flukiness about it. You can never be *quite* sure which way the cat will jump. But if you know your cat well (*Hom. sap.* I mean), and if you know the ground well, you can't go far wrong in the long run.'

By the use of his new technique John gradually, throughout the earlier part of his adolescence, amassed a very imposing fortune, much of which was legally owned by me. It may seem strange that he never told his parents about his wealth until the time came for him to use it on a lavish scale. 'I don't want to upset their lives sooner than I need,' he said, 'and I don't want to give them the worry of trying not to blab.' On the other hand he allowed them to know that *I* had come in for a lot of money (supposed to be entirely due to luck on the Stock Exchange), and he was glad that I should help his parents in a number of ways, such as paying for the education of his brother and sister, and taking them all (John included) on foreign holidays. The parental gratitude, I may say, was extremely embarrassing. John made it more so by joining unctuously in the chorus, and dubbing me 'The Benefactor', which title he soon shortened aggravatingly to 'The Benny', and subsequently to 'The Bean'.

VIII
Scandalous Adolescence

Although during a large part of his fourteenth year finance constituted John's main occupation, his attention was never wholly absorbed by it; and after his period of intensive study and speculation he was able to continue the business of gaining monetary power while giving the best of his energies to very different matters. He was increasingly intrigued by the new experiences consequent on adolescence. At the same time he was very seriously engaged on the study of the potentialities and limitations of *Homo sapiens* as manifested in contemporary world-problems. And as his opinion of the normal species became more and more unflattering, he began to turn his attention to the search for other individuals of his own calibre. Though all these activities were pursued together, it will be convenient to deal with them separately.

The onset of John's adolescence was very late compared with that of the normal human being, and its duration was extremely prolonged. At fourteen he was physically comparable with a normal child of ten. When he died, at twenty-three, he was still in appearance a lad of seventeen. Yet, though physically he was always far behind his years, mentally, and not merely in intelligence but also in temperament and sensibility, he often seemed to be incredibly advanced beyond his actual age. This mental precocity, I should say, was entirely due to imaginative power. Where as the normal child clings to the old interests and attitudes long after more developed capacities have actually begun to awaken in him, John seemed to seize upon every budding novelty in his own nature and 'force' it into early bloom by the sheer intensity and heat of his imagination.

This was obvious, for instance, in the case of his sexual experience. It should be said that his parents were for their time exceptional in their attitude to sex in their children. All three grew up unusually free from the common shames and obsessions.

Doc took a frankly physiological view of sexual development; and Pax treated the sexual curiosity and experimentation of her children in a perfectly open and humorous way.

Thus John may be said to have had an exceptionally good start. But the use which he made of it was very different from that which satisfied his brother and sister. They were exceptional only in being permitted to develop naturally, and in thus escaping the normal distortions. They did all that most children were solemnly forbidden to do, and they were not condemned. I have no doubt that they practised whatever 'vices' they happened to think of, and then passed light-heartedly to other interests. In the home circle they would prattle about sex and conception in a shameless manner; but not in public, 'because people don't understand yet that it doesn't matter'. Later they obviously had romantic attachments. And later still they both married, and are seemingly well content.

The case of John was strikingly different. Like them, he passed in infancy through a phase of intense interest in his own body. Like them he found peculiar gratification in certain parts of his body. But whereas with them sexual interest began long before consciousness of personality had become at all precise, with John self-consciousness and other-consciousness were already vivid and detailed long before the onset of adolescence. Consequently, when that great change first began to affect him, and his imagination seized upon its earliest mental symptoms, he plunged headlong into kinds of behaviour that might have been deemed far beyond his years.

For instance, when John was ten, but physiologically much younger, he went through a phase of sexual interest more or less equivalent to the infantile sexuality of the normal type, but enlivened by his precocious intelligence and imagination. For some weeks he amused himself and outraged the neighbours by decorating walls and gate-posts with 'naughty' drawings in which particular adults whom he disliked were caricatured in the act of committing various 'wicked' practices. He also enticed his friends into his evil ways, and caused such a storm among the local parents that his father had to intervene. This phase, I take it, was due largely to a sense of impotence and consequent inferiority. He was trying to be sexually mature before his body was ready. After a week or two he apparently worked through this interest, as he had worked through the interest in personal combat.

But as the months advanced into years, he obviously felt an increasing delight in his own body, and this came in time to change his whole attitude to life. At fourteen he was generally taken for a strange child of ten, though it was not unusual for an observer sensitive to facial expression to suppose him some kind of 'genius' of eighteen with arrested physique. His general proportions were those of a ten-year-old; but over a childlike skeleton he bore a lean and knotted musculature about which his father used to say that it was not quite human, and that there ought to be a long prehensile tail to complete the picture. How far this muscular development was due to nature, and how far to his deliberate physical culture, I do not know.

His face was already changing from the infantile to the boyish in underlying structure; but the ceaseless expressive movements of mouth and nostrils and brows were already stamping it with an adult, alien, and almost inhuman character. Thinking of him at this period, I recall a creature which appeared as urchin but also as sage, as imp but also as infant deity. In summer his usual dress was a coloured shirt, shorts and sandshoes, all of them fairly grubby. His large head and close platinum wool, and his immense green-rimmed, falcon eyes, gave one a sense that these commonplace clothes had been assumed as a disguise.

Such was his general appearance when he began to discover a vast attractiveness in his own person, and a startling power of seducing others to delight in him no less luxuriously than he did himself. His will to conquest was probably much exaggerated by the knowledge that from the point of view of the normal species there was something grotesque and repellent about him. His narcissism was also, I imagine, aggravated and prolonged by the fact that, from his own point of view, there was no other to meet him on an equal footing, none fit for him to regard with that blend of selfishness and devotion which is romantic love.

I must make it clear that in reporting John's behaviour at this time I do not seek to defend it. Much of it seems to me outrageous. Had it been perpetrated by anyone other than John, I should have unhesitatingly condemned it as the expression of a self-centred and shockingly perverted mind. But in spite of the most reprehensible incidents in his career, I am convinced that John was far superior to the rest of us in moral sensibility, as in intelligence. Therefore, even in respect of the seemingly disgraceful conduct which I have now to describe, I feel that the right course is not to condemn but to suspend judgement and try to understand. I tell myself that, if John was indeed a superior being, much of his conduct would certainly outrage us, simply because we, with our grosser sensibility, would never be able to apprehend its true nature. In fact, had his behaviour been simply an idealization of normal human behaviour, I should have been *less* disposed to regard him as of an essentially different and superior type. On the other hand it should be remembered that, though superior in capacity, he was also juvenile, and may well have suffered in his own way from the inexperience and crudity of the juvenile mind. Finally, his circumstances were such as to warp him, for he found himself alone in a world of beings whom he regarded as only half human.

It was in his fourteenth year that John's new consciousness of himself first appeared, and shortly after his fourteenth birthday that it expressed itself in what I can only call an orgy of ruthless vamping. I myself was one of the few persons within his circle at whom he never 'set his cap', and I was exempt only because he could not regard me as fair game. I was his slave, his hound, toward whom he felt a certain responsibility. One other who escaped was Judy; for there again he felt no need to enforce his attractiveness, and there again he felt responsibility and affection.

So far as I know, his first serious affair was with the unfortunate Stephen, now a consciously grown-up young man who went to business every day. Stephen had a girl friend whom he took out on Saturdays on his motor-bike. One Saturday, when John and I were returning from a business trip in my car (we had visited a rubber factory), we stopped for tea at a popular road-side café. We found Stephen and his girl inside, almost ready to leave. John persuaded them to 'stay and talk to us for a bit'. The girl was obviously reluctant, having perhaps already had reason to dislike John's behaviour toward her man; but Stephen delayed departure. Then began a most distressing scene. John behaved toward Stephen in a manner calculated to eclipse the young woman at his side. He prattled. He sparkled with just the right standard of wit to fascinate Stephen and pass over the head of his simple companion. He kept the whole conversation well beyond her powers, occasionally appealing to her in a manner likely to trap her into making herself ridiculous. He faced Stephen now with the shy hauteur of a deer, now with seductiveness. He found excuses to move about the room and display his curiously feline, though also coltish, grace. Stephen was obviously captivated against his will, and, I feel sure, not for the first time. Toward the girl his gallantry grew laboured and false. She, poor out-classed little creature, could not conceal her distress, but Stephen never noticed it, for he was hypnotized. At last she looked at her watch and tremulously snapped, 'It's frightfully late. Please take me home.' But even as they were leaving the room John enticed Stephen back for a final sally.

When the couple had gone I told John very emphatically what I thought of his behaviour. He looked at me with the offensive complacency of a cat, then drawled, '*Homo sapiens!*' Whether he was referring to me or to Stephen was not clear. But presently he said, 'Tickle him the right way, and you've got him.'

A week later people were talking about the change in Stephen. They said 'he ought to be ashamed to carry on that way with the boy', and that John would be ruined. When I saw the two of them together, I felt that Stephen was struggling heroically against an obsession. He shunned all physical contact with John, but when contact came, either by accident or through John's contrivance, he was electrified, and could not help prolonging it under a pretence of ragging. John himself appeared to be suffering from a conflict of luxury and disgust. It was clear that he was gratified by his conquest, but at the same time he was repelled. Often he would terminate an amatory brawl with harshness, venting his repulsion by some unexpected piece of brutality, pushing his thumb fiercely into Stephen's eye, or tearing at his ear. As on an earlier occasion, my disgust and indignation at this kind of behaviour seemed to lead John to self-criticism. He was not above learning from his inferiors. His attitude to Stephen changed back to 'man to man' comradeship, tempered by an almost humble gentleness. Stephen, too, slowly woke from his infatuation, but he woke with lasting scars.

For some weeks John refrained, so far as I know, from activities of this kind. But his behaviour toward his elders had become definitely more self-conscious and more body-conscious. He was evidently discovering in his own person an interest which had hitherto escaped him. He studied the art of displaying the bizarre attractiveness of his young body to the best advantage in the eyes of the inferior species. Of course he was far too intelligent to indulge in those excesses of adornment which so often render the adolescent ludicrous. Indeed, I doubt whether any but the most intimate and persevering observer would have guessed that the artistry of his behaviour was at all conscious. That it actually was so I inferred from the fact that it varied according to the standards of his audience, now expressing the crudest sort of self-delight and shameless seductiveness, now attaining to that unadorned and steely grace which was to characterize the later John.

During the eighteen months before he reached the age of sixteen John indulged in occasional and abortive love-affairs with older boys and young men. He was still sexually undeveloped, but imagination forestalled his physique, and made him capable of amatory sensitiveness beyond his years. Throughout this phase, however, he seemed indifferent to the fact that most girls showed some degree of physical repulsion in his presence.

But when he was sixteen, and in appearance a queer sort of twelve-year old, he turned his attention to women. For some weeks the girls with whom he came in contact had shown a more positive, often a positively vindictive, attitude to him. This suggests at least that they were being forced to take note of him with new eyes, and that he had already begun to study a new technique of behaviour, directed toward the opposite sex.

Having perfected his technique, he proceeded to use it with cold deliberation upon one of the acknowledged stars of local society. This haughty young woman, who bore the surprising name of Europa, was the daughter of a wealthy shipowner. She was fair, large, athletic. Her normal expression was a rather contemptuous pout, tempered by a certain cow-like wistfulness about the eyes. She had been engaged twice, but rumour affirmed that her experience of the opposite sex had been far more intimate than was justified by mere betrothal.

One afternoon down at the bathing place accident (seemingly) brought John to the notice of Europa. She was lying in the sun, attended by her admirers. Unwitting, she had settled herself close to John's towel. Her elbow was on the corner of it. John, needing to dry himself after a swim, approached her from behind, mildly tugged at the towel and murmured, 'Excuse me.' She turned, found a grotesque young face close to her own, gave a start of repulsion, hastily released the towel, and recovered her composure by remarking to her audience, 'Heavens! What an imp!' John must have heard.

Later, when Europa executed one of her admirable dives from the top board, John evidently managed to get entangled with her under water, for they came up together in close contact. John laughed, and broke away. Europa was left gasping for a moment, then she, too, laughed, and returned to the diving platform. John, looking like a gargoyle, was already squatting on one of the boards. As she stretched her arms for the dive, she remarked with kindly contempt, 'You won't catch me this time, little monkey.' John dropped like a stone, and entered the water half a second behind her. After a considerable time they appeared together again. Europa was seen to smack his face, break from his clinging arm, and make for shore. There, she sunned and preened herself.

John now disported himself in her view, diving and swimming. He had invented a stroke of his own, very different from the 'trudgeon' which was still at this time almost unchallenged in the remote northern provinces. Lying on his stomach in the water and flicking his feet alternately, while his arms behaved in the ordinary 'trudgeon' manner, he was able to out-strip many experts older than himself. Some said that if he would only learn a decent stroke he would develop into a really fine swimmer. No one in the little provincial suburb realized that John's eccentric stroke, or something very like it, a product of Polynesia, was even then ousting the 'trudgeon' from the more advanced swimming circles of Europe and America, and even England.

With this eccentric stroke John displayed his prowess before the reluctantly attentive eyes of Europa. Presently he came out of the water and played ball with his companions, running, leaping, twisting, with that queer grace which few could detect, but by which those few were strangely enthralled. Europa, talking to her swains, watched and was evidently intrigued.

In the course of the game John threw the ball, seemingly by accident, so that it knocked her cigarette from her hand. He leapt to her, sank on one knee, took the outraged fingers and kissed them, with mock gallantry and a suggestion of real tenderness. Everyone laughed. Still holding Europa's hand, he brought his great eyes to bear upon her face, inquiringly. The proud Europa laughed, unaccountably blushed, withdrew her hand.

This was the beginning. There is no need to follow the stages by which the urchin captured the princess. It is enough to dwell for a moment on their relations when the affair was at its height. Little knowing what was in store for her, Europa encouraged the juvenile philanderer, not only at the swimming pool, where they gambolled together, but also by taking him out in her car. John, I should say, was much too wise, and much too occupied with other matters, to make his society cheap. Their meetings were not very frequent; but they were frequent enough to secure his prey.

The metaphor is perhaps unjust. I do not pretend to be able to analyse John's motives adequately, even the comparatively simple motives of his adolescence. Though I feel fairly sure that the origin of his attack upon Europa was his new craving to be admired by a woman in her prime, I can well believe that, as the relationship developed, he came to regard her in a much more complex manner. He sometimes watched her with an expression in which aloofness struggled not only with contempt but with genuine admiration. His delight in her caresses was doubtless in part due to dawning sexual appreciation. But though he could imaginatively judge her and enjoy her from the point of view of the male of her species, he was, I think, always conscious of her biological and spiritual inferiority to himself. The delight of conquest and the luxury of physical contact with a full-blooded and responsive woman were always for him poisoned by the sense that this contact was with a brute, with something which could never satisfy his deeper needs, and might debase him.

On Europa the relationship had striking effects. The swains found themselves spurned. Bitter taunts were flung. It was said that she had 'fallen for a kid, and a freak kid, too'. She herself was obviously torn between the need to preserve her dignity and the half-sexual, half-maternal hunger which John had inspired. Horror at her plight and revulsion from the strangeness of the thing that had enthralled her made matters worse. She once said something to me which revealed the nerve of her feeling for John. It was at a tennis party. She and I were alone for a few minutes. Examining her racquet, she suddenly asked, 'Do *you* blame me, about John?' While I was trying to reply, she added, 'I expect *you* know what a power he has. He's like – a god pretending to be a monkey. When you've been noticed by him, you can't bother about ordinary people.'

The climax of this strange affair must have happened very shortly after that incident. I heard the story from John himself several years later. He had laughingly threatened to invade Europa's bedroom one night by way of the window. It seemed to her an impossible feat, and she dared him to do it. In the small hours of the following morning she woke to a soft touch on her neck. She was being kissed. Before she had time to scream a well-known boyish voice made known that the invader was John. What with astonishment, amusement, defiance and sexual-maternal craving, Europa seems to have made but a half-hearted resistance to the boy's advances. I can imagine that in the grip of his still childish arms she found an intoxicating blend of the innocent and the virile. After some protest and sweet struggle she threw prudence to the winds and responded with passion. But when she began to cling to him, revulsion and horror invaded him. The spell was broken.

The caressing fingers, which at first had seemed to open up for him a new world of mutual intimacy, affection, trust, in relation with a spirit of his own stature, became increasingly sub-human, 'as though a dog were smelling round me, or a monkey'. The impression became so strong that he finally sprang from the bed and disappeared through the window, leaving his shirt and shorts behind him. So hasty was his retreat that he actually bungled the descent in a most un-John-like manner, fell heavily into a flower-bed, and limped home in the darkness with a sprained ankle.

For some weeks John was painfully torn between attraction and repulsion, but never again did he climb into Europa's window. She, for her part, was evidently horrified at her own behaviour, for she deliberately avoided her boy-lover, and when she encountered him in public she acted the part of the remote though kindly adult. Presently, however, she realized that John's attitude to her had changed, that his ardour had apparently cooled and given place to a gentle and disconcerting protective-ness.

When John took me into his confidence about his relations with Europa, he said, if I remember rightly, something like this. 'That one night gave me my first real shaking. Before, I had been sure of myself; suddenly I found myself swept this way and that by currents that I could neither stem nor understand. I had done something that night which I knew deeply I was *meant* to do, but it was somehow all *wrong*. Time after time, during the next few weeks, I went to Europa intending to make love to her, but when I found her I just didn't. Before I reached her I'd be all full of the recollection of that night, and her vital responsiveness, and her so-called beauty; but when I saw her – well, I felt as Titania felt when she woke to see that Bottom was an ass. Dear Europa

65

seemed just a nice old donkey, a fine one of course, but rather ridiculous and pitiable because of her soullessness. I felt no resentment against her, just kindness and responsibility. Once, for the sake of experiment, I started being amorous, and she, poor thing, rejoiced like an encouraged dog. But it wouldn't do. Something fierce in me rose up and stopped me, and filled me with an alarming desire to get my knife into her breasts and smash up her face. Then something else woke in me that looked down on the whole matter from a great height and felt a sort of passion of contemptuous affection for us both; but gave me a mighty scolding.'

At this point, I remember, there was a long silence. At last John told me something which it is better not to report. I did, indeed, write a careful account of this most disturbing incident in his career; and I confess that at the time I was so deeply under the spell of his personality that I could not feel his behaviour to have been vile. I recognized, of course, that it was flagrantly unconventional. But I had so deep an affection and respect for both the persons concerned that I gladly saw the affair as John wished me to see it. Years later, when I innocently showed my manuscript to others of my species, they pointed out that to publish such matter would be to shock many sensitive readers, and to incur the charge of sheer licentiousness.

I am a respectable member of the English middle class, and wish to remain so. All I will say, then, is that the *motive* of the behaviour which John confessed seems to have been double. First, he needed soothing after the disastrous incident with Europa, and, therefore, he sought delicate and intimate contact with a being whose sensibility and insight were not wholly incomparable with his own; with a being, moreover, who was beloved, who also loved him deeply, and would gladly go to any lengths for his sake. Second, he needed to assert his moral independence of *Homo sapiens*, to free himself of all deep unconscious acquiescence in the conventions of the species that had nurtured him. He needed, therefore, to break what was one of the most cherished of all the taboos of that species.

IX
Methods of a Young Anthropologist

John had been engaged in studying his world ever since he was born; but from fourteen to seventeen this study became much more earnest and methodical than it had been, and took the form of a far-reaching examination of the normal species in respect of its nature, achievement and present plight.

This vast enterprise had to be carried on in secret. John was determined not to attract attention to himself. He had to behave as a naturalist who studies the habits of some dangerous brute by stalking it with field-glass and camera, and by actually insinuating himself among the herd under a stolen skin, and an assumed odour.

Unfortunately, I cannot give at all a full account of this phase of John's career, for I played but a minor part in it. His disguise was always the precocious but naïve 'schoolboy' character which had served him so well in making contact with financiers; and his approach was very often a development of the 'gate-crashing' tactics which he had used in the same connection. This technique was combined with his diabolically skilled vamping. Always his methods were nicely adjusted to the mentality of the particular quarry. I will mention only a few examples, to give the reader some idea of the procedure, and then I will pass on to record some of the ruthless judgements which his researches enabled him to make.

He effected contact with a Cabinet minister by being taken ill outside the great man's private residence at the moment when the minister's wife was entering the house. It will be remembered that John had remarkable control over his organic reflexes, and could influence his glandular secretions, his temperature, his digestive processes, the rate of his heart-beat, the distribution of blood in his body, and so on. By careful manipulation of these controls he was able to produce a disorder the symptoms of which were sufficiently alarming though its after-effects were not serious. A pale pathetic wreck, he was laid on a couch and mothered by the minister's wife while the minister himself phoned for the family doctor. Before the physician arrived, John was already an intriguing little convalescent, and was busy attaching the minister to himself with subtle bonds of compassion and interest. The medical pundit did his best to conceal his bewilderment, and recommended that the boy should rest where he was till his parents were found. But John wailed that his parents were away for the day, and the house would be shut till the evening. Might he stay until their return, and then go home in a taxi? By the time he left the house he had already gained some insight into the mind of his host, and had secured an invitation to come again.

The artificial illness had proved so successful that it became one of his favourite methods. He used it, for instance, to make contact with a Communist leader, supplementing it with an account of his shocking home conditions since his father 'got the sack for organizing a strike'. Variants of the same method of artificial illness, with appropriate religious trimmings, were used also upon a bishop, a Catholic priest, and several other clerical gentlemen. It also proved effective with a woman MP.

As an example of a different approach I may mention that John bagged an eminent astronomer-physicist by writing him a schoolboyish letter of the naïve-brilliant kind, begging to be shown over an observatory. The request was granted, and John turned up at the appointed *rendezvous* equipped with schoolcap and a pocket telescope. This meeting led to other connections among physicists, biologists, physiologists.

The epistolary method was also used upon a well-known Cambridge philosopher and social writer. This time the handwriting was disguised; and, when finally John called on his man, he turned up with dyed hair, dark glasses and a Cockney accent. He intended to assume a very different character from that which had served with the astronomer; and he was anxious to avoid all possibility that the philosopher might identify him as the lad whom the astronomer had encountered.

The letter by which he effected this contact was nicely adapted to its purpose. It combined crude handwriting, bad spelling, dislike of religion, scraps of striking though crude philosophical analysis, and enthusiasm for the philosopher's books. I quote a characteristic passage:

My father beet me for saying if god made the world he made a mess. I said you said it was silly to beet children, so he beet me again for knowing you said it. I said being abel to beet a fellow didn't proove he was wrong. He said I was evil to answer back on my father. I said wots good and evil anyhow but just wot I like and dont like. He said it was blastphemy. *Please* let me call and ask you some questiuns about how a mind works and wot it is.

John had already made several visits to the philosopher's rooms in Cambridge, when he received a note from the astronomer. I should have explained that a young schoolmaster in a London suburb was allowing John to use his flat as a postal address. The astronomer asked John to come and meet 'another very wide-awake boy', who lived in Cambridge and was a friend of the philosopher. The ingenuity and relish which John displayed in defeating the repeated efforts of both men to bring about this meeting afforded me an amusing sidelight on his character, but I have not space to describe it.

The epistolary approach was used with equal effect upon a well-known modern poet. In this case the style of the letter and the *persona* which John assumed in the subsequent interviews were very different from those which had served for the astronomer and the philosopher. They were adjusted, moreover, not precisely to the conscious mentality of the poet as he was then known to the public and to himself, but to a mood or attitude in him which was *subsequently* to dominate his work. I quote the most striking passage from John's letter:

In all my hideous frustration of spirit, at home, at school, and in my confused attempts to come to terms with the modern world, the greatest comfort and source of strength is your poetry. How is it, I wonder, that, although you seem simply to describe a tortured and degenerate civilization, the very describing lends it dignity and significance, as though revealing it to be, after all, not *mere* frustration, but the necessary darkness before some glorious enlightenment.

John's efforts were not directed solely upon the intelligentsia and the leaders of political and social movements. Using appropriate methods, he made friends with engineers, artisans, clerks, dock-labourers. He acquired first-hand information about the mental differences between South Wales and Durham coal-miners. He was smuggled into Trade Union meetings. He had his soul saved in Baptist chapels. He received messages from a mythical dead sister in spiritualists' *séances*. He spent some weeks attached to a gipsy caravan, touring the southern counties. This post he apparently gained by showing his proficiency at petty theft and at repairing pots and pans.

One activity he repeated again and again, spending on it a length of time which seemed to me disproportionate to its significance. He became very friendly with the owner of a fishing smack near home, and would often spend days or nights with this man and his mate on the estuary or the open sea. When I asked John why he gave so much attention to the fishing community and these two men in particular, he said, 'Well, they're damned fine stuff, these fishermen, and Abe and Mark are two of the best. You see, when *Homo sapiens* is up against the sort of job and the sort of life that's not really beyond him, he's all right. It's only when civilization gives him a job that's too much for his intelligence or too much for his imagination that he fails. And then the failure poisons him through and through.' It was not till long afterwards that I realized his ulterior purpose in giving so much attention to the sea. At one time he became very friendly with the skipper of a coasting schooner, and made several voyages with him up and down the narrow seas. I ought to have realized that one motive of these adventures was the desire to learn how to handle a ship.

One other matter should be mentioned here. John's study of *Homo sapiens* now extended to the European Continent. In my capacity of family benefactor I was charged with the task of persuading Doc and Pax to join me on excursions to France, Germany, Italy, Scandinavia. John always accompanied us, with or without his brother and sister. Since Doc could not leave his practice frequently or for long at a time, these occasional family holidays had to be supplemented by trips in which the parents did not participate. I would announce that I had to 'run over to Paris to a journalists' conference,' or to Berlin to see a newspaper proprietor, or to Prague to report on a conference of philosophers, or to Moscow to see what they were doing about education. Then I would ask the parents to let me take John. Consent was certain, and our plans were often laid in detail before it was given. In this way John was enabled to carry on abroad the researches that he was already pursuing in the British Isles.

Foreign travel in John's company was apt to be a humiliating experience. Not only did he learn to speak a new language in an incredibly short time and in a manner indistinguishable from that of the native; he was also amazingly quick at learning foreign customs and intuiting foreign attitudes of mind. Consequently, even in countries with which I was familiar I found myself outclassed by my companion within a few days after his arrival.

When it was a case of learning a language entirely new to him, John simply read through a grammar and a dictionary, took concentrated courses of pronunciation from one or two natives or from gramophone records, and proceeded to the country. At this stage he would be regarded by natives as a native child who had been in foreign parts for some time and had lost touch somewhat with his own speech. At the end of a week or so, in the case of most European languages, no one would suspect that he had ever been out of the country. Later in his career, when his travels took him farther afield, he reckoned that even an Eastern language, such as Japanese, could be thoroughly mastered in a fortnight from his landing in the country.

Travelling with John on the European Continent I often asked myself why I allowed this strange being to hold me perpetually as his slave. I had much time for thought, for John was as often as not away hunting some writer or scientist or priest, some politician or popular agitator. Or else he was getting in touch with the workers by travelling in third or fourth class railway carriages, or talking to navvies. While he was thus engaged he often preferred to be without me. Every now and then, however, I was needed to act the part of guardian or travelling tutor. Sometimes, when John was particularly anxious to avoid giving any suggestion of his unique superiority, he would coach me carefully before the interview, priming me with questions to ask and observations to make.

On one occasion, for instance, he persuaded me to take him to an eminent psychiatrist. John himself played the part of a backward and neurotic child while I discussed his case with the professional man. This interview led to a course of treatment for John, and occasional meetings between the psychiatrist and myself to discuss progress. The poor man remained throughout ignorant that his small patient, seemingly so absorbed in his own crazy fantasies, was all the while experimenting on the physician, and that my own intelligent, though often provoking, questions had all originated in the mind of the patient himself.

Why did I let John use me thus? Why did I allow him to occupy so much of my time and attention, and to interfere so seriously with my career as a journalist? It could hardly be said that he was lovable. Of course, he was unique material for the journalist or the biographer, and I had already decided that some day I would tell the world all that I knew of him. But it is clear that even at this early stage the unfledged spirit of John exercised over me a fascination more subtle than that of novelty. I think I felt already that he was groping towards some kind of spiritual re-orientation which would put the whole of existence in a new light. And I hoped that I myself should catch some gleam of this illumination. Not till much later did I realize that his vision was essentially beyond the range of normal human minds.

For the present the only kind of illumination which came to John was apparently a devastating conviction of the futility of the normal species. To this discovery he reacted sometimes with mere contempt, sometimes with horror at the doom which awaited the human world, and with terror at his own entanglement in it. But on other occasions his mood was compassion, and on others again sardonic delight, and yet on others delight of a more serene kind in which compassion and horror and grim relish were strangely transmuted.

X
The World's Plight

I shall now try to give some idea of John's reactions to our world by setting down, more or less at random, some of his comments on individuals and types, institutions and movements, which he studied during this period.

Let us begin with the psychiatrist. John's verdict on this eminent manipulator of minds seemed to me to show both his contempt for *Homo sapiens* and his sympathetic appreciation of the difficulties of beings that are neither sheer animal nor fully human.

After our last visit to the consulting-room, indeed before the door was closed behind us, John indulged in a long chuckling laugh that reminded me of the cry of a startled grouse. 'Poor devil!' he cried. 'What else could he do anyhow? He's got to *seem* wise at all costs, even when he's absolutely blank. He's in the same fix as a successful medium. He's not just a quack. There's a lot of real sound stuff in his trade. No doubt when he's dealing with straightforward cases of a fairly low mental order, with troubles that are at bottom primitive, he fixes them up all right. But even then he doesn't really know *what* he's doing or *how* he gets his cures. Of course, he has his theories, and they're damned useful, too. He gives the wretched patient doses of twaddle, as a doctor might give bread pills, and the poor fool laps it all up and feels hopeful and manages to cure himself. But when another sort of case comes along, who is living habitually on a mental storey about six floors above our friend's own snug little flat, so to speak, there must be a glorious fiasco. How can a mind of his calibre possibly understand a mind that's at all aware of the really human things? I don't mean the highbrow things. I mean subtle human contacts, and world-contacts. He *is* a sort of highbrow, with his modern pictures and his books on the unconscious. But he's not human in the full sense, even according to the standards of *Homo sapiens*. He's not really grown up. And so, though he doesn't know it, the poor man is all at sea when he comes up against really grown-up people. For instance, in spite of his modern pictures, he hasn't a notion what art is after, though he thinks he has. And he knows less of philosophy, real philosophy, than an ostrich knows about the upper air. You can't blame him. His wings just wouldn't carry his big fleshy pedestrian mind. But that's no reason why he should make matters worse by burying his head in the sand and kidding himself he sees the foundations of human nature. When a really *winged* case comes along, with all sorts of troubles due to not giving his wings exercise, our friend hasn't the slightest perception what's the matter. He says in effect, "Wings? What's wings? Just flapdoodle. Look at mine. Get 'em atrophied as quick as possible, and bury your head in the sand to make sure." In fact he puts the patients into a sort of coma of the spirit. If it lasts, he's permanently "cured", poor man, and completely worthless. Often it *does* last, because your psychiatrist is an extremely good suggestionist. He could turn a saint into a satyr by mere sleight of mind. God! Think of a civilization that hands over the cure of souls to toughs like that! Of course, you can't blame him. He's a decent sort on his own plane, and doing his bit. But it's no use expecting a vet to mend a fallen angel.'

If John was critical of psychiatry, he was no less so of the churches. It was not only with the purpose of studying *Homo sapiens* that he had begun to take an interest in religious practices and doctrines. His motive was partly (so he told me) the hope that some light might be thrown upon certain new and perplexing experiences of his own which might perhaps be of the kind that the normal species called religious. He actually attended a few services at churches and chapels. He always returned from these expeditions in a state of excitement, which found outlet sometimes in ribald jests about the proceedings, sometimes in almost hysterical exasperation and perplexity. Coming out from an emotional chapel service of the Bethel type he remarked, 'Ninety-nine *per cent.* slush and one *per cent.* – something else, *but what?*' A tensity about his voice made me turn to look at him. To my amazement I saw tears in his eyes. Now John's lachrymatory reflexes were normally under absolute voluntary control. Since his infancy I had never known him weep except by deliberate policy. Yet these were apparently spontaneous tears, and he seemed unconscious of them. Suddenly he laughed and said, 'This soul-saving! If one were God, wouldn't one laugh at it, or squirm! What *does* it matter whether we're saved or not? Sheer blasphemy to want to be, *I* should say. But what is it that *does* matter, and comes through all the slush like light through a filthy window?'

On Armistice Day he persuaded me to go with him to a service in a Roman Catholic cathedral. The great building was crowded. Artificiality and insincerity were blotted out by the solemnity of the occasion. The ritual was somehow disturbing even to an agnostic like me. One felt a rather terrifying sense of the power which worship in the grand tradition could have upon massed and susceptible believers.

John had entered the cathedral in his normal mood of aloof interest in the passions of *Homo sapiens*. But as the service proceeded, he became less aloof and more absorbed. He ceased to look about him with his inscrutable hawklike stare. His attention, I felt, was no longer concentrated on individuals of the congregation, or on the choir, or on the priest, but on the totality of the situation. An expression strangely foreign to all that I knew of him now began to flicker on his face, an expression with which

I was to become very familiar in later years, but cannot to this day satisfactorily interpret. It suggested surprise, perplexity, a kind of incredulous rapture, and withal a slightly bitter amusement. I naturally assumed that John was relishing the folly and self-importance of our kind; but when we were leaving the cathedral he startled me by saying, 'How splendid it might be, if only they could keep from wanting their God to be human!' He must have seen that I was taken aback for he laughed and said, 'Oh, of course I see it's nearly all tripe. That priest! The way he bows to the altar is enough to show the sort he is. The whole thing is askew, intellectually and emotionally; but – well, don't *you* get the echo of something *not* wrong, of some experience that happened ages ago, and was right and glorious? I suppose it happened to Jesus and his friends. And something remotely like it was happening to about a fiftieth of that congregation. Couldn't you feel it happening? But, of course, as soon as they got it they spoilt it by trying to fit it all into the damned silly theories their Church gives them.'

I suggested to John that this excitement which he and others experienced was just the sense of a great crowd and a solemn occasion, and that we should not 'project' that excitement, and persuade ourselves we were in touch with something superhuman.

John looked quickly at me, then burst into hearty laughter. 'My dear man,' he said, and this I believe was almost the first time he used this devastating expression, 'even if *you* can't tell the difference between being excited by a crowd and the other thing, I can. And a good many of your own kind can, too, till they let the psychologists muddle them.'

I tried to persuade him to be more explicit, but he only said, 'I'm just a kid, and it's all new to me. Even Jesus couldn't really say what it was he saw. As a matter of fact, he didn't try to say much about *it*. He talked mostly about the way it could change people. When he *did* talk about it, itself, he nearly always said the wrong thing, or else they reported him all wrong. But how do I know? I'm only a kid.'

It was in a very different mood that John returned from an

interview with a dignitary of the Anglican Church, one who was at the time well known for his efforts to revitalize the Church by making its central doctrines live once more in men's hearts. John had been away for some days. When he returned he seemed much less interested in the Churchman than in an earlier encounter with a Communist. After listening to a disquisition on Marxism I said, 'But what about the Reverend Gentleman?' 'Oh, yes, of course, there was the Reverend Gentleman, too. A dear man, so sensible and understanding. I wish the Communist bloke could be a bit sensible, and a bit dear. But *Homo sapiens* evidently can't be that when he has any sort of fire in him. Funny how members of your species, when they do get any sort of real insight and grasp some essential truth, like Communism, nearly always go crazy with it. Funny, too, what a religious fellow that Communist really is. Of course, he doesn't know it, and he hates the word. Says men ought to care for Man and nothing else. A moral sort of cove, he is, full of "oughts". Denies morality, and then damns people for not being Communist saints. Says men are all fools or knaves or wasters unless you can get 'em to care for the Class War. Of course, he tells you the Class War is needed to emancipate the Workers. But what really *gets* him about it isn't that. The fire inside him, though he doesn't know it, is a passion for what he calls dialectical materialism, for the dialectic of history. The one selfishness in him is the longing to be an instrument of the Dialectic, and oddly enough what he really *means* by that, in his heart of hearts, is what Christians so quaintly describe as the law of God, or God's will. Strange! He says the sound element in Christianity was love of one's fellow men. But *he* doesn't really love them, not as actual persons. He'd slaughter the lot of them if he thought that was part of the Dialectic of History. What he really shares with Christians, real Christians, is a most obscure but teasing, firing awareness of something super-individual. Of course, he thinks it's just the mass of individuals, the group. But he's wrong. What's the group anyhow, but just everybody lumped together, and nearly all fools or limps or knaves? It's not simply the *group* that fires him. It's justice, righteousness, and the whole spiritual music that ought to be made by the group. Damned funny that! Of course, I know all Communists are not religious, some are merely – well, like that bloody little man the other day. But this fellow *is* religious. And so was Lenin, I guess. It's not enough to say his root motive was desire to avenge his brother. In a sense that's true. But one can feel behind nearly everything he said a sense of being the chosen instrument of Fate, of the Dialectic, of what might almost as well be called God.'

'And the Reverend Gentleman?' I queried. 'The Reverend Gentleman? Oh, him! Well, he's religious in about the same sense as firelight is sunshine. The coal-trees once lapped up the sun's full blaze, and now in the grate they give off a glow and a flicker that snugs up his room nicely, so long as the curtains are drawn and the night kept at arm's length. Outside, everyone is floundering about in the dark and the wet, and all he can do is to tell them to make a nice little fire and squat down in front of it. One or two he actually fetches into his own beautiful room, and they drip all over the carpet, and leave muddy marks, and spit into the fire. He gets very unhappy about it, but he puts up with it nobly because, though he hasn't a notion what *worship* is, he does up to a point try to love his neighbours. Funny, that, when you think of the Communist who doesn't. Of course, if people get really nasty, the Reverend would phone the police.'

Lest the reader should suppose that John was not critical of the Communists, I will quote some of his comments on that other Communist, referred to above. 'He knows in an obscure way that he's an utter waster, though he pretends to himself that he's noble and unfortunate. Of course he is unfortunate, frightfully unfortunate, in being the sort he is. And of course that's society's fault as much as his own. So the wretched creature has to spend his life putting out his tongue at society, or at the powers that be in society. He's just a hate-bag. But even his hate isn't really sincere. It's a posture of self-defence, self-justification, not like the hate that smashed the Tsar, and turned creative and made Russia. Things haven't got bad enough for that in England yet. At present all that can be done by blokes like this is to spout hate and give the other side a fine excuse for repressing

Communism. Of course, hosts of well-off people and would-be-well-off people are just as ashamed of themselves subconsciously as that blighter, and just as full of hate, and in need of a scapegoat to exercise their hate upon. He and his like are a godsend to them.'

I said there was more excuse for the have-nots to hate than for the haves. This remark brought from John a bit of analysis and prophecy that has since been largely justified.

'You talk,' he said, 'as if hate were rational, as if men only hated what they had reason to hate. If you want to understand modern Europe and the world, you have to keep in mind three things that are really quite distinct although they are all tangled up together. First there's this almost universal need to hate something, rationally or irrationally, to find something to unload your own sins on to, and then smash it. In perfectly healthy minds (even of your species) this need to hate plays a small part. But nearly all minds are damnably unhealthy, and so they must have something to hate. Mostly, they just hate their neighbours or their wives or husbands or parents or children. But they get a much more exalted sort of excitement by hating foreigners. A nation, after all, is just a society for hating foreigners, a sort of super-hate-club. The second thing to bear in mind is the obvious one of economic disorder. The people with economic power try to run the world for their own profit. Not long ago they succeeded, more or less, but now the job has got beyond them, and, as we all know, there's the hell of a mess. This gives hate a new outlet. The have-nots with very good reason exercise their hate upon the haves, who have made the mess and can't clean it up. The haves fear and therefore zestfully hate the have-nots. What people can't realize is that if there were no deep-rooted *need* to hate in almost every mind the social problem would be at least intelligently faced, perhaps solved. Then there's the third factor, namely, the growing sense that there's something all wrong with modern solely-scientific culture. I don't mean that people are intellectually doubtful about science. It's much deeper than that. They are simply finding that modern culture isn't enough to live by. It just doesn't work in practice. It has got a screw loose somewhere. Or some vital bit of it is dead. Now this horror against modern culture, against science and mechanization and standardization, is only just beginning to be a serious factor. It's newer than Bolshevism. The Bolshies, and all the socially left-wing people, are still content with modern culture. Or rather, they put all its faults down to capitalism, dear innocent theorists. But the essence of it they still accept. They're rationalistic, scientific, mechanistic, brass-tack-istic. But another crowd, scattered about all over the place, are having the hell of a deep revulsion against all this. They don't know what's the matter with it, but they're sure it's not enough. Some of them, feeling that lack, just creep back into church, specially the Roman Church. But too much water has passed under the bridge since the churches were alive, so that's no real use. The crowds who can't swallow the Christian dope are terribly in need of something, though they don't know what, or even know they're in need at all. And this deep need gets mixed up with their hate-need; and, if they're middle class, it gets mixed up also with their fear of social revolution. And this fear, along with their hate-need, may get played on by any crook with an axe to grind, or by any able man with an itch for bossing. That's what happened in Italy. That sort of thing will spread. I'd bet my boots that in a few years there'll be a tremendous anti-lift movement all over Europe, inspired partly by fear and hate, partly by that vague, fumbling suspicion that there's something all wrong with scientific culture. It's more than an intellectual suspicion. It's a certainty of the bowels, call it a sort of brute-blind religious hunger. Didn't you *feel* the beginnings of it in Germany last year when we were there? A deep, still-unconscious revulsion from mechanism, and from rationality, and from democracy, and from sanity. That's it, a confused craving to be mad, possessed in some way. Just the thing for the well-to-do haters to use for their own ends. *That's* what's going to get Europe. And its power depends on its being a hotch-potch of self-seeking, sheer hate, and this bewildered hunger of the soul, which is so worthy and so easily twisted into something bloody. If Christianity could hold it in and discipline it, it might do wonders. But Christianity's played out. So these folk will probably invent some ghastly religion of their own. Their God will be the God of the hate-club, the nation. That's what's coming. The new Messiahs (one for each tribe) won't triumph by love and gentleness, but by hate and ruthlessness. Just because *that's* what you all really *want*, at the bottom of your poor diseased bowels and crazy minds. Jesus Christ!'

I was not much impressed by this tirade. I said the best minds had outgrown that old tribal god, and the rest would follow the best minds in the long run. John's laughter disconcerted me.

'The best minds!' he said. 'One of the main troubles of your unhappy species is that the best minds can go even farther astray than the second best, much farther than the umpteenth best. That's what has been happening during the last few centuries. Swarms of the best minds have been leading the populace down blind alley after blind alley, and doing it with tremendous courage and resource. Your trouble, as a species, is that you can't keep hold of everything at once. Anyone who is very wide awake toward one set of facts invariably loses sight of all the other equally important sets. And as you have practically no inner experience to orientate you, compass-wise, to the cardinal points of reality, there's no telling how far astray you'll go, once you start in the wrong direction.'

Here I interjected, 'Surely that is one of the penalties of being gifted with intelligence; it may lead one forward, but it may lead one badly astray.'

John replied, 'It's one of the penalties of being more than beast and less than fully human. Pterodactyls had a great advantage over the old-fashioned creepy crawly lizards, but they had their special dangers. Because they could fly a bit, they could crash. Finally, they were outclassed by birds. Well, I'm a bird.'

He paused, and then said, 'Centuries ago all the best minds were in the Church. In those days there was nothing to compare with Christianity for practical significance and theoretical interest. And so the best minds swarmed upon it, and generation after generation of them used their bright intelligences on it. Little by little they smothered the actual living spirit of religion, with their busy theorizing. Not only so but they also used their religion, or rather their precious doctrines, to explain all physical events. Presently there came along a generation of best minds that found all this ratiocination very unconvincing, and began watching how things really did happen in physical nature. They and their successors made modern science, and gave man physical power, and changed the face of the earth. All this was as impressive in its own way as the effects of religion had been, real live religion, in a quite different way, centuries earlier. So now nearly all the best minds buzzed off to science, or to the job of working out a new scientific view of the universe and a new scientific way of feeling and acting. And being so impressed by science and by industry and the business attitude to life, they lost whatever trace of the old religion they ever had, and also they became even more blind to their own inner nature than they need have been. They were too busy with science, or industry, or empire-building, to bother about interior things. Of course, a few of the best minds, and some ordinary folk, had mistrusted fashionable thought all the way through. But after the war mistrust became widespread. The war made Nineteenth Century culture look pretty silly, didn't it? So what happened? Some of the best minds (the *best* minds, mind you) tumbled helter-skelter back to the Churches. Others, the most social ones, declared that we ought all to live to improve mankind, or to make the future generations happy. Others, feeling that mankind was really past hope, just struck a fine attitude of despair, based either on contempt and hate of their fellows or on a compassion which was at bottom self-pity. Others, the bright young things of literature and art, set out to enjoy themselves as best they might in a crashing world. They were out for pleasure at any price, pleasure not entirely un-refined. For instance, though they demanded unrestrained sex-ual pleasure, it was to be highly conscious and discriminating. They also demanded aesthetic pleasure of a rather self-indulgent sort, and the thoroughly self-indulgent pleasure of tasting ideas, just for their spiciness or tang, so to speak. Bright young things! Yes, blowflies of a decaying civilization. Poor wretches! How

82

they must hate themselves, really. But damn it, after all, they're mostly good stuff gone wrong.'

John had recently spent some weeks studying the intelligentsia. He had made his entry into Bloomsbury by acting the part of a precocious genius, and allowing a well-known writer to exhibit him as a curio. Evidently he flung himself into the life of these brilliant and disorientated young men and women with characteristic thoroughness, for when he returned he was something of a wreck. I need not retail his account of his experiences, but his analysis of the plight of the leaders of our thought is worth reporting.

'You see,' he said, 'they really are in a sense the leaders of thought, or leaders of fashion in thought. What they think and feel today, the rest think and feel next year or so. And some of them really are, according to the standards of *Hom. sap.*, first-class minds, or might have been, in different circumstances. (Of course, most are just riff-raff, but they don't count.) Well, the situation's really very simple, and very desperate. Here is the centre to which nearly all the best sensibility and best intellect of the country gets attracted in the expectation of meeting its kind and enriching its experience; but what happens? The poor little flies find themselves caught in a web, a subtle mesh of convention, so subtle in fact that most of them are unaware of it. They buzz and buzz and imagine they are free fliers, when as a matter of fact each one is stuck fast on his particular strand of the web. Of course, they have the reputation of being the most unconventional people of all. The centre imposes on them a convention of unconventionality, of daring thought and conduct. But they can only be "daring" within the limits of their convention. They have a sameness of intellectual and moral taste which makes them fundamentally all alike in spite of their quite blatant superficial differences. That wouldn't matter so much if their taste were really discriminate taste, but it's not, in most cases; and such innate powers of precision and delicacy as they actually have get dulled by the convention. If the convention were a sound one, all might be well, but it's not. It consists in trying to be "brilliant" and "original", and in craving "experience". Some of them *are* brilliant and original according to the standards of your species; and some of them *have* the gift for experience. But when they do achieve brilliance and experience, this is *in spite* of the web, and consists at best in a certain flutter and agitation, not in flight. The influence of the all-pervading convention turns brilliance into brightness, originality into perversity, and deadens the mind to all but the cruder sorts of experience. I don't mean merely crudity in sex-experience and personal relations, though indeed their quite sound will to break the old customs and avoid sentimentality at all costs *has* led them in the end to a jading and coarsening extravagance. What I mean is crudity of – well, of spirit. Though they are often very intelligent (for your species) they haven't got any of the finer aspects of experience to use their intelligence *on*. And that seems to be due partly to a complete lack of spiritual discipline, partly to an obscure, half-conscious funk. You see they're all very sensitive creatures, very susceptible to pleasure and pain; and early in their lives, whenever they bumped into anything like a fundamental experience, they found it terribly upsetting. And so they formed habits of avoiding that sort of thing. And they made up for this persistent avoidance by drenching themselves in all sorts of minor and superficial (though sensational) experiences; and also by talking big about Experience with a capital E, and buzzing intellectually.'

This analysis made me feel uncomfortable, for though I was not one of 'them' I could not disguise from myself that the same sort of condemnation might apply to me. John evidently saw my thoughts, for he grinned, and moreover indulged in an entirely vulgar wink. Then he said, 'Strikes home, old thing, doesn't it? Never mind, you're not *in* the web. You're an outsider. Fate has kept you safely fluttering in the backward North.'

Some weeks after this conversation John's mood seemed to change. Hitherto he had been light-hearted, sometimes even ribald, both in the actual pursuit of his investigation and in his comments. In his more serious phases he displayed the sympathetic though aloof interest of an anthropologist observing the customs of a primitive tribe. He had always been ready to talk about his experiences and to defend his judgements. But now he began to be much less communicative, and, when he did condescend to talk, much more terse and grim. Banter and friendly contemptuousness vanished. In their place he developed a devastating habit of coldly, wearily pulling to pieces whatever one said to him. Finally this reaction also vanished, and his only response to any remark of general interest was a steady gloomy stare. So might a lonely man gaze at his frisking dog when the need of human intercourse was beginning to fret him. Had anyone other than John treated one in that way, the act would have been offensive. Coming from John it was merely disturbing. It roused in me a painful self-consciousness, and an irresistible tendency to look away and busy myself with something.

Once only did John express himself freely. By appointment I had met him in his subterranean workshop to discuss a financial project which I proposed to undertake. He was lying in his little bunk, swinging one leg over the side. Both hands were behind his head. I embarked on my theme, but his attention was obviously elsewhere. 'Damn it, can't you listen?' I said. 'Are you inventing a gadget or what?' 'Not inventing,' he replied, 'discovering.' There was such solemnity in his voice that a wave of irrational panic seized me. 'Oh, for God's sake do be explicit. What's up with you these days? Can't you tell a fellow?' He transferred his gaze from the ceiling to my face. He stared. I started to fill my pipe.

'Yes, I'll tell you,' he said, 'if I can, or as much as I can; some time ago I asked myself a question, namely this. Is the plight of the world today a mere incident, an illness that might have been avoided and may be cured? Or is it something inherent in the very nature of your species? Well, I have got my answer. *Homo sapiens* is a spider trying to crawl out of a basin. The higher he crawls, the steeper the hill. Sooner or later, down he goes. So long as he's on the bottom, he can get along quite nicely, but as soon as he starts climbing, he begins to slip. And the higher he climbs the farther he falls. It doesn't matter which direction he tries. He can make civilization after civilization, but every time, long before he begins to be really civilized, skid!'

I protested against John's assurance. 'It *may* be so,' I said, 'but how can you possibly *know*? *Hom. sap.* is an inventive animal. Might not the spider some time or other contrive to make his feet sticky? Or – well, suppose he's not a spider at all but a beetle. Beetles have wings. They often forget how to use them, but – aren't there signs that *Hom. sap.*'s present climb is different from all the others? Mechanical power is a stickiness for his feet. And I believe his wing-cases are stirring, too.'

John regarded me in silence. Pulling himself together, he said, as if from a great distance, 'No wings. No wings.' Then, in a more normal voice, 'And as for mechanical power, if he knew how to use it, it might help him up a few steps farther, but he doesn't. You see, for every type of creature there's a limit of *possible* development of capacity, a limit inherent in the ground plan of its organization. *Homo sapiens* reached his limit a million years ago, but he has only recently begun to use his powers dangerously. In achieving science and mechanism he has brought about a state of affairs which cannot be dealt with properly save by capacity which is much more developed than his. Of course, he *may* not slip just yet. He *may* succeed in muddling through this particular crisis of history. But if he does, it will only be muddling through to stagnation, not to the soaring that even he in his own heart is desperately craving. Mechanical power, you see, is indeed vitally necessary to the full development of the human spirit; but to the sub-human spirit it is lethal.'

'But, how *can* you know that? Aren't you being a bit too confident in your own judgement?'

John's lips compressed themselves and assumed a crooked smile. 'You're right,' he said. 'There's just one possibility that I have not mentioned. If the species as a whole, or a large proportion of the world population, were to be divinely inspired, so that their nature became truly human at a stride, all would soon be well.'

I took this for irony, but he went on to say, 'Oh, no, I'm quite serious. It's possible; if you interpret "divinely inspired" to mean lifted out of their pettiness by a sudden and spontaneous access

86

of strength to their own rudimentary spiritual nature. It happens again and again in individuals here and there. When Christianity came, it happened to large numbers. But they were a very small proportion of the whole, and the thing petered out. Short of that kind of thing, or rather something much more widespread and much more powerful than the Christian miracle, there's no hope. The early Christians, you see, and the early Buddhists and so on, remained at bottom what I should call sub-human, in spite of their miracle. In intelligence they remained what they were before the miracle; and in will, though they were profoundly changed by the new thing in them, the change was insecure. Or rather the new thing seldom managed to integrate their whole being into a new and harmonious order. Its rule was precarious. The new psychological compound, so to speak, was a terribly unstable compound. Or, putting it in another way, they managed to become saints, but seldom angels. The sub-human and the human were always in violent conflict in them. And so they mostly got obsessed with the idea of sin, and saving their souls, instead of being able to pass on to live the new life with fluency and joy, and with creative effect in the world.'

At this point we fell silent. I relit my pipe, and John remarked, 'Match number nine, you funny old thing!' It was true. There lay the eight burnt matches, though I had no recollection of using them. John from his position on the bed could not see the ash-tray. He must have noticed the actual re-lightings. It was simply that he observed whatever happened however engrossed he might be. 'You funnier young thing!' I retorted.

Presently he began talking again. He kept his eye on me, but I felt that he was talking rather to himself than to me. 'At one time,' he said, 'I thought I should simply take charge of the world and help *Homo sapiens* to remake himself on a more human plan. But now I realize that only what men call "God" could do that. Unless perhaps a great invasion of superior beings from another planet, or another dimension, could do it. But I doubt if they would trouble to do it. They would probably merely use the Terrestrials as cattle or museum pieces or pets, or just vermin. All the same, if they wanted to make a better job of *Hom. sap.* I expect they could. But *I* can't do it. I believe, if I set my mind to it, I *could* fairly easily secure power and take charge of the normal species; and, once in charge, I could make a much more satisfactory world, and a much happier world; but always I should have to accept the ultimate limitations of capacity in the normal species. To make them try to live beyond their capacity would be like trying to civilize a pack of monkeys. There would be worse chaos than ever, and they would unite against me, and sooner or later destroy me. So I'd just have to accept the creature with all its limitations. And that would be to waste my best powers. I might as well spend my life chicken-farming.'

'You arrogant young cub!' I protested. 'I don't believe we are as bad as you think.'

'Oh, don't you! Of course not, you're one of the pack,' he said. 'Look here, now! I've spent some time and trouble poking about in Europe, and what do I find? In my simplicity I thought the fellows who had come to the top, the best minds, the leaders in every walk, would be something like real human beings, fundamentally sane, rational, efficient, self-detached, loyal to the best in them. Actually they are nothing of the sort. Mostly they're even below the average. Their position has underminded them. Think of old Z (naming a Cabinet minister). You'd be amazed if you could see him as I have seen him. He simply can't experience anything clearly and correctly, except things that bear on his petty little self-esteem. Everything has to penetrate to him through a sort of eider-down of pre-conceived notions, *clichés*, diplomatic phrases. He has no more idea of the real issues in politics today than a mayfly has of the fish in the stream it's fluttering on. He has, of course, the trick of using a lot of phrases that *might* mean very important things, but they don't mean them to *him*. They are just counters for him, to be used in the game of politics. He's simply not *alive*, to the real things. That's what's the matter with him. And take Y, the Press magnate. He's just a nimble-witted little guttersnipe who has found out how to hoax the world into giving him money and power. Talk to him about the real things, and he just hasn't a notion what you're driving at. But it's not only that sort that terrify me with their combination of power and inanity. Take the real leaders, take young X, whose revolutionary ideas are going to have a huge effect on social thought. He's got a brain, and he's using it on the right side, and he has nerve, too. But – well, I've seen enough of him to spot his *real* motive, hidden from himself, of course. He had a thin time long ago, and now he wants to get his own back, he wants to make the oppressor frightened of him. He wants to *use* the have-nots to break the haves, for his own satisfaction. Well, *let* him get his own back, and good luck to him. But fancy taking that as your life's goal, even unconsciously! It has made him do damned good work, but it has crippled him, too, poor devil. Or take that philosopher bloke, W, who did so much toward showing up the old school with their simple trust in words. He's really in much the same fix as X. I know him pretty well, the perky old bird. And knowing him I can see the mainspring of all that brilliant work quite clearly, namely, the idea of *himself* as bowing to no man and no god, as purged of prejudice and sentimentality, as faithful to reason yet not blindly trustful of it. All that is admirable. But it obsesses him, and actually warps his reasoning. You can't be a real philosopher if you have an obsession. On the other hand, take V. He knows all about electrons and all about galaxies, and he's first class at his job. Further, he has glimmers of spiritual experience. Well, what's the mechanism this time? He's a kind creature, very sympathetic. And he likes to think that the universe is all right from the human point of view. Hence all his explorations and speculations. Well, so long as he sticks to science he is sound enough. But his spiritual experience tells him science is all very superficial. Right, again; but his is not very deep spiritual experience, and it gets all mixed up with kindliness, and he tells us things about the universe that are sheer inventions of his kindliness.'

John paused. Then with a sigh he resumed. 'It's no good going on about it. The upshot is simple enough. *Homo sapiens* is at the end of his tether, and I'm not going to spend my life tinkering a doomed species.'

'You're mighty sure of yourself, aren't you?' I put in. 'Yes,' he said, 'perfectly sure of myself in some ways, and still utterly unsure in others, in ways I can't explain. But one thing is stark clear. If I were to take over *Hom. sap.* I should freeze up inside, and grow quite incapable of doing what is my *real* job. *That* job is what I'm not yet sure about, and can't possibly explain. But it begins with something very *interior to me*. Of course, it's not just saving my soul. I, as an individual, might damn myself without spoiling the world. Indeed, my damning myself *might* happen to be an added beauty to the world. I don't matter on my own account, but I have it in me to do something that does matter. This I *know*. And I'm pretty sure I have to begin with – well, interior discovery of objective reality, in preparation for objective creation. Can you make anything of that?'

'Not much,' I said, 'but go on.'

'No,' he said, 'I won't go on along that line, but I'll tell you something else. I've had the hell of a fright lately. And I'm not easily frightened. This was only the second time, ever. I went to the Cup Tie Final last week to see the crowd. You remember, it was a close fight (and a damned good game from beginning to end) and three minutes before time there was trouble over a foul. The ball went into goal before the referee's whistle had got going for the foul, and that goal would have won the match. Well, the crowd got all het up about it, as you probably heard. That's what frightened me. I don't mean I was scared of being hurt in a row. No, I should have quite enjoyed a bit of a row, if I'd known which side to be on, and there'd been something to fight about. But there wasn't. It clearly *was* a foul. Their precious, "sporting instinct" ought to have kept them straight, but it didn't. They just lost their heads, went brute-mad over it. What got me was the sudden sense of being different from everyone else, of being a human being alone in a vast herd of cattle. Here was a fair sample of the world's population, of the sixteen hundred millions of *Homo sapiens*. And this fair sample was expressing itself in a thoroughly characteristic way, an inarticulate bellowing and braying, and here was I, a raw, ignorant, blundering little creature, but human, *really* human, perhaps the only real human being in the world; and just because I was really human, and had in me the possibility of some new and transcendent spiritual achievement, I was more important than all the rest of the sixteen hundred million put together. That was a terrifying thought in itself. What made matters worse was the bellowing crowd. Not that I was afraid of *them*, but of the thing they were a sample of. Not that I was afraid as a private individual, so to speak. The thought was very exhilarating from that point of view. If they had turned on me I'd have made a damned good fight for it. What terrified me was the thought of the immense responsibility, and the immense odds against my fulfilling it.'

John fell silent; and I was so stunned by his prodigious self-importance that I had nothing to say. Presently he began again.

'Of course I know, Fido old thing, the whole business must seem fantastic to you. But, perhaps, by being a bit more precise on one point I may make the thing clearer. It's already pretty common knowledge of course that another world-war is likely, and that if it does come it may very well be the end of civiliza-tion. But I know something that makes the whole situation look much worse than it's generally thought to be. I don't really *know* what will happen to the species in the long run, but I do know that unless a miracle happens there is *bound* to be a most ghastly mess in the short run for psychological reasons. I have looked pretty carefully into lots of minds, big and little, and it's devastatingly clear to me that in big matters *Homo sapiens* is a species with very slight educable capacity. He has entirely failed to learn his lesson from the last war. He shows no more practical intelligence than a moth that has fluttered through a candle-flame once and will do so again as soon as it has recovered from the shock. And again and yet again, till its wings are burnt. Intellectually many people realize the danger. But they are not the sort to act on the awareness. It's as though the moth *knew* that the flame meant death, yet simply couldn't stop its wings from taking it there. Then what with this new crazy religion of nationalism that's beginning, and the steady improvement in the technique of destruction, a huge disaster is simply inevitable, barring a miracle, which of course *may* happen. There *might* be some sort of sudden leap forward to a more human mentality, and therefore a world-wide social and religious revolution. But apart from that possibility I should give the disease fifteen to twenty years to come to a head. Then one fine day a few great powers will attack one another, and – phut! Civilization will have gone in a few weeks. Now, of course, if I took charge I could probably stave off the smash. But, as I say, it would mean chucking the really *vital* thing I can do. Chicken-farming is not worth such a sacrifice. The upshot is, Fido, I'm through with your bloody awful species. I must strike out on my own, and, if possible, in such a way as to avoid being smashed in the coming disaster.'

XI
Strange Encounters

The grave decision about the plight of *Homo sapiens* seems to have occurred at a time when John's own development had ripened him for a far-reaching spiritual crisis. Some weeks after the incident which I have just described he seemed to retire within himself more than ever, and to shun companionship even with those who had counted themselves among his friends. His former lively interest in the strange creatures among whom he lived apparently evaporated. His conversation became perfunctory; save on rare occasions when be flared up into hostile arrogance. Sometimes he seemed to long for intimacy and yet be quite unable to attain it. He would persuade me to go off with him for a day on the hills or for an evening at the theatre, and after a brave effort to restore our accustomed relationship, he would fall miserably silent, scarcely listening to my attempts at conversation. Or he would dog his mother's footsteps for a while, and yet find nothing to say to her. She was thoroughly frightened about his state, and indeed feared that 'his brain was giving out,' so blankly miserable and speechless could he be. One night, so she told me, she heard sounds in his room and crept in to see what was the matter. He was 'sobbing like a child that can't wake from a bad dream'. She stroked his head and begged him to tell her all about it. Still sobbing, he said, 'Oh, Pax, I'm so *lonely*.'

When this distressful state of affairs had lasted many weeks, John disappeared from home. His parents were well used to absences of a few days, but this time they received a postcard, bearing a Scottish postmark, saying that he was going to have a holiday in the mountains, and would not be back 'for quite a long time'.

A month later, when we were beginning to feel anxious about him, an acquaintance of mine, Ted Brinston, who knew that John had disappeared, told me that a friend of his, McWhist, who was a rock-climber, had encountered 'a sort of wild boy in the mountains of northern Scotland'. He offered to put me in touch with McWhist.

After some delay Brinston asked me to dine with him to meet McWhist and his climbing companion, Norton. When the occasion arrived I was surprised and disconcerted to find that both men seemed reluctant to speak frankly about the incident that had brought us four together. Alcohol, however, or my anxiety about John, finally broke down their reluctance. They had been exploring the little-known crags of Ross and Cromarty, pitching their tent for a few days at a time beside a handy burn or loch. One hot day, as they were climbing a grassy spur of a mountain (which they refused to name) they heard a strange noise, apparently coming from the head of the glen to the right of them. They were so intrigued by its half-animal, half-human character that they went in search of its cause. Presently they came down to the stream and encountered a naked boy sitting beside a little waterfall and chanting or howling 'in a way that gave me the creeps,' said McWhist. The lad saw them and fled, disappearing among the birch-trees. They searched, but could not find him.

A few days later they told this story in a little public-house. A red-bearded native, who had not drunk too little, immediately retailed a number of yarns about encounters with such a lad – if it *was* a lad, and not some sort of kelpie. The good man's own sister-in-law's nephew said he had actually chased him and seen him turn into a wisp of mist. Another had come face to face with him round a rock, and the creature's eyes were as large as cannon balls, and black as hell.

Later in the week the climbers came upon the wild boy again. They had been climbing a rather difficult chimney, and had reached a point where further direct ascent seemed impossible. McWhist, who was leading, had just brought his second man up, and was preparing to traverse round a very exposed buttress in search of a feasible route. Suddenly a small hand appeared round the far side of the buttress, feeling for a hold. A moment later a lean brown shoulder edged its way round into view, followed by the strangest face that McWhist had ever seen. From his description I judged confidently that it was John. I was disturbed by the stress that McWhist laid on the leanness of the face. The cheeks seemed to have shrunk to pieces of leather, and there was a startling brightness about the eyes. No sooner had John appeared than his face took on an expression of disgust almost amounting to horror, and he vanished back round the buttress. McWhist traversed out to catch a view of him again. John was already half-way down a smooth face of rock which the climbers had attempted on the way up and then rejected in favour of the chimney. Recounting the incident, McWhist ejaculated. 'God! The lad could climb! He *oozed* from hold to hold.' When John reached the bottom of the bad pitch, he cut away to the left and disappeared.

Their final encounter with John was more prolonged. They were groping their way down the mountain late one evening in a blizzard. They were both wet through. The wind was so violent that they could hardly make headway against it. Presently they realized that they had missed their way in the cloud, and were on the wrong spur of the mountain. Finally they found themselves hemmed in by precipices, but they roped themselves and managed to climb down a gully or wide chimney, choked with fallen rocks. Halfway down, they were surprised to smell smoke, and saw it issuing from behind a great slab jammed in an angle of rocks beside their route. With considerable difficulty McWhist worked his way by rare and precarious holds over to a little platform near the smoking slab, and Norton followed. Light came from under it and behind it. A step or two of scrambling brought them to the illuminated space between one end of the slab and the cliff. The sides and opposite end of the slab were jammed in a mass of lesser rocks, and held in position by the two sides of the chimney. Stooping, they peered through the bright hole into a little irregular cave, which was lit by a fire of peat and heather. Stretched on a bed of dried grass and heather lay John. He was gazing into the fire, and his face was streaming with tears. He was naked, but there was a jumble of deer-skin beside him. By the fire was part of a cooked bird on a flat stone.

Feeling unaccountably abashed by the tears of this strange lad, the climbers quietly withdrew. Whispering together, however, they decided that they really must do something about him. Therefore, making a noise on the rocks with their boots as though in the act of reaching the cave, they remained out of sight while McWhist demanded, 'Is anyone there?' No answer was given. Once more they peered through the tiny entrance. John lay as before, and took no notice. Near the bird lay a stout bone knife or dirk, obviously 'home-made', but carefully pointed and edged. Other implements of bone or antler were scattered about. Some of them were decorated with engraved patterns. There was also a sort of pan-pipe of reeds and a pair of hide sandals or moccasins. The climbers were struck by the fact that there were no traces whatever of civilization, nothing, for instance, that was made of metal.

Cautiously they spoke again, but still John took no notice. McWhist crept through the entrance, noisily, and laid a hand on the boy's bare foot, gently shaking it. John slowly looked round and stared in a puzzled way at the intruder; then suddenly his whole form came alive with hostile intelligence. He sprang into a crouching posture, clutching a sort of stiletto made of the largest tine of an antler. McWhist was so startled by the huge glaring eyes and the inhuman snarl that he backed out of the cramping entrance of the cave.

'Then,' said McWhist, 'an odd thing happened. The boy's

anger seemed to vanish, and he stared intently at me as though I were a strange beast that he had never seen before. Suddenly he seemed to think of something else. He dropped his weapon, and began gazing into the fire again with that look of utter misery. Tears welled in his eyes again. His mouth twisted itself in a kind of desperate smile.'

Here McWhist paused in his narrative, looking both distressed and awkward. He sucked violently at his pipe. At last he proceeded.

'Obviously we couldn't leave the kid like that, so I asked cautiously if we could do anything for him. He did not answer. I crept in again, and squatted beside him, waiting. As gently as I could I put a hand on his knee. He gave a start and a shudder, looked at me with a frown, as if trying to get things straight in his mind, made a quick movement for the stiletto, checked himself, and finally broke into a wry boyish grin, remarking, "Oh, come in, please. Don't knock, it's a shop." He added, "Can't you blighters leave a fellow alone?" I said we had come upon him quite by accident, but of course we couldn't help being puzzled about him. I said we'd been very struck with his climbing, the other day. I said it seemed a pity for him to be stuck up here alone. Wouldn't he come along with us? He shook his head, smiling, and said he was quite all right there. He was just having a bit of a rough holiday, and thinking about things. At first it had been difficult feeding himself, but now he'd got the technique, and there was plenty of time for the thinking. Then he laughed. A sudden sharp crackle it was that made my scalp tingle.'

Here Norton broke in and said, 'I had crawled into the cave by then, and I was terribly struck by the gaunt condition he was in. There wasn't a bit of fat on him anywhere. His muscles looked like skeins of cord under his skin. He was covered with scars and bruises. But the most disturbing thing was the look on his face, a look that I have only seen on someone that had just come out of the anaesthetic after a bad op. – sort of purified. Poor kid, he'd evidently been through it all right, but through what?'

'At first,' said McWhist, 'we thought he was mad. But now

I'm ready to swear he wasn't. He was possessed. Something that we don't know anything about had got him, something good or bad, I don't know which. The whole business gave me the creeps, what with the noise of the storm outside, and the dim firelight, and the smoke that kept blowing back on us down the sort of chimney he'd made for it. We were a bit light-headed with lack of food, too. He offered us the rest of his bird, by the way, and some bilberries, but of course we didn't want to run him short. We asked if there wasn't *anything* we could do for him, and he answered, yes, there was, we could make a special point of not telling anyone about him. I said, couldn't we take a message to his people. He grew very serious and emphatic, and said, "No, don't tell a soul, not a soul. Forget. If the papers get on to my tracks," he said very slowly and coldly, "I shall just have to kill myself." This put us in a hole. We felt we really ought to do something and yet somehow we felt we *must* promise.'

McWhist paused, then said crossly, 'And we did promise. And then we cleared out, and floundered about in the dark till we reached our tent. We roped to get down the rock, and the lad went in front, unroped, to show us the way.' He paused again, then added, The other day when I happened to hear from Brinston about your lost lad, I broke my promise. And now I'm feeling damned bad about it.'

I laughed, and said, 'Well, no harm's done. *I* shan't tell the Press.'

Norton spoke again. 'It's not as simple as that. There's something McWhist hasn't told you yet. Go on, Mac.'

'Tell him yourself,' said McWhist, 'I'd rather not.'

There was a pause, then Norton laughed awkwardly, and said, 'Well, when one tries to describe it in cold blood over a cup of coffee, it just sounds crazy. But damn it, if the thing *didn't* happen, something mighty queer must have happened to *us*, for we both saw it, as clearly as you see us now.'

He paused. McWhist rose from his armchair and began examining the rows of books on shelves behind us.

Norton proceeded: 'The lad said something about making us realize we'd come up against something big that we couldn't understand, said he'd give us something to remember, and help us to keep the secret. His voice had changed oddly. It was very low and quiet and composed. He stretched his skinny arm up to the roof, saying, "This slab must weigh fifty tons. Above it there's just blizzard. You can see the raindrops in the doorway there." He pointed to the cave entrance. "What of it?" he said in a cold proud voice. "Let us see the stars." Then, my God, you won't believe it, of course, but the boy lifted that blasted rock up on his finger-tips like a trap door. A terrific gust of wind and sleet entered, but immediately died away. As he lifted he rose to his feet. Overhead was a windless, clear, starry sky. The smoke of the fire rose as a wavering column, illuminated at the base, and spreading dimly far above us, where it blotted out a few stars with a trail of darkness. He pushed the rock back till it was upright, then leaned lightly against it with one arm, crooking the other on his hip. "There!" he said. In the starlight and firelight I could see his face as he gazed upwards. Transfigured, I should call it, bright, keen, peaceful.

'He stayed still for perhaps half a minute, and silent; then, looking down at us, he smiled, and said, "Don't forget. We have looked at the stars together." Then he gently lowered the rock into position again, and said, "I think you had better go now. I'll take you down the first pitch. It's difficult by night." As we were both pretty well paralyzed with bewilderment we made no immediate sign of quitting. He laughed, gently, reassuringly, and said something that has haunted me ever since. (I don't know about McWhist.) He said, "It was a childish miracle. But I am still a child. While the spirit is in the agony of outgrowing its childishness, it may solace itself now and then by returning to its playthings, knowing well that they are trivial." By now we were creeping out of the cave, and into the blizzard.'

There was a silence. Presently McWhist faced us again, and glared rather wildly at Norton. 'We were given a great sign,' he said, 'and we have been unfaithful.'

I tried to calm him by saying, 'Unfaithful in the letter, perhaps, but not in the spirit. I'm pretty sure John wouldn't mind *my* knowing. And as to the miracle, I wouldn't worry about that,' I said, with more confidence than I felt. 'He probably hypnotized you both in some odd sort of way. He's a weird kid.'

Toward the end of the summer Pax received a postcard, saying 'Home late tomorrow. Hot bath, please. John.'

On the first opportunity I had a long talk with John about his holiday. It was a surprise to me to find that he was ready to talk with perfect frankness, and that he had apparently quite got over the phase of uncommunicative misery which had caused us so much anxiety before his flight from home. I doubt if I really understood what he told me, and I am sure there was a good deal that he didn't tell me because he knew I wouldn't understand. I had a sense that he was all the while trying to *translate* his actual thoughts into language intelligible to me, and that the translation seemed to him very crude. I can give only so much of his statement as I understood.

XII
John in the Wilderness

John said that when he had begun to realize the tragic futility of *Homo sapiens* he was seized with 'a panicky sense of doom,' and along with that 'a passion of loneliness'. He felt more lonely in the presence of others than in isolation. At the same time, apparently, something strange was happening to his own mind. At first he thought perhaps he was going mad, but clung to the faith that he was after all merely growing up. Anyhow he was convinced that he must cut right adrift and face this upheaval in himself undisturbed. It was as though a grub were to feel premonitions of dissolution and regeneration, and to set purposefully about protecting itself with a cocoon.

Further, if I understood him, he felt spiritually contaminated by contact with the civilization of *Homo sapiens*. He felt he must for a while at least strip away every vestige of it from his own person, face the universe in absolute nakedness, prove that he could stand by himself, without depending in any way whatever on the primitive and debased creatures who dominated the planet. At first I thought this hunger for the simple life was merely an excuse for a boyish adventure, but now I realize that it did have for him a grave importance which I could only dimly comprehend.

Of some such kind were the motives that drove him into the wildest region of this island. The thoroughness with which he carried out his plan amazed me. He simply walked out of a Highland railway station, had a good meal in an inn, strode up on to the moors toward the high mountains, and, when he judged himself safe from interruption, took off all his clothes, including his shoes, and buried them in a hole among the rocks. He then took his bearings carefully, so as to be able to recover his property in due season, and moved away in his nakedness, seeking food and shelter in the wilderness.

His first days were evidently a terrible ordeal. The weather turned wet and cold. John, it must be remembered, was an extremely hardy creature, and he had prepared himself for this adventure by a course of exposure, and by studying beforehand all possible means of securing food in the valleys and moors of Scotland without so much as a knife or a piece of string to aid him. But fate was at first against him. The bad weather made shelter a necessity, and in seeking it he had to spend much time that might otherwise have been spent in the search for food.

He passed the first night under a projecting rock, wrapped in heather and grass that he had collected before the weather broke. Next day he caught a frog, dismembered it with a sharp stone, and ate it raw. He also ate large quantities of dandelion leaves, and other green stuff which from previous study he knew to be edible. Certain fungi, too, contributed to his diet on that day, and indeed throughout his adventure. On the second day he was feeling 'pretty queer'. On the third evening he was in a high fever, with a bad cough and diarrhoea. On the previous day, foreseeing possible illness, he had greatly improved his shelter, and laid by a store of such food as he considered least indigestible. For some days, he didn't know how long, he lay desperately sick, scarcely able to crawl to the stream for water. 'I must have been delirious at one time,' he said, 'because I seemed to have a visit from Pax. Then I came to and found there wasn't any Pax, and I thought I was dying, and I loved myself desperately, knowing I was indeed a rare bright thing. And it was torture to be just wasted like that. And then that unspeakable joy came, that joy of seeing things as it were through God's eyes, and finding them after all *right*, fitting, in the picture.' There followed a few days of convalescence, during which, he said, 'I seemed to have lost touch completely with all the motives of my adventure. I just lay and wondered why I had been such a self-important fool. Fortunately, before I was strong enough to crawl back to civilization I lashed myself into facing this spiritual decay. For even in my most abject state I vaguely *knew* that somewhere there was another "I", and a better one. Well, I set my teeth and determined to go on with the job even if it killed me.'

Soon after he had come to this decision some local boys with a dog came up the hill right on to his hiding-place. He leapt up and fled. They must have caught a glimpse of his small naked figure, for they gave chase, hallooing excitedly. As soon as he was on his feet he realized that his legs were like water. He collapsed. 'But then,' he said, 'I suddenly managed to tap some deep reserve of vitality, so to speak. I simply jumped up and ran like hell round a corner of hillside, and farther, to a rocky place. There I climbed a pretty bad pitch into a hole I knew of and had counted on. Then I must have fainted. In fact, I think I must have lain unconscious for almost twenty-four hours, for when I came to, the sun seemed to have gone back to early morning. I was cold as death, and one huge ache, and so weak I couldn't move from the twisted position I was in.'

Later in the day he managed to crawl back to his lair, and with great difficulty moved his bedding to a safer but less comfortable spot. The weather was now hot and bright. For ten days or so he spent nearly all his time creeping about in search of frogs, lizards, snails, birds' eggs and green stuff, or just lying in the sun recovering his strength. Sometimes he managed to catch a few fish by 'tickling' them in a pool in the river. The whole of one day he spent in trying to get a flame by striking sparks from stones on a handful of dry grass. At last he succeeded, and began to cook his meal, in an ecstasy of pride and anticipation. Suddenly he noticed a man, far away but obviously interested in the smoke of his fire. He put it out at once and decided to go much farther into the wilds.

Meanwhile, though his feet had been hardened with long practice at home, they were now terribly sore, and quite unfit for 'a walking tour'. He made moccasins out of ropes of twisted grass which he bound round his feet and ankles. They kept in place for a while, but were always either coming undone or wearing through. After many days of exploration, and several nights without shelter, two of which were wet, he found the high cave where later the climbers discovered him. 'It was only just in time,' he said. 'I was in a pretty bad state. Feet swollen and bleeding, ghastly cough, diarrhoea. But in that cave I soon felt snugger than I had ever felt in my life, by contrast with the past few weeks. I made myself a *lovely* bed, and a fireplace, and I felt fairly safe from intrusion, because mine was a remote mountain, and anyhow very few people could climb those rocks. Not far below there were grouse and ptarmigan; and deer. On my first morning, sitting in the sun on my roof, positively happy, I watched a herd of them crossing a moor, stepping so finely, ears spread, heads high.'

The deer seem to have become his chief interest for a while. He was fascinated by their beauty and freedom. True, they now depended for their existence on a luxurious civilization; but equally they had existed before there was any civilization at all. Moreover, he coveted the huge material wealth that the slaughter of one stag would afford him. And he had apparently a queer lust to try his strength and cunning against a worthy quarry. For at this time he was content to be almost wholly the primitive hunter, 'though with a recollection, away at the back of my mind, that all this was just a process of getting clean in spirit for a very different enterprise.'

For ten days or so he did little but devise means for catching birds and hares, and spent all spare time in resting, recuperating, and brooding over the deer. His first hare, caught after many failures, he took by arranging a trap in its runway. A huge stone was precariously held in position by a light stick, which the creature dislodged. Its back was broken. But a fox ate most of it in the night. From its skin, however, he made a rough bow-string, also soles and thongs for his foot-gear. By splitting its thigh bones and filing them on the rock he made some fragile little knives to help him in preparing his food. Also he made some minute sharp arrow-heads. With a diversity of traps, and his toy bow and arrows, and vast patience and aptitude, he managed to secure enough game to restore him to normal strength. Practically his whole time was spent in hunting, trapping, cooking, making little tools of bone or wood or stone. Every night he rolled himself in his grass bedding dead tired, but at peace. Sometimes he took his bedding outside the cave and slept on a ledge of the precipice, under stars and driving cloud.

But there were the deer; and beyond them the spiritual problem which was the real motive of his adventure, and had not yet been consciously faced at all. It was clear that if he did not greatly improve his way of life, he would have no time for that concentrated meditation and spiritual exercise which he so greatly needed. The killing of the stag became a symbol for him. The thought of it stirred unwonted feelings in him. 'It was as though all the hunters of the past challenged me,' he said, 'and as though, as though – well, as though the angels of God ordered me to do this little mighty deed in preparation for mightier deeds to come. I dreamt of stags, of their beauty and power and speed. I schemed and plotted, and rejected every plan. I stalked the herd, weaponless, intent only on learning their ways. One day I came upon some deer-stalkers, and I stalked them too, until they brought down a stag of ten; and how I despised them for their easy slaughter. To me they were just vermin preying upon *my* game. But when I had thought that thought, I laughed at myself; for *I* had no more right to the creatures than anyone else.'

The story of how John finally took his stag seemed to me almost incredible, yet I could not but believe it. He had marked down as his quarry the finest beast of the herd, an eight-year-old monarch, bearing besides his brow, bay and tray, 'three on top' on the right, and four on the left. The weight of antler gave his head a superb poise. One day John and the stag met one another face to face round a shoulder of moor. They stood for full three seconds, twenty paces apart, gazing at one another, the stag's wide nostrils taking the scent of him. Then the beast swung round and cantered easefully away.

When John described that meeting, his strange eyes seemed to glow with dark fire. He said, I remember, 'With my soul I saluted him. Then I pitied him, because he was doomed, and in the prime. But I remembered that I too was doomed. I suddenly knew that I should never reach my prime. And laughed aloud, for him and for me, because life is brief and wild, and death too is in the picture.'

John took long to decide on the method of his attack. Should he dig a pit for him, or lasso him with a cord of hide, or set a mighty stone to fell him, or pierce him with a bone-pointed arrow? Few of these devices seemed practicable; all but the last seemed ugly, and that last was not practicable. For some time he busied himself making dirks of various kinds, of wood, of the fragile bones of hares, of keen stone splinters from a neighbouring mountain. Patient experiment produced at last a preposterous little stiletto of hard wood pointed with bone, the whole 'streamlined' by filing upon the rock. With this fantastic weapon and his knowledge of anatomy, he proposed to leap on the stag from a hiding-place and pierce its heart. And this in the end he did, after many days of fruitless stalking and waiting. There was a little glade where the deer sometimes grazed, and beside it a rock some ten feet high. On the top of this rock he secreted himself early one morning, when the wind was such that his scent would not betray him. The great stag came round the shoulder of hill, attended by three binds. Cautiously they sniffed and peered; then, at last, lowered their heads and peacefully grazed. Hour after hour John lay, waiting for the right beast to stray below the rock. But it was as though the stag deliberately avoided the danger-spot. Finally the four deer left the glade. Two more days were spent in vain watching. Not till the fourth day did John leap from the rock upon the back of the grazing stag, bringing it down with its right flank to the ground. Before the creature could regain its feet John had thrust his primitive weapon home with all his weight. The stag half righted itself, wildly swung its antlers, tearing John's arm, then collapsed. And John, to his own surprise, behaved in a style most unseemly in a hunter. For the third time in his life, he burst into spontaneous tears.

For days afterwards he struggled to dismember the carcass with his inadequate implements. This task proved even more difficult than the killing, but in the end he found himself with a large quantity of meat, an invaluable hide, and the antlers, which, with desperate efforts, he smashed in pieces with a great stone and worked up as knives and other tools, by scraping them on the rocks.

At the end he could hardly lift his hands with fatigue, and they were covered with bleeding blisters. But the deed was accomplished. The hunters of all the ages saluted him, for he had done what none of them could have done. A child, he had gone naked into the wilderness and conquered it. And the angels of heaven smiled at him, and beckoned him to a higher adventure.

John's way of life now changed. It had become a fairly easy matter for him to keep himself alive, and even in comfort. He set his traps, and let fly his arrows, and gathered his green things; but all was now routine work. He was able to carry it out while giving his best attention to the strange and disturbing events which were beginning to occur within his own mind.

It is obviously quite impossible for me to give anything like a true account of the spiritual side of John's adventure in the wilderness. Yet to ignore it would be to ignore all that was most distinctive in John. I must at least try to set down as much of it as I was able to understand, for that little seems to me to have real significance for beings of my own species. Even if as a matter of fact I have merely misunderstood what he told me, my misunderstanding afforded at least to me a real enlightenment.

For a time he seems to have been chiefly concerned with art. He 'sang against the waterfall'. He made and played his pan-pipes, apparently adopting some weird scale of his own. He played strange themes and figures on the shores of the loch, in the woods, on the mountain-tops, and in his rock home. He decorated his tools with engraved angles and curves consonant with their form and use. On pieces of bone and stone he recorded symbolically his adventures with fish and birds; and with the stag. He devised strange shapes which epitomized for him the tragedy of *Homo sapiens*, and the promise of his own kind. At the same time he was allowing the perceptual forms with which he was surrounded to work themselves deeply into his mind. He accepted with insight the quality of moor and sky and crag. From the bottom of his heart he gave thanks for all these subtle contacts with material reality; and found in them a spiritual refreshment which we also find, though confusedly and grudgingly. He was also constantly, and ever surprisingly, illuminated by the beauty of the beasts and birds on which he preyed, a beauty significant of their power and their frailty, their vitality and their obtuseness. Such perceived organic forms seem to have moved him far more deeply than I could comprehend. The stag, in particular, that he had killed and devoured, and now daily used, seems to have had some deep symbolism for him which I could but dimly appreciate, and will not attempt to describe. I remember his exclaiming, 'How I knew him and praised him! And his death was his life's crown.'

This remark epitomized, I believe, some new enlightenment which John was now receiving about himself and about *Homo sapiens* and indeed about all living things. The actual nature of that enlightenment I find it impossible to conceive, but certain dim reflections of it I do seem able to detect, and must try to record.

It will be remembered that John had shown, even as an infant, a surprising detachment and strange relish in situations in which he himself was the sufferer. Referring to this, he now said, 'I could always enjoy the "realness" and the *neatness* of my own pains and griefs, even while I detested them. But now I found myself faced with something of quite a new order of horribleness, and one which I could not get into place. Hitherto my distresses had been merely isolated smarts and temporary frustrations, but now I saw my whole future as something at once much more vivid and much more painfully frustrated than anything I had conceived. You see, I knew so clearly by now that I was a unique being, far more awake than other people. I was beginning to understand myself and discover all sorts of new and exquisite capacities in myself; and at the same time I saw now all too clearly that I was up against a savage race which would never tolerate me or my kind, and would sooner or later smash me with its brute weight. And when I told myself that after all this didn't really matter, and that I was just a little self-important microbe making a fuss over nothing, something in me cried out imperiously that, even if *I* was of no account, the things I could *do*, the *beauty* I could make, and the *worship* that I was now beginning to conceive, did most emphatically matter, and *must* be brought to fruition. And I saw that there would be no fruition, that the exquisite things that it was my office to do would never be done. This was a sort of agony altogether different from anything that my adolescent mind had ever known.'

While he was wrestling with this horror, and before he had triumphed over it, there came upon him the realization that for members of the normal species *every* pain, *every* distress of body and of mind, had this character of insurmountable hideousness which he himself had found only in respect of the highest reach of his experience, and was determined to conquer even there. It came as a shocking revelation to him that normal human beings were quite incapable of detachment and zest even in sufferings upon the personal plane. In fact he realized clearly for the first time the torture that lies in wait at every turn for beings who are more sensitive and more awakened than the beasts and yet not sensitive enough, not fully awakened. The thought of the agony of this world of nightmare-ridden half-men crushed him as nothing else had ever done.

His attitude to the normal species was undergoing a great change. When he had fled into the wilderness his dominant reaction was disgust. One or two of us he unreasonably cherished, but as a species he loathed us. He had recently seen too much, lived at too close quarters, been fouled and poisoned. His researches into the world of men had been too devastating for a mind which, though superior in quality, was immature and delicate. But the wild had cleansed him, healed him, brought him to sanity again. He could now put *Homo sapiens* at arm's length for study and appreciation. And he saw that, though no divinity, the creature was after all a noble and even a lovable beast, indeed the noblest and most lovable of them all; nay further, that its very repulsiveness lay in its being something more than beast, but not enough more. A normal human being, he now ungrudgingly admitted, was indeed a spirit of a higher order than any beast, though in the main obtuse, heartless, unfaithful to the best in himself.

Realizing all this, and realizing for the first time the incapacity of *Homo sapiens* to accept his pains and sorrows with equanimity, John was overwhelmed with pity, a passion which he had not hitherto experienced in any intensity; save on particular occasions, as when Judy's dog was run over by a car, and when Pax was ill and in great pain. And even then his pity was always tempered by his assumption that everyone, even little Judy, could always 'look at it from outside and enjoy it', as he himself could do.

For many days John seems to have been at grips with this newly realized problem of the absoluteness of evil, and the novel fact that beings that were tissues of folly and baseness could yet be pitiable and, in their kind, beautiful. What he sought was not an intellectual solution but an emotional enlightenment. And this, little by little, he seems to have gained. When I pressed him to tell me more of this strange enlightenment, he said it was just 'seeing my own fate and the piteous plight of the normal species in the same way as I had always, since I was a kid, seen bumps and burns and disappointments. It was a case of delighting in their clear-cut form, and in their unity with the rest of things, and the way they – how shall I put it? – deepened and quickened the universe.' Here, I remember, John paused, then repeated, 'Yes, deepened and quickened the universe – that's the main point. But it wasn't a case of *understanding* that they did so, but just *seeing* and *feeling* that they did so.'

I asked him if what he meant was some kind of coming face to face with God. He laughed, and said, 'What do I know about God? No more than the Archbishop of Canterbury, and that's nothing whatever.'

He said that when McWhist and Norton came upon him in the cave he was 'still desperately puzzling things out', and that their presence filled him just for a moment with the old disgust at their species, but that he had really done with all that long ago, and when he saw them there, looking so blank, he remembered his first close meeting with the stag. And suddenly the stag seemed to symbolize the whole normal human species, as a thing with a great beauty and dignity of its own, and a rightness of its own, so long as it was not put into situations too difficult for it. *Homo sapiens*, poor thing, *had* floundered into a situation too difficult for him, namely the present world-situation. The thought of *Homo sapiens* trying to run a mechanized civilization suddenly seemed to him as ludicrous and pathetic as the thought of a stag in the driving-seat of a motorcar.

I took this opportunity of asking him about the 'miracle' with which he had so impressed his visitors. He laughed again. 'Well,' he said, 'I had been discovering all sorts of odd powers. For instance I found that by a kind of telepathy I could get in touch with Pax and talk to her. It's true. You can ask her about it. Also I could sometimes feel what *you* were thinking about, though you were too dull to catch my messages and respond to me. And I had made queer little visits to events in my own past life. I just lived them again, with full vividness, as though they were "now". And in a telepathic way I had begun to get something very like evidence that after all I was not the only one of my kind in the world, that there were in fact quite a number of us scattered about in different countries. And then again, when McWhist and Norton appeared in the cave I found that by looking at them I could read the whole of their past lives in their faces, and I saw how thoroughly sound they both were within the limitations of their kind! And I *think* I saw something about their future, something that I won't tell you. Then, when it was necessary to impress them, I suddenly got the idea of lifting the roof and clearing away the blizzard so that we could see the stars. And I knew perfectly well that I could do it, so I did it.'

I looked at John with misgiving. 'Oh yes,' he said, 'I know you think I'm mad, and that all I did was to hypnotize them. Well, put it that I hypnotized myself too, for I *saw* the whole thing as clearly as they did. But, believe me, to say I hypnotized us all is no more true and no less true than to say I actually shifted the rock and the blizzard. The truth of the matter was something much more subtle and tremendous than any plain little physical miracle could ever be. But never mind that. The important thing was that, when I did see the stars (riotously darting in all directions according to the caprice of their own wild natures, yet in every movement confirming the law), the whole tangled horror that had tormented me finally presented itself to me in its true and beautiful shape. And I knew that the first, blind stage of my childhood had ended.'

I had indeed sensed a change in John. Even physically he had altered strikingly during his six months' absence. He was harder, more close-knit; and there were lines on his face suggestive of ordeals triumphantly passed. Mentally, though still capable of a most disconcerting impishness, he had also acquired that indefinable peacefulness and strength which is quite impossible to the adolescent of the normal species, and is very seldom acquired even by the mature. He himself said that his 'discovery of sheer evil' had fortified him. When I asked, 'how fortified?' he said, 'My dear, it is a great strength to have faced the worst and to have *felt* it a feature of beauty. Nothing ever after can shake one.'

He was right. By what magic he did it I do not know, but in all his future, and in the final destruction of all that he most cherished, he accepted the worst not with resignation, merely, but with a strange joy that must remain to the rest of us incomprehensible.

I will mention one other point that emerged in my long talk with John. It will be remembered that after performing his 'miracle' he apologized for it. I questioned him on this matter, and he said something like this: 'To enjoy exercising one's powers is healthy. Children enjoy learning to walk. Artists enjoy painting pictures. As a baby I exulted in the tricks I could do with numbers, and later in my inventions, and recently in killing my stag. And of course the full exercise of one's powers really is part of the life of the spirit. But it is only a part, and sometimes we are inclined to take it as the whole purpose of our existence, especially when we discover new powers. Well, in Scotland, when I began to come into all those queer powers that I mentioned just now, I was tempted to regard the exercise of them as the true end of my life. I said to myself, "Now at last, in these wonderful ways, I shall indeed advance the spirit." But after the momentary exaltation of lifting the rock I saw clearly that such acts were in no sense the goal of the spirit, but just a by-play of true life, amusing, and sometimes useful, and often dangerous, but never themselves the goal.'

'Then tell me,' I said, perhaps rather excitedly, 'what *is* the goal, the true life of the spirit?' John suddenly grinned like a boy of ten, and laughed that damnably disturbing laugh of his. 'I'm afraid I can't tell you, Mr Journalist,' he said. 'It is time your interview was concluded. Even if I *knew* what the true life of the spirit was, I couldn't put it into English, or any "sapient" language. And if I could, you wouldn't understand.' After a pause he added, 'Perhaps we might safely say this much about it anyhow. It's not doing any one particular kind of thing, like miracles, or even good deeds. It's doing everything that comes along to be done, and doing it not only with all one's might but with – spiritual taste, discrimination, *full* consciousness of what one is doing. Yes, it's that. And it's more. It's – praise of life, and of all things in their true setting.' Once more he laughed, and said, 'What stuff! To describe the spiritual life, we should have to remake language from the foundations upwards.'

XIII
John Seeks his Kind

For many weeks after his return from the wilderness John spent a good deal of his time at home, or in the neighbouring city. Apparently he was content to sink back into the interests of the normal adolescent. He resumed his friendship with Stephen, and with Judy. Often he took the child to a picture show, a circus, or any entertainment suited to her years. He acquired a motorbicycle, on which, upon the very day of the purchase, Judy was treated to a wild ride. The neighbours said that John's holiday had done him good. He was much more normal now. With his brother and sister too, on the rare occasions when he met them, John became more fraternal. Anne was married. Tom was a successful young architect. The two brothers had generally maintained a relation of restrained hostility to one another, but now hostility seemed to have mellowed into mutual tolerance. After a family reunion Tom remarked, 'Our infant prodigy's positively growing up.' Doc was delighted by John's new companionableness, and often talked to him at great length. Their main topic was John's future. Doc was anxious to persuade him to take to medicine and become 'a greater Lister'. John used to attend to those exhortations thoughtfully, seeming to be almost persuaded. Once Pax was present. She shook her head, smilingly but reprovingly at John. 'Don't believe him, Doc,' she said, 'he's pulling your leg.' In this period, by the way, John and Pax often went together to a theatre or concert. Indeed, mother and son were now seeing a great deal of each other. Pax's interest in the drama, and in 'persons', seemed to afford him an unfailing common platform. Occasionally they even went up to London together for a weekend, 'to see the shows'.

There came a time when I began to feel a certain curiosity as to the meaning of this prolonged period of relaxation. John's behaviour seemed now almost completely normal. There was, indeed, one unusual but unobtrusive feature about it. In the midst of conversation or any other activity he would sometimes give a noticeable start of surprise. He would then perhaps repeat the immediately preceding remark, whether his own or the other person's; and then he would look around him with amused interest. I fancied that for some time after such an incident he was more alert than before it. Not that in the earlier stage he had seemed at all absent-minded. He was at all times thoroughly adjusted to his surroundings. But after these curious jerks the current of his life seemed to reach a higher tension.

One evening I accompanied the three Wainwrights to the local Repertory Theatre. During an interval, while we were drinking coffee in the foyer and discussing the play, John gave a more violent start than usual, spilling his coffee into the saucer. He laughed, and looked about him with surprised interest. After a moment's awkward silence, in which Pax regarded her boy with veiled solicitude, John continued his comments on the play, but (as it seemed to me) with new penetration. 'My point is just this,' he said. 'The thing's too lifelike to be really alive. It's not a portrait but a death mask.'

Next day I asked him what had happened when he spilt his coffee. We were in my flat. John had come to inquire if the post had brought information about some patent or other. I was at my writing-table. He was standing at the window, looking out across the deserted promenade to the wintry sea. He was chewing an apple that he had picked up from a dish on my table. 'Yes,' he said, 'it's time you were told, even if you can't believe. At present I am looking for other people more or less like me, and to do it I become a sort of divided personality. Part of me remains where my body is, and behaves quite correctly, but the other, the essential I, goes off in search of *them*. Or if you like, I stay put all the time, but *reach out* in search of them. Anyhow, when I come back, or stop the search, I get a bit of a jolt, taking up the threads of ordinary life again.'

'You never seem to *lose* the threads,' I said.

'No,' he answered. 'The incoming "I" comes slick into possession of all the past experiences of the residential one, so to speak.

But the sudden jump from God knows where to here gives a bit of a jar, all the same.'

'And when you're away,' I asked, 'where do you go, what do you find?'

'Well,' he said, 'I had better begin at the beginning. I told you before that when I was in Scotland I used to find myself in telepathic touch with people, and that some of the people seemed queer people, or people in a significant way more like me than you. Since I came home I've been working up the technique for tuning in to the people I want. Unfortunately it's much easier to pick up the thoughts of folk one knows well than of strangers. So much depends on the general form of the mind, the matrix in which the thoughts occur, so to speak. To get you or Pax I have only to think of you. I can get your actual consciousness, and if I want to, I can get a good bit of the deeper layers of you too.'

I was seized with horror, but I comforted myself with incredulity.

'Oh, yes, I can,' said John. 'While I've been talking, half your mind was listening and the other half was thinking about a quarrel you had last night with—' I cut him short with an expostulation.

'Righto, don't get excited,' said John. '*You* haven't much to be ashamed of. And anyhow I don't want to pry. But just now – well, you kept fairly shouting the stuff at me, because while you were attending to me you were thinking about it. You'll probably soon learn how to shut me out at will.'

I grunted, and John continued: 'As I was saying, it's much harder to get in touch with people one doesn't know, and at first I didn't know any of the people I was looking for. On the other hand, I found that the people of my sort make, so to speak, a much bigger "noise" telepathically than the rest. At least they do when they want to, or when they don't care. But when they want *not* to, they shut themselves off completely. Well, at last I managed to single out from the general buzz of telepathic "noise", made by the normal species, a few outstanding streaks or themes that seemed to have about them something or other of the special quality that I was looking for.'

John paused, and I interjected, 'What sort of quality?'

He looked at me for some seconds in silence. Believe it or not, but that prolonged gaze had a really terrifying effect on me. I am not suggesting that there was something magical about it. The effect was of the same kind as any normal facial expression may have. But knowing John as I did, and remembering the strange events of his summer in Scotland, I was no doubt peculiarly susceptible. I can only describe what I felt by means of an image. It was as though I was confronted with a mask made of some semi-transparent substance, and illuminated from within by a different and a *spiritually luminous* face. The mask was that of a grotesque child, half monkey, half gargoyle, yet wholly urchin, with its huge cat's eyes, its flat little nose, its teasing lips. The inner face – obviously it cannot be described, for it was *the same* in every feature, yet wholly different. I can only say that it seemed to me to combine the august and frozen smile of a Buddha with the peculiar creepy grimness that the battered Sphinx can radiate when the dawn first touches its face. No, these images fail utterly. I cannot describe the symbolical intention that John's features forced upon me in those seconds. I can only say that I longed to look away and could not, or dared not. Irrational terror welled up in me. When one is under the dentist's drill, one may endure a few moments of real torture without flinching. But as the seconds pile up, it becomes increasingly difficult not to move, not to scream. And so with me, looked at by John. With this difference, that I was bound, and could not stir, that I had passed the screaming point and could not scream. I believe my terror was largely a wild dread that John was about to laugh, and that his laugh would annihilate me. But he did not laugh.

Suddenly the spell broke, and I leapt up to put more coal on the fire. John was gazing out of the window, and saying, in his normal friendly voice, 'Well, of course I can't *tell* you what that special quality is, can I? Think of it this way. It's seeing each thing, each event, on its *eternal* side, instead of *merely* as a dated thing; seeing it as a living leaf on the tree Yggdrasill, flushed with the sap of eternity, and not *merely* as a plucked and dried and dated specimen in the book of history.'

There was a long silence, then he continued his report. 'The first trace of mentality like my own gave me a lot of trouble. I could only catch occasional glimpses of this fellow, and I couldn't make him take any notice of me. And the stuff that did come through to me was terribly incoherent and bewildering. I wondered whether this was the fault of my technique, or whether his was a mind too highly developed for me to understand. I tried to find out where he was, so I could go and see him. He was evidently living in a large building with lots of rooms and many other people. But he had very little to do with the others. Looking out of his window, he saw trees and houses and a long grassy hill. He heard an almost continuous noise of trains and motor traffic. At least *I* recognized it as that, but it didn't seem to mean much to him. Clearly, I thought, there's a main line and a main road quite close to where he lives. Somehow I must find that place. So I bought the motorbike. Meanwhile I kept on studying him. I couldn't catch any of his thoughts, but only his perceptions, and the way he felt about them. One striking thing was his music. Sometimes when I found him he was outside the house in a sloping field with trees between it and the main road; and he would be playing a pipe, a sort of recorder, but with the octave very oddly divided. I discovered that each of his hands had *five* fingers and a thumb. Even so, I couldn't make out how he managed all the extra notes. The kind of music he played was extraordinarily fascinating to me. Something about it, the mental pose of it, made me quite sure the man was really my sort. I discovered, by the way, that he had the not very helpful name of James Jones. Once when I got him he was out in the grounds and near a gap in the trees, so that he could see the road. Presently a bus flashed past. It was a "Green Line" bus, and it was labelled "BRIGHTON". I noticed with surprise that these words apparently meant nothing to James Jones. But they meant a lot to me. I went off on the bike to search the Green Line routes out of Brighton. It took me a couple of days to find the right spot – the big buildings, the grassy hill, and so on. I stopped and asked someone what the building was. It was a lunatic asylum.'

John's narrative was interrupted by my guffaw of relief. 'Funny,' he said, 'but not quite unexpected. After pulling lots of wires I got permission to see James Jones, who was a relative of mine, I said. They told me at the Asylum that there was a family likeness, and when I saw James Jones I knew what they meant. He's a little old man with a big head and huge eyes, like mine. He's quite bald, except for a few crisp white curls above the ears. His mouth was smaller than mine (for the size of him) and it had a sort of suffering sweetness about it, specially when he let it do a peculiar compressed pout, which was a characteristic mannerism of his. Before I saw him they had told me a bit about him. He gave no trouble, they said, except that his health was very bad, and they had to nurse him a lot. He hardly ever spoke, and then only in monosyllables. He could understand simple remarks about matters within his ken, but it was often impossible to get him to attend to what was said to him. Yet oddly enough, he seemed to have a lively interest in everything happening around him. Sometimes he would listen intently to people's voices; but not, apparently, for their significance, simply for their musical quality. He seemed to have an absorbing interest in perceived rhythms of all sorts. He would study the grain of a piece of wood, poring over it by the hour; or the ripples on a duck-pond. Most music, ordinary music invented by *Homo sapiens*, seemed at once to interest and outrage him; though when one of the doctors played a certain bit of Bach, he was gravely attentive, and afterwards went off to play oddly twisted variants of it on his queer pipe. Certain jazz tunes had such a violent effect on him that after hearing one record he would sometimes be prostrate for days. They seemed to tear him with some kind of conflict of delight and disgust. Of course the authorities regarded his own pipe-playing as the caterwauling of a lunatic.

'Well, when we were brought face to face, we just stood and looked at one another for so long that the attendant found it uncomfortable. Presently James Jones, keeping his eyes on mine, said one word, with quiet emphasis and some surprise, "Friend!" I smiled and nodded. Then I felt him catch a glimpse of my mind, and his face suddenly lit up with intense delight and surprise. Very slowly, as if painfully searching for each word, he said, "You – are – not – mad, NOT MAD! We two, NOT MAD! But these—" (slowly pointing at the attendant and smiling) "All mad, quite, quite mad. But kind and clever. He cares for me. I cannot care for self. Too busy with – with—" The sentence trailed into silence. Smiling seraphically, he nodded slowly, again and again. Then he came forward and laid a hand for an instant on my head. That was the end. When I said yes, we were friends, and he and I saw things the same way, he nodded again; but when he tried to speak, an expression of almost comic perplexity came over his face. Looking into his mind, I saw that it was already a welter of confusion. He perceived, but he could not find any mundane significance in what he perceived. He saw the two human beings that confronted him, but he no longer connected my visible appearance with human personality, with the mind that he was still striving to communicate with. He didn't even see us as physical objects at all, but just as colour and shape, without any meaning. I asked him to play to me. He could not understand. The attendant put the pipe in to his hand, closing the fingers over it. He looked blankly at it. Then with a sudden smile of enlightenment he put it to his ear, like a child listening to a shell. The attendant took it again, and played a few notes on it, but in vain. Then I took it and played a little air that I had heard him play before I found him. His attention was held. Perplexity cleared from his face. To our surprise he spoke, slowly but without difficulty. "Yes, John Wainwright," he said, "you heard *me* play that the other day. I knew some *person* was listening. Give me my pipe."

'He took it, seated himself on the edge of the table, and played, with his eyes fixed on mine.'

John startled me with one sharp gasp of laughter. 'God! it was music,' he said. 'If you could have heard it! I mean if you could have *really* heard it, and not merely as a cow might! It was lucid. It straightened out the tangles of my mind. It showed me just precisely the true, appropriate attitude of the adult human spirit to its world. Well, he played on, and I went on listening, hanging on to every note, to remember it. Then the attendant interrupted. He said this sort of noise always upset the other patients. It wasn't as if it was real *music*, but such crazy stuff. That was why J. J. was really only allowed to play out of doors.

'The music stopped with a squawk. J. J. looked with a kindly but tortured smile at the attendant. Then he slid back into insanity. So complete was his disintegration that he actually tried to eat the mouthpiece.'

I believe I saw John shudder. He was now standing at the window once more, and he stood silent, while I wondered what to say. Then he exclaimed, 'Where's your field-glass, quick! Damned if that's not a grey phalarope. Priceless little devil, isn't he!' In turn we watched the small silvery bird as it swam hither and thither in search of food, heedless of the buffeting wavecrests. Beside the gulls it was a yacht amongst the liners. 'Yes,' said John, answering my thoughts, 'the way you feel when you watch that little blighter, just observant and delighted, and – well, curiously pious yet aloof – yes, that's the starting-point, the very first moment, of what J. J. was working out in his music. If you could hold that always, and fill it out with a whole world of overtones, you'd be well on the way to "us".'

In the tone of John's 'us' there was something of the shy audacity with which a newly married couple first speak of 'us'. It began to dawn on me that the discovery of his own kind, even in a lunatic asylum, must have been for John a deeply moving experience. I began to realize that, having lived for nearly eighteen years with mere animals, he had at last discovered a human being.

John sighed, and took up his narrative. 'Well, of course James Jones was no good as a partner in the job of founding a new world. I've seen him several times since, and he always plays to me, and I come away a little clearer in my head, and a little more grown up. But he's incurably mad, all the same. So I started "listening in" again; rather gloomily, for I was afraid they might all turn out to be mad. And really the next one almost cured me of looking any more. You see, I was trying to get in touch with the near ones first, because they were handier. I had already spotted a strain of French thinking that must be one of us, and also an Egyptian, and a Chinese or Tibetan. But for the present I left these alone. Well, my next was an infant more or less, the son of a crofter in South Uist (Outer Hebrides). He's a ghastly cripple; no legs, and arms like a newt's arms. And there's something wrong with his mouth, so that he can't talk. And he's always sick, because his digestion doesn't work properly. In fact he's the sort any decent society would drown at birth. But the mother loves him like a tigress; though she's scared stiff of him too, and loathes him. Neither parent has any idea he's – what he is. They think he's just an ordinary little cripple. And because he's a cripple, and because they treat him all wrong, he's brewing the most murderous hate imaginable. Within the first five minutes of my visit he spotted me as different from the others. He got me telepathically. I got him too, but he shut his mind up immediately. Now you'd think that finding a kindred spirit for the first time ever would be an occasion for thanksgiving. But he didn't take it that way at all. He evidently felt at once there wasn't room for him and me together on the same planet. But he didn't let on he was going to do anything about it. He kept his mind shut like an oyster, and his face as blank as a piece of paper. I began to think I had made a mistake, that he was not one of us after all. Yet all the circumstances corresponded with my earlier telepathic glimpses of him, – the minute room with a flagged floor, the peat fire, his mother's face, with one eye slightly bigger than the other, and traces of a moustache at the corners of her lips. By the way, his parents were quite old people, both grey. This made me curious, because the kid looked about a three-year-old. I asked how old the baby was, but they seemed unwilling to say. I tactfully said the child had a terribly wise face, not like a baby's. The father blurted out that he was eighteen years old, and the mother gave a high-pitched hysterical sort of laugh. Gradually I succeeded in making friends with his parents. (I had told them, by the way, that I was on a fishing holiday with a party on the neighbouring island.) I flattered them by telling them I had read in a book that deformed children sometimes turned out to be great geniuses. Meanwhile I was still trying to get behind the kid's defences to see what his mind was like inside. It's impossible to give you a clear idea of the murderous trick he played on me. He must have made up his mind as soon as he saw me that he'd do me in. He chose the only effective weapon he had, and it was a diabolic one. It happened this way, so far as I can tell you. I had turned from his parents and was talking to him, trying to make friends. He just stared at me blankly. I tried harder and harder to open the oyster, and was just about ready to give up in disgust when, my God, the oyster opened wide, and I – well, this is the indescribable thing. I can only carry on with the image. The mental oyster opened wide and tried to swallow me into itself. And itself was – just the bottomless black pit of Hell. Of course, that sounds silly and romantic to you. But that's what it was like. I felt myself dropping plumb into the most appalling gulf of darkness, of mental and spiritual darkness, in which there was nothing whatever but eternally unsatisfied black hate; a sort of dank atmosphere of poison, in which everything that I had ever cared for seemed to moulder away into nastiness. I can't explain, I can't explain.'

John had been sitting on the corner of my writing-table. He got up suddenly and walked to the window. 'Thank God for light,' he said, looking at the grey sky. 'If there was someone who could understand, I could tell it all and be rid of it, perhaps. But half-telling it just makes it all come welling up again. And some say there's no Hell!'

He remained silent for some time, looking out of the window, Then he said, 'Look at that cormorant, He's got a conger fatter than his own neck.' I came up beside him, and we watched the fish writhing and lashing. Sometimes bird and prey disappeared together under water. Once the conger got away, but was speedily recovered. After many failures, the cormorant caught it by the head, and swallowed it, slick, so that nothing was to be seen of it but its tail, and a huge swelling in the bird's neck.

'And now,' said John, 'he'll be digested. That's what nearly happened to me. I felt my whole mind being disintegrated by the digestive juices of that Satanic young mollusc. I don't know what happened next. I remember seeing a perfectly diabolic expression on the kid's face; and then I must have saved myself somehow, for presently I found myself lying on the grass some way from the house, alone and in a cold sweat. The very sight of the house in the distance gave me the creeps. I couldn't think. I kept seeing that infantile grin of hate, and turning stupid again. After a while I realized I was cold, so I got up and walked toward the little bay where the boats were. Presently I began to ask myself what sort of a devil this baby Satan really was. Was he one of "us", or something quite different? But there was very little doubt in my mind, actually. Of course he was one of us, and probably a much mightier one than either J. J. or myself. But everything had gone wrong with him, from conception onwards. His body had failed him, and was tormenting him, and his mind was as crippled as his body, and his parents were quite unable to give him a fair chance. So the only self-expression possible to him was hate. And he had specialized in hate pretty thoroughly. But the oddest thing about it all was this. The further I got away from the experience, the more clearly it was borne in on me that his ecstasy of hate was really quite self-detached. He wasn't hating *for* himself. He hated himself as much as me. He hated everything, including hate. And he hated it all with a sort of sacred fervour. And why? Because, as I begin to discover, there's a sort of minute, blazing star of *worship* right down in the pit of his hell. He sees everything from the side of eternity just as clearly as I do, perhaps more clearly; but – how shall I put it? – he conceives his part in the picture to be the devil's part, and he's playing it with a combination of passion and detachment like a great artist, and for the glory of God, if you understand what I mean. And he's right. It's the only thing he *can* do, and he does it with style. I take off my hat to him, in spite of everything. But it's pretty ghastly, really. Think of the life he's living; just like an infant's, and with his powers! I dare say he'll manage to find some trick for blowing up the whole planet some day, if he lives much longer. And there's another thing. I've got to keep a sharp look out or he'll catch me again. He can reach me anywhere, in

Australia or Patagonia. God! I can feel him now! Give me another apple, and let's talk about something else.'

Crunching his second Cox, John became calm again. Presently he went on with his narrative. 'I haven't done much since that affair. It took me some time to get my mind straight, and then I felt depressed about the chances of ever finding any one anywhere that was really my sort and yet also sane. But after ten days or so I began the search again. I found an old gipsy woman who was a sort of half-baked one of "us". But she's always having fits. She tells fortunes, and perhaps has some sort of glimpses of the future. But she's as old as the hills, and cares for nothing but fortune-telling and rum. Yet she's quite definitely one of us, up to a point; not intellectually, though she has the reputation of being damnably cunning, but in insight. She sees things on their eternal side all right, though not very steadily. Then there are several others in asylums, quite hopeless. And a hermaphrodite adolescent in a sort of home for incurables. And a man doing a life-sentence for murder. I fancy he might have been the real thing if he hadn't had a bit of his skull knocked in when he was a kid. Then there's a lightning calculator, but he doesn't seem to be anything else. He's not really one of us at all, but he's got just *one* of the essential factors in his make up. Well, that's all there is of *Homo superior* in these islands.'

John began pacing the room, quickly, methodically, like a polar bear in its cage. Suddenly he stopped, and clenched his fists and cried out, 'Cattle! Cattle! A whole world of cattle! My God, how they stink!' He stared at the wall. Then he sighed, and turning to me he said, 'Sorry, Fido, old man! That was a lapse. What do you say to a walk before lunch?'

XIV
Engineering Problems

Not long after John told me of his efforts to make contact with other supernormals he took me into his confidence about his plans for the future. We were in the subterranean workshop. He was absorbed in a new invention, a sort of generator-accumulator, he said. His bench was covered with test-tubes, jars, bits of metal, bottles, insulated wires, voltmeters, lumps of stone. He was so intent on his work that I said, 'I believe you're regressing to childhood. This sort of thing has got hold of you again and made you forget all about – Scotland.'

'No, you're wrong,' he said. 'This gadget is an important part of my plan. When I have finished this test I'll tell you.' Silently he proceeded with the experiment. Presently, with a little shout of triumph, he said, 'Got it, this time!'

Over a cup of coffee we discussed his plans. He was determined to search the whole world in the hope of discovering a few others of his kind, and of suitable age for joining with him in the founding of a little colony of supernormals in some remote part of the earth. In order to do this without loss of time, he said, he must have an ocean-going yacht and a small aeroplane, or flying machine of some kind, which could be stowed on the yacht. When I protested that he knew nothing about flying and less about designing planes, he replied, 'Oh yes, I do. I learned to fly yesterday.' It seems he had managed to persuade a certain brilliant young airman to give him not only a joy-ride but a long spell in control of the machine. 'Once you get the feel of it,' he said, 'it's easy enough. I landed twice, and took off twice, and did a few stunts. But of course there's a good deal more to learn. As for designing, I'm on the job already, and on the yacht design too. But a lot depends on this new gadget. I can't explain it very well. At least, I can explain, in a way, but you just won't believe it. I've been looking into nuclear chemistry lately, and in the light of my Scottish experiences an idea struck me. Probably even you know (though you have a genius for keeping out of touch with science) that there's the hell of a lot of energy locked up in every atomic nucleus, and that the reason why you can't release it is that the unlocking would take a fantastically powerful electric current, to overcome the forces that hold the electrons and protons, and so on, together. Well, I've found a much handier key. But it's not a physical key at all but a psychical one. It's no use trying to *overcome* those terrific interlocking forces. You must just *abolish* them for the time being; send them to sleep, so to speak. The interlocking forces, and the disruptive forces too, are just the spontaneous urges of the basic physical units, call them electrons and protons, if you like. What I do, then, is to hypnotize the little devils so that they go limp for a moment and loosen their grip on one another. Then when they wake up they barge about in hilarious freedom, and all you have to do is to see that their barging drives your machinery.'

I laughed, and said I liked his parable. 'Parable be damned,' he said. 'It's only a parable in the sense that the protons and electrons themselves are merely fictitious characters in a parable. They're not *really* independent entities at all, but determinations within a system – the cosmos. And they're not *really* just physical, but determinations within a psychophysical system. Of course if you take "sapient" physics as God's truth, and not as an abstraction from a more profound truth, the whole idea seems crazy. But I thought it worth looking into, and I find it works. Of course there are difficulties. The main one is the psychological one. The "sapient" mind could never do the trick; it's not awake enough. But the supernormal has the necessary influence, and practice makes the job reasonably safe and easy. The physical difficulties,' he said, glancing at his apparatus, 'are all connected with selecting the most favourable atoms to work on, and with tapping the flood of energy as it comes into action. I'm working on those problems now. Ordinary mud from the estuary is pretty good for the job. There's a minute percentage of a very convenient element in it.'

With a pair of tweezers he took a pinch of mud from a test-tube and put it in a platinum bowl. He opened the trapdoor of the workshop and placed the bowl outside, then returned, almost closing the trapdoor. We both looked through the opening at the little bowl. Smiling, he said, 'Now all you little electrons and protons go to sleep, and don't wake up till Mummy tells you.' Turning to me, he added, 'The patter, I may say, is for the audience, not for the rabbits in the conjurer's hat.'

An expression of grave concentration came over his face. His breathing quickened. 'Now!' he said. There was a terrific flash, and a report like a gun.

John wiped his forehead with a grubby pocket handkerchief, and remarked, 'Alone I did it!' We returned to our coffee, and his plans.

'I've still got to find some really good way of bottling the energy till it's wanted. You can't be at one and the same time hypnotizing electrons *and* navigating a ship. I may simply have to use the energy to drive a dynamo and charge an accumulator. But there's a more interesting possibility. I *may* be able, when I have hypnotized the little beggars, to give them a sort of "post-hypnotic suggestion", so that they can only wake up and barge about again in response to some particular stimulus. See?'

I laughed. We both sipped our coffee. I may as well say at once that the 'post-hypnotic' system turned out ultimately to be feasible, and was adopted.

'Well, you can see,' he said, 'there are great possibilities in this new dodge of mine. Now, while the yacht and plane are building, you are to come on the Continent with me. (I'm sure Bertha will be glad to have a holiday from you.) I want to do a bit of research. There's an obviously supernormal mind in Paris, and one in Egypt, and perhaps others, not too far away. When I have the yacht and plane I'll do the world tour in search of the rest. If I find a few suitable young things, I'll voyage in the Pacific to find a satisfactory island for the Colony.'

During the next two months John was absorbed in the practical work of designing the yacht and the plane, perfecting the new power technique, and improving his flying.

At this time he was often to be seen 'playing at boats' on the Park Lake or the more boisterous Estuary, like any ordinary boy. He was now over eighteen, but in appearance under fifteen. Thus his behaviour seemed quite normal. He produced a large number of models and fitted them out with electric motors or steam engines. These he dispatched across the lake in all weathers, observing their performance with great care. The design was largely determined by the necessity of stowing the plane on board, with wings folded, and by the need for extreme sea-worthiness. John's final choice was an extraordinary craft which local yachtsmen regarded as a mere caricature of a ship. John made a special three-foot model to this design, and fitted her out in great detail. In general shape she was ludicrously broad in the beam, and of shallow draft, in fact an exaggeration of the speed-boat hull; a sort of cross between a speed-boat and a life-boat, with a saucer somewhere in her ancestry, and perhaps a flat pebble of the 'ducks and drakes' type. She was certainly a delightful toy; and I feel sure that John thoroughly enjoyed her simply as a toy, and had put much more work into her than was needed for mere experimentation. She represented a vessel the size of a small tug. No detail was omitted from her equipment. There were bunks for nine persons, but twenty could sleep on board at a pinch, and she could be handled comfortably by a single navigator. There was a realistic dining-saloon, with tables, chairs, cupboards. There was a latrine, glass portholes, minute navigation controls. These controls could be operated by some sort of radio device on shore. The engine was a fairly detailed replica of the sub-atomic engine that John intended for the actual ship.

Much entertainment was afforded by the antics which John made his model perform. On the Park Lake he would send her in leisurely pursuit of the terrified ducks. On the estuary, when the tide was in, he would stop her far out at sea, and persuade some kindly member of the sailing club to salvage her in a dinghy. When the sweating oarsman had reached the little derelict, and was putting out his hand to seize her, John (on shore, and half a mile away) would set her going for a yard or two and watch the man's repeated efforts to recover her. Finally he would let her out at full speed for the shore, and she would return to her master's hand like a well-trained dog.

John had also been at work on several model planes. He used to spend much time flying them; but in secret, for he feared that, if they were seen performing their surprising antics, they would attract too much attention. He therefore used to retire with them into the wilds of North Wales, by means of his motor-bike or my car. There he would try out his models in the fickle mountain winds, their sub-atomic power enabling them to perform feats which no elastic-driven model could possibly achieve.

His final choice was a surprising mechanism, made on the same scale as the model yacht, and capable of being dismantled and stowed on board. With this stub-winged instrument he would amuse himself and me by the hour, making it rise from the surface of a 'llyn' (it had both wheels and floats), and climb heavenwards, till we had to use a field-glass to follow it. It maintained its equilibrium automatically, but was steered by radio from the ground. When he had become adept in the management of this mechanical bird, he sometimes used it for a modern sort of hawking, sending the sparrow-like little object in chase of curlews, buzzards and ravens. This sport needed very delicate perception as well as control. As a rule the quarry would hurry away as soon as it realized it was being chased. The plane would then chevy it, or even swoop upon its back. But one old raven turned to fight, and before John could bring his toy's superior speed into operation for escape, the raven's horny neb had slashed one of the silken wings, and the plane came tumbling to the heather.

The plans for the yacht and the plane were finished before John reached the age of nineteen. I need not describe how I negotiated with shipbuilders and aeroplane manufacturers, and finally placed orders for the actual construction. I gained the reputation of being a mad millionaire; for the designs appeared to be quite unworkable, and I would not consider any of the objections raised against them. The main trouble was that in both plane and yacht the space allotted to the generation of power was by all ordinary standards quite insufficient. Contracts for the generators and machinery were distributed among several engineering firms in such a manner as to arouse as little curiosity as possible.

XV
Jacqueline

When these problems of engineering had been solved, John was able to turn his attention once more to his telepathic researches. As he still looked too young to be wandering about the Continent by himself, he insisted on taking me with him to Paris. When we were approaching our destination he showed signs of eagerness. Well might he, for he expected to find a being who could meet him as an equal and afford him a far more satisfying companionship than any he had yet known. But when we had lodged ourselves in a little hotel in the rue Bertholet (off the avenue de Claude Bernard) he became almost disheartened. When I questioned him he laughed awkwardly, and said, 'I'm having a new sensation. I'm feeling shy! She doesn't seem particularly keen on my coming. She won't help me to find her. I know she's somewhere in the Quartier Latin. She passes the end of this street quite often. I know she knows someone is looking for her, and yet she won't help. Also, she's evidently very old and wise. She remembers the Franco-Prussian War. I've been trying to see what she sees when she looks in a mirror, so as to get her face; but I can't catch her at the right time.'

At that moment his head jerked, and he said without any pause, 'While I was talking to you, *I*, the real I, was in touch with her. She's in a certain café. She'll be there for some time. Let's find her.'

He had an obscure feeling that the café was near the Odéon, so thither we hastened. After some hesitation he selected a certain establishment, and we entered. As soon as he had passed through the door, he whispered excitedly, 'This is it all right.

This is the room she is seeing at the moment.' He stood for a second or two, a queer little foreigner, jostled by waiters and a stream of guests. Then he made his way to an empty table at the far side of the room.

'There she is,' said John, with surprise in his voice, almost with awe. Following his gaze I saw at a near table two women. One had her back to us, but I judged that she was under thirty, for her figure was slim and the curve of her cheek almost juvenile. The other was extravagantly old. Her face was a relief map; all ridges and valleys. I studied her with disappointment, for she had a dull and peevish face, and she was looking at John with offensive curiosity.

But now the other woman turned her head and looked about the room. There was no mistaking those large eyes. They were John's, though heavy-lidded. For a moment they rested on me, then on John. The drooping lids were lifted to reveal two black and lofty caverns more abysmal even than John's. The whole face lit up with intelligence and amusement. She rose, and advanced toward John, who also rose. They faced one another in silence. Then the woman said, 'Alors c'est toi qui me cherches toujours!'

She was not what I had expected. In spite of the great eyes, she might almost have passed for a normal woman, an eccentric specimen of the normal species. Her head, though large, did not look noticeably out of proportion to her body, for she was tall, and the black hair which scarcely showed under her close-fitting hat added little to its size. Her ample mouth, I guessed, had been skilfully reduced by painting.

But though passably 'human,' according to the standards of *Homo sapiens*, she was strange. Were I an imaginative writer, and not merely a journalist, I might be able to suggest symbolically something of the almost 'creepy' effect she had on me, something of its remote and sleepy power. As it is I can only record certain obvious features, and in general that curious combination of the infantile, or even the foetal, with the mature. The protruding brow, the short broad nose, the great distance between the great eyes, the surprising breadth of the whole face, the marked furrow from nose to lips – all these characters were definitely foetal; and yet the precisely chiselled lips themselves and the delicate moulding of the eyelids produced an expression of subtle experience suggestive of an ageless divinity. To me at least, prepared of course by familiarity with John's own strangeness, this strange face seemed to combine idiosyncrasy and universality. Here, in spite of a vaguely repulsive uncouthness, was a living symbol of womanhood. Yet here also was a being utterly different from any other, something unique and individual. When I looked from her to the most attractive girl in the room I was shocked to find that it was the normal beauty that was repulsive. With something like vertigo I looked once more at the adorable grotesque.

While I was watching her, she and John stood regarding one another in complete silence. Presently the New Woman, as I had already cynically named her for my private amusement, asked us to move to her table, which we accordingly did. Her real name was given as Jacqueline Castagnet. The old lady, introduced as Mme Lemaître, regarded us with hostility, but had to put up with us. She was thoroughly commonplace; yet I was struck with certain points of likeness with Jacqueline, certain indescribable traits of expression and of voice. I guessed that the two women were mother and daughter. Later it turned out that I was right; and yet also quite wrong.

There followed a few aimless remarks, and then Jacqueline began speaking in a language quite unknown to me. For a second John looked surprised, then laughed, and answered, apparently in the same tongue. For half an hour or so they continued speaking, while I laboured to maintain conversation with Mme Lemaître in very bad French.

Presently the old lady reminded Jacqueline that they were both due elsewhere. When the two women had left us, John and I remained at the table for a while. He was silent and absorbed. I asked what language they had been talking. 'English,' he said. 'She wanted to tell me a lot about herself, and didn't want the old one to know about it, so she started in on English-back-to-front I've never tried that before, but it's quite easy, for us.'

There was a faint stress on the 'us'. John evidently knew that I felt 'left out', for he continued: 'I had better tell you the gist of what she said. The old lady is her daughter, but doesn't know it. Jacqueline was married to a man called Cazé eighty-three years ago, but she cleared out when the child was four. A few days ago she came across this old thing, and recognized her as her baby daughter, and made friends with her. Mme Lemaître showed her a photograph "of my mother who died when I was quite little – strangely like you, my dear. Perhaps you are some sort of great niece of mine." Jacqueline herself was born in 1765.'

John's account of the amazing life story of Jacqueline I can only summarize. It deserves to be recorded in a fat volume, but my concern is with John.

Her parents were peasants of that bleak country called 'Lousy Champagne,' between Chalons-sur-Marne and the Forest of Argonne. They were thrifty even to miserliness. Jacqueline, with her supernormal intelligence and sensibility and her ravenous capacity for life, was brought up in very cramping circumstances. This was probably a cause of the passion for pleasure and power which played so great a part in the earlier phases of her career. Like John, she took an unconscionable time a-growing up. This was a grievance to her parents, who were impatient for her to help in the house and on the land, and later were indignant that at an age when other girls were ready for marriage she was still a breastless child. The life which she was compelled to lead was physically healthy, but devastating to her spirit. She soon realized that she had capacities for all manner of subtle experience beyond the reach of her fellow mortals, and that the sane course was to devote herself to the exercise of these capacities; but her monotonous and dour existence made it impossible for her to detach herself from the less developed cravings of her nature, the increasing hunger for luxury and power. The fact that she inhabited a world of half-wits was borne in on her most obviously in the perception that the neighbouring peasants' daughters, though they eclipsed her in normal sexual appeal, were too stupid to make full use of this asset as a means to dominance.

Before adolescence had properly begun, when she was only

nineteen, she had already determined to beat them all at their own game, and indeed to become a queen among women. In the neighbouring town of Ste Menehould she sometimes saw fine ladies passing through in their coaches on their way to Paris, or breaking their journey at the local inn. She observed them with scientific care, and laid the foundations of her future technique.

When she was on the threshold of womanhood, her parents betrothed her to a neighbouring farmer. She ran away. Making full use of her only two weapons, sex and intelligence, she struggled through from the humblest and most brutish sort of prostitution to become the mistress of a wealthy Parisian merchant For some years she lived upon him, latterly giving him nothing in return but the terrible charm of her society once a week at dinner.

When she had reached the age of thirty-five she fell in love, for the first time in her life, with a young artist, one of those who were preparing the way for the vital and triumphant movement of Parisian painting. This novel experience brought to a climax the great conflict which tormented her. She who had followed the most ancient profession without repugnance was now horrified at herself. For the young man had wakened in her those dormant capacities which had perforce been thwarted by her career. She used her technique to capture him, and easily succeeded. They lived together. For a few months both were happy.

Gradually, however, she came to realize that, after all, she was mated to something which, from her point of view, was little better than an ape. She had known, of course, that her peasant clients, her Parisian clients, and her amiable wealthy patron, were 'subhuman'; the artist, she had persuaded herself, was an exception. Yet she still clung to her man. To break with the being to whom she had given her soul, even though in error, would, she felt, have killed her. Moreover, she still genuinely, though irrationally, loved him. He was her almost-human animal. She cared for him as a huntswoman and a spinster might care for her horse. He was *not* human, and could never be the mate of her spirit; but he was a noble animal and she was proud of his animal attainments, namely of his triumphs in the sphere of 'subhuman' art. She entered into his work with enthusiasm. She was not merely his source of inspiration; increasingly she took command of his artistic faculty. The more she possessed him, the more clearly the unhappy man realized that his native genius was being overborne and suffocated by the flood of her fertile imagination. His was a complex tragedy. He seems to have recognized that the pictures which he produced under her influence were more daring and aesthetically more triumphant than anything he could produce without her; but he realized also that he was losing his reputation, that even the most sensitive of his fellow-artists could not appreciate them. He made a stand for independence, and began to regain his self-respect and reputation. On her this turn of affairs had the effect of rousing all her suppressed disgust. Each was striving to be rid of the other, yet each craved the other. There was a quarrel, in which she played the part of the divinity who had come down to raise him to her own level, and was rejected. Next day he shot himself.

This tragedy evidently had a profound effect on her still juvenile mind. The finality of the deed bred in her a new tenderness and respect for the subhuman beings who surrounded her. Somehow this death lessened the distance between her and them. Though her passion for self-expression soon returned, and though she sometimes indulged it ruthlessly, it was tempered by the recollection that she had killed the one being in the world who for a whole month had seemed to her superior to herself.

For a few years after the death of the artist Jacqueline lived in great poverty on savings which she had accumulated in her association with the merchant. She tried to make a name for herself as a writer, under a masculine pseudonym; but the stuff which she produced was too remote to be appreciated, and she could not bring herself to write in a different vein. When she was in her forties, and still in the first flush of maturity, her obsessive craving for luxury and power returned with such insistence that, in a panic, she became a nun. She did not believe any of the explicit doctrines of the Church; but she made up her mind to pay lip service to all its superstitions for the sake of its flicker of genuine and corporate religious experience, which, she felt, she needed for the strengthening of her better nature. Her presence in the nunnery, however, very soon caused such an upheaval that the institution was finally disbanded, and Jacqueline, with bitter laughter in her heart, returned to her original calling.

But to her own surprise prostitution now afforded her something more than the means to wealth and power. Her experience in the nunnery had not been wholly barren. She had learned a good deal about the spiritual cravings of the subhuman kind; and this knowledge she now put to good use. Her motive in returning to prostitution had been purely self-regarding, but she soon discovered that the more human of her clients were suffering from an unconscious need for something more than carnal satisfaction. And she found exaltation in ministering to this essentially spiritual need. Carnal satisfaction she gave ungrudgingly. Her own initial distaste at intercourse with beings of a lowly order gave way to delight in her new office. Many a man whose real need was not merely copulation but intimacy with a sensitive yet fearless woman, many who needed moreover help in the seemingly hopeless task of 'coming to terms with the universe', found in Jacqueline a well of strength. As her reputation grew, ever greater demands were made on her. Hoping to save herself from a breakdown, she chose disciples, young women who were ready to live her life and give themselves as she gave herself. Some of them were partially successful, but none could do as she had done. The strain increased until at last she fell seriously ill.

When she recovered, her old self-seeking passion was once more uppermost. Using all her prowess she fought her way up the social ladder of Europe, till, at fifty-seven and on the threshold of full maturity, she married a Russian prince. She did so knowing that he was a worthless creature and a half-wit, even by normal standards. So skilfully did she play her cards during the next fifteen years that she had a good prospect of setting him on the throne. Increasing disgust and horror, however, flung her into another mental disorder. From this she emerged once more her true self. She cut adrift, disguised herself, and fled back to Paris to carry on her old profession. Occasionally she met one or other of her former clients, now well advanced in years. But as she herself had retained her youthful appearance, and indeed seemed to have the full flower of womanhood still ahead of her, she easily persuaded them that she was the former Jacqueline's young niece.

All this while she had never had a child, never conceived. In her early years she had taken precaution to avoid such a disaster; but in maturity, though she had felt no craving for motherhood, she had been less reluctant to risk it, and less cautious. As the decades passed and her remaining caution dwindled out, she came to suspect that she was sterile, and in the end she ceased to take any precautions at all. On her return from Russia an obscure sense that in missing motherhood she had missed a valuable experience developed into a definite hunger to have a baby of her own.

Not a few of her clients had tried to persuade her to accept marriage. Hitherto she had laughed at these suitors, but when she had passed her eightieth year, she began to be seriously attracted by the prospect of a spell of quiet married life. Among her clients was a young Parisian lawyer, Jean Cazé. Whether he was in fact the father of her child she did not know; but when, to her amazement, she found that she had conceived, she singled him out as a suitable husband. He, it so happened, had never thought of marrying her; but when she had slipped the idea into his mind, he pressed her ardently, overcame her feigned reluctance and carried her off in pride. After eleven months of pregnancy she bore her daughter, and very nearly died in the ordeal. Four years of maternal duties and of companionship with the faithful Cazé were enough for her. Jean, she knew, would treasure the infant; and indeed he did, to the extent of spoiling her for life. Jacqueline fled not only from Paris but from France, and started all over again in Dresden.

Throughout the last two-thirds of the nineteenth century Jacqueline appears to have had alternating spells of exalted prostitution and marriage. She counted among her husbands, she said, a British ambassador, a famous writer, and a West African negro who was a private in the French colonial army. Never again did she conceive. Probably John was right in surmising that she had the power of preventing conception by an act of volition though she had no idea how she exercised this power.

Since the close of the nineteenth century Jacqueline had not indulged in marriage. She had preferred to carry on her profession, because of her 'great affection for the dear children', by which she meant her clients. Hers must have been a strange life. Of course she gave herself for money, like any member of her profession, or of any other profession. Nevertheless, her heart was in her work, and she chose her clients, not according to their power to pay, but according to their needs and their capacity to benefit by her ministrations. She seems to have combined in her person the functions of harlot, psycho-analyst and priest.

During the war of 1914–18 she was drawn into overstraining herself once more. So many tragic cases came her way. And after the war, being wholly without national prejudices, she moved to Germany, where the need was greater. It was in Germany, in 1925, that she had once more collapsed, and was forced to spend a year in a 'mental home'. When we met her she was again established in Paris, and again at work.

On the day after our meeting in the café John had left me to amuse myself as best I could while he visited Jacqueline. He stayed away four days, and when he returned he was haggard and obviously in great distress. Not till long afterwards could he bring himself to tell the cause of his misery, and then he said only, 'She's glorious, and hurt, and I can't help her, and she won't help me. She was terribly kind and sweet to me. Said she had never met any one like me, wished we'd met a hundred years ago. She says my work is going to be great. But *really* she thinks it's just schoolboy adventure, no more.'

XVI
Adlan

John continued his search. I accompanied him. I shall not at this stage describe the few suitable supernormal youngsters whom he discovered and persuaded to prepare themselves for the great adventure. There was a young girl in Marseilles, an older girl in Moscow, a boy in Finland, a girl in Sweden, another in Hungary, and a young man in Turkey. Save for these, John found nothing but lunatics, cripples, invalids, and inveterate old vagabonds in whom the superior mentality had been hopelessly distorted by contact with the normal species.

But in Egypt John actually met his superior. This incident was so strange that I hesitate to record it, or even to believe it myself.

John had for long been convinced that a very remarkable mind was secreted somewhere in the Levant or the Nile Delta. From Turkey we took ship to Alexandria. Thence, after further investigation, we moved to Port Saïd. Here we spent some weeks. As far as I was concerned, they were weeks of idleness. There was nothing for me to do but to play tennis, bathe and indulge in mild flirtations. John himself seemed to be idling. He bathed, rowed in the harbour, wandered about the town. He was unusually absent-minded, and sometimes almost irritable.

When Port Saïd was beginning to bore me excessively, I suggested that we should try Cairo. 'Go yourself,' said John, 'if you want to, but I'm staying here. I'm busy.' I therefore took him at his word, and crossed the Delta by train. Long before we reached Cairo the Great Pyramids came into view, overtopping the palm trees and the unseen city. I shall not forget that first glimpse of them, for later it seemed to symbolize the experience that John himself was passing through in Port Saïd. They were grey-blue, in the blue sky. They were curiously simple, remote, secure.

I took a room at Shepheard's Hotel, and gave myself over to sight-seeing. One day, about three weeks after I left Port Saïd, a telegram came from John. It said merely, 'Home, John.' Nothing loath, I packed my traps and took the next train for Port Saïd.

As soon as I arrived, John made me book accommodation for *three* to Toulon by an Orient boat that was due to pass through the Canal a few days later. The new member of the party, he said, was on his way from Upper Egypt, and would join us as soon as he could. Before giving details of our future fellow passenger I must try to report what John told me of the very different being with whom he was in contact during my absence in Cairo.

'You see,' he said, 'the fellow I was after (Adlan, by name) turned out to have died thirty-five years ago. He was trying to get me from his place in the past, and at first I didn't realize. When at last we effected some sort of communication, he managed to show me what he was seeing, and I noticed that the steamers in the harbour were all little low old things with yards on the masts. Also there wasn't any Canal Company's Building where it ought to have been. (You know, the green-domed thing.) You can imagine how exciting this was. It took me a long time to get myself into the past instead of his coming to me in the present.'

John's story must be condensed. In order to secure a less precarious footing in the past, John, under Adlan's direction, made the acquaintance of a middle-aged Englishman, a ship-chandler, who had spent much of his childhood in Port Saïd in Adlan's time. This Anglo-Egyptian, Harry Robinson, was easily persuaded to talk about his early experiences, and to describe Adlan, whom he used at one time to meet almost daily. John soon made himself familiar with Robinson's mind to such an extent that he was able to reach back and establish himself quite firmly in the child and in the Port Saïd that had long since vanished.

Seen through Harry's eyes, Adlan turned out to be an aged and poverty-stricken native boatman. His face, John said, was like a mummy's, black and pinched and drawn, but very much alive, with a frequent and rather grim smile. His gigantic head bore upon its summit a fez which was ridiculously small for it. When, as occasionally happened, this covering fell off, his cranium was seen to be perfectly bald. John said it reminded him of a dark and polished and curiously moulded lump of wood. He had the typical great eyes, one of which was bloodshot, and running with yellow mucus. Like so many natives, he had suffered from ophthalmia. His bare brown legs and feet were covered with scars. Several toe-nails had been lost.

Adlan made his living by ferrying passengers between the liners and the shore, and by transporting European residents to and from the 'bath-houses' – wooden erections built out over the sea on angle-irons. The Robinson family hired Adlan and his boat several times a week to row them across the harbour to their 'bath house.' He had to wait while they bathed and lunched. Then he would row them back to the town. It was while Adlan was tugging at the oars in his long-prowed and gaily painted boat, and while Harry was prattling to his parents or his sister or even to Adlan himself, that John, regarding the scene through Harry's eyes, carried on his telepathic conversations with the unique Egyptian.

John's projection of his mind into the past took him back to the year 1896. At this time Adlan claimed that he was three hundred and eighty-four years old. John would have been less inclined to believe this before he met Jacqueline, but by now he was ready to accept it. Adlan, then, was born in 1512, somewhere in the Soudan. Most of his first century was spent as the wise man of his tribe, but in the end he resolved to exchange his primitive environment for something more civilized. He travelled down the Nile, and settled in Cairo, where in time he gained a reputation as a sorcerer. During the seventeenth century he played an active part in the turbulent political life of Egypt, and was at one time the power behind the throne. But political activities could not satisfy him. He was drawn into them much as an intelligent spectator might be drawn into a game of chess played by blockheads. He could not help seeing how the game might be played most effectively, and presently he found himself playing it. Toward the end of the eighteenth century, he became more and more absorbed in the development of his 'occult' powers, and chiefly his most recent art, that of projecting himself into the past.

A few years before Napoleon's Egyptian expedition Adlan broke with his political life entirely by faking a suicide. For some years he continued to live in Cairo, but in complete obscurity and very humble circumstances. He made his living as a water-carrier, driving his ass, laden with swollen and dripping skins, along the dusty streets. Meanwhile he continued to improve his supernormal powers, and would sometimes use them to practise psycho-therapy upon his fellow-proletarians. But his chief interest was exploration of the past. At this time the knowledge of Ancient Egypt was extremely scanty, and Adlan's passion was to gain direct experience of the great race of long ago. Hitherto his powers had only enabled him to reach a few years back, to events which occurred in an environment similar to his own. But presently he determined to bury himself in some obscure village and till the soil of the Delta, entering into the life of the primitive agriculturalists whose customs and culture had probably changed little since the days of the Pharaohs. For many decades he wielded the hoe and the shadoof; and in due course he learned to be almost as familiar with ancient Memphis as with modern Cairo.

In the second quarter of the ninteenth century, however, when he was still in appearance no more than middle-aged, he conceived the need to explore other cultures. For this purpose he settled in Alexandria, and took up his old profession of water-carrier. Here, with less ease and less success than in his study of Ancient Egypt, he made his entry into Ancient Greece, learning to project himself into the era of the great Library, and even into Greece itself of the age of Plato.

Not till the last quarter of the nineteenth century did Adlan ride his donkey along the strip of sand between Lake Menzaleh and the sea, and settle in Port Saïd, once more as a water-carrier. He did not practise his old profession exclusively. Sometimes he would hire out his donkey to a European passenger, ashore for the day. Then he would run barefoot behind the tall white ass, affectionately whacking its hindquarters, and crying 'Haa! Haa!'

Once when his beast, which he called 'Two Lovely Black Eyes,' was stolen, he ran thirty miles in chase of it, following its footprints in the moist shore. When at last he overtook the thief, he battered him, and returned in triumph on the ass. Sometimes he would board the liners and amuse the passengers with conjuring tricks with rings and balls and restless little yellow chicks. Sometimes he would sell them silk or jewellery.

Adlan's object in moving to Port Saïd had been to put himself into touch with contemporary European life and thought, and if possible to make some kind of contact with India and China. The Canal was by now the most cosmopolitan spot in all the world. Levantines, Greeks, Russians, Lascars, Chinese firemen, Europeans on their way to the East, Asiatics on their way to London and Paris, Moslem pilgrims on their way to Mecca, – all passed through Port Saïd. Scores of races, scores of languages, scores of religions and cultures jostled one another in that most flagrantly mongrel town.

Adlan soon learned how to get the best out of his new environment. His methods were diverse, but all depended chiefly on telepathy and extreme intelligence. He constructed little by little in his own mind a very clear picture of European, and even Indian and Chinese culture. He did not, indeed, find any culture ready to hand in the minds of the beings with whom he made contact in Port Saïd, for they, residents and passengers alike, were nearly all quite philistine. But by a brilliant process of inference from the meagre and incoherent traces of thought in these migrants he was able to reconstruct the cultural matrix in which they had developed. This method he supplemented by reading books lent him by a shipping agent who had a liking for literature. He learned also to extend his telepathic reach to such an extent that, by conjuring up all that he knew of John Ruskin (let us say), he could make contact with that didactic sage in his remote home by Coniston Water.

Presently it became evident to Adlan that the really interesting period of European thought lay in the future. Could he, then, explore the future as he had explored the past? This proved a far more difficult task, and one which he could never have performed at all effectively had he not, by great good luck, discovered John, a mind of somewhat the same calibre as his own. He conceived the idea of teaching that fellow-supernormal to reach back into the past to him, so that he himself might learn about the future without the precarious and dangerous labour of projecting himself into it.

I was surprised to hear from John, that, though only a few weeks had passed since our arrival in Egypt, he had in that period spent many months with Adlan. Or perhaps I should say that his interviews with Adlan (through the mind of Harry) were distributed over a period of many months in Adlan's life. Day after day the old man would ferry the Robinsons to their bath house, pulling steadily at his battered oars, and prattling in kitchen Arabic to Harry about ships and camels. And at the same time he would be carrying on a most earnest and subtle telepathic conversation with John about relativity or the quantum theory or the economic determination of history. John was soon convinced that he had encountered a mind which either through native superiority or through prolonged meditation was far in advance of his own, even in ability to cope with Western European culture. But Adlan's brilliance made his way of life seem all the more perplexing. With some complacency John assured himself that if he were to live as long as Adlan he would not have to spend his old age toiling for a pittance from *Homo sapiens*. But before he parted from Adlan he began to take a humbler view of himself and a more respectful attitude to Adlan.

The old man was greatly interested in John's biological knowledge, and its bearing upon himself and John. 'Yes,' he said, 'we are very different from other men. I have known since I was eight. Indeed these creatures that surround us are scarcely men at all. But perhaps, my son, you take that difference too seriously. No, I should not say that. What I mean is that though for you this project of founding the new species is the true way, for me there is another way. And each of us must serve Allah in the way that Allah demands of him.'

It was not, John explained, that Adlan threw cold water on his great adventure. On the contrary he entered into it with sympathy and made many helpful suggestions. Indeed one of his favourite occupations, as he plied his oars, was to expound to John with prophetic enthusiasm the kind of world that 'John's New Men' would make, and how much more vital and more happy it would be than the world of *Homo sapiens*. This enthusiasm was undoubtedly sincere, yet, said John, there was a delicate mockery behind it. It was not wholly unlike the zeal with which grown men enter into the games of children. One day John deliberately challenged him by referring to his project as the greatest adventure that man could ever face. Adlan was resting on his oars before crossing the harbour, for an Austrian Lloyd steamer was passing into the Canal. Harry was intent upon the liner, but John induced him to turn his eyes on the old boatman. Adlan was lookingly gravely at the lad. 'My son, my dear son,' he said, 'Allah wills of his creatures two kinds of service. One is that they should toil to fulfil his active purpose in the world, and that is the service which you have most at heart. The other is that they should observe with understanding and praise with discriminate delight the excellent form of his handiwork. And this is my service, to lay at Allah's feet such a life of praise that no man, not even you, my very dear son, can give him. He has fashioned you in such a manner that you may serve him best in action, though in action inspired always by deep-searching contemplation. But me he has fashioned such that I must serve him directly through contemplation and praise, though for this end I had first to pass through the school of action.'

John protested that the end of praise would be far better served by a world of the New Men than by a few isolated lofty spirits in a world of subhuman creatures; and that, therefore, the most urgent of all tasks was to bring such a world into being.

But Adlan replied, 'It seems so to you, because you are fashioned for action, and because you are young. And indeed it *is* so. Spirits of my kind know well that in due season spirits of your kind will in fact create the new world. But we know also that for us there is another task. It may even be that part of my task is actually to peer so far into the future that I may see and praise those great deeds which you, or some other, are destined to perform.'

When John had reported this speech to me he said, 'Then the old man broke off his communication with me, and also ceased prattling to Harry. Presently he thought to me again. His mind embraced me with grave tenderness, and he said, "It is time for you to leave me, you very dear and godlike child. I have seen something of the future that lies before you. And though you could bear the foreknowledge without faltering from the way of praise, it is not for me to tell you." Next day I met him again, but he was uncommunicative. At the end of the trip, when the Robinsons were stepping out of the boat, he took Harry in his arms and set him on the land, saying in the lingo that passed as Arabic with European residents, " 'L hwaga swoia, quaïs ketír!" (the little master, very nice). To me he said in his thoughts, "Tonight, or perhaps tomorrow, I will die. For I have praised the past and the present, and the near future too, with all the insight that Allah has given me. And peering into the farther future I have been able to see nothing but obscure and terrible things which it is not in me to praise. Therefore it is certain that I have fulfilled my task, and may now rest." '

Next day another boat took Harry and his parents to the bath houses.

XVII
Ng-Gunko and Lo

It will be remembered that we booked passages for three persons by Orient to Toulon and England. The third member of the party turned up three hours before the ship sailed.

John explained that in discovering this amazing child, who went by the name of Ng-Gunko, he had been helped by Adlan. The old man in the past had been in touch with this contemporary of John's, and had helped the two to make contact with one another.

Ng-Gunko was a native of some remote patch of the forest-clad mountain in or near Abyssinia; and though only a child he had at John's request found his way from his native country to Port Saïd by a series of adventures which I will not attempt to describe.

As time advanced and he failed to appear, I became more and more sceptical and impatient, but John was confident that he would arrive. He turned up at our hotel as I was trying to shut my cabin trunk. He was a grotesque and filthy little blackamoor, and I resented the prospect of sharing accommodation with him. He appeared to be about eight years old, but was in fact over twelve. He wore a long, blue and very grubby caftan and a battered fez. These clothes, we subsequently learned, he had acquired on his journey, in order to attract less attention. But he could not help attracting attention. My own first reaction to his appearance was frank incredulity. 'There ain't no such beast,' I said to myself. Then I remembered, that, when a species mutates, it often produces a large crop of characters so fantastic that many of the new types are not even viable. Ng-Gunko was decidedly viable, but he was a freak. Though his face was a dark blend of the negroid and the semitic with an unmistakable reminiscence of the Mongolian, his negroid wool was not black but sombre red. And though his right eye was a huge black orb not inappropriate to his dark complexion, his left eye was con-siderably smaller, and the iris was deep blue. These dis-crepancies gave his whole face a sinister comicality which was borne out by his expression. His full lips were frequently stretched in a grin which revealed three small white teeth above and one below. The rest had apparently not yet sprouted.

Ng-Gunko spoke English fluently but incorrectly, and with an uncouth pronunciation. He had picked up this foreign tongue on his six-weeks' journey down the Nile valley. By the time we reached London his English was as good as our own.

The task of making Ng-Gunko fit for a trip on an Orient liner was arduous. We scrubbed him all over and applied insecticide.

On his legs there were several festering sores. John sterilized the sharpest blade of his penknife and cut away all the bad flesh, while Ng-Gunko lay perfectly still, but sweating, and pulling the most hideous grimaces, which expressed at once torture and amusement. We purchased European clothes, which, of course, he detested. We had him photographed for his passport, which John had already arranged with the Egyptian authorities. In triumph we took him off to the ship in his new white shorts and shirt.

Throughout the voyage we were busy helping him to acquire European ways. He must not pick his nose in public, still less blow it in the natural manner. He must not take hold of his meat and vegetables with his hands. He had to acquire the technique of the bathroom and the water-closet. He must not relieve himself in inappropriate places. He must not, though a mere child, saunter into the crowded dining-saloon without his clothes. He must not give evidence that he was excessively intelligent. He must not stare at his fellow-passengers. Above all, he must, we said, restrain his apparently irresistible impulse to play practical jokes on them.

Though frivolous, Ng-Gunko was certainly of superior intelligence. It was, for instance, remarkable that a child who had lived his fourteen years in the forest should easily grasp the principle of the steam turbine, and should be able to ask the chief engineer (who showed us round the engine room) questions which made that experienced old Scot scratch his head. It was on this expedition that John had to whisper fiercely to the little monster, 'If you don't take the trouble to bottle up your blasted curiosity I'll pitch you overboard.'

When we reached our northern suburb Ng-Gunko was installed in the Wainwright household. As we did not want him to cause more of a sensation than need be, we dyed his hair black and made him wear spectacles with a dark glass for one eye. Only in the house might he be without them. Unfortunately he was too young to be able to resist the temptation of startling the natives. Walking along the street with John or me, muffled to the eyes against the alien climate, duly spectacled and demure, he would sometimes drop a pace behind as we were approaching some old lady or child. Then, projecting his chin above his scarf, he would whip off his glasses and assume a maniacal grin of hate. How often he did this without being caught I do not know; but on one occasion he was so successful that the victim let out a scream. John turned upon his protégé and seized him by the throat. 'Do that again,' he said, 'and I'll have that eye of yours right out, and step on it.' Never again did Ng-Gunko play the trick when John was present. But with me he did, knowing I was too amiable to report him.

In a few weeks, however, Ng-Gunko began to enter more seriously into the spirit of the great adventure. The conspiratorial atmosphere appealed to him. And the task of preparing himself to play his part gradually absorbed his attention. But he remained at heart a little savage. Even his extraordinary passion for machinery suggested the uncritical delight of the primitive mind in its first encounter with the marvels of our civilization. He had a mechanical gift which in some ways eclipsed even John's. Within a few days of his arrival he was riding the motor-bicycle and making it perform incredible 'stunts'. Very soon he took it to pieces and put it together again. He mastered the principles of John's psychophysical power unit, and found, to his intense delight, that he could perform the essential miracle of it himself. It began to be taken for granted that he would be the responsible engineer of the yacht, and of the future colony, leaving John free for more exalted matters. Yet in all Ng-Gunko's actions, and in his whole attitude to life, there was an intensity and even a passion which was very different from John's invariable calm. Indeed I sometimes wondered whether he was emotionally a true supernormal, whether he had anything unusual in his nature beyond brilliant intelligence. But when I suggested this to John he laughed. 'Ng-Gunko's a kid,' he said, 'but Ng-Gunko's all right. Among other things he has a natural gift for telepathy, and when I have trained him a bit he may beat me in that direction. But we are both beginners.'

Not long after our return from Egypt another supernormal arrived. This was the girl whom John had found in Moscow.

Like others of her kind, she looked much younger than she was. She seemed a child, not yet on the threshold of womanhood, but was actually seventeen. She had run away from home, taken a job as stewardess on a Soviet steamer, and slipped ashore at an English port. Thence, equipped with a sufficiency of English money, which she had secured in Russia, she had found her way to the Wainwrights.

Lo was at first glance a much more normal creature than either Ng-Gunko or John. She might have been Jacqueline's youngest sister. No doubt her head was strikingly large, and her eyes occupied more of her face than was normal, but her features were regular, and her sleek black hair was long enough to pass for a 'shingle'. She was clearly of Asiatic origin, for her cheek bones were high, and her eyes, though great, were deeply sunk within their half-closed and slanting lids. Her nose was broad and flat, like an ape's, her complexion definitely 'yellow'. She suggested to me a piece of sculpture come to life, something in which the artist had stylized the human in terms of the feline. Her body, too, was feline, 'so lean and loose,' said John. 'It feels breakable, and yet it's all steel springs covered with loose velvet.'

During the few weeks which passed before the sailing of the yacht, Lo occupied the room which had once belonged to Anne, John's sister. Relations between her and Pax were never easy, yet always amicable. Lo was exceptionally silent. This, I am sure, would not trouble Pax, for she was generally drawn to silent persons. Yet with Lo she seemed to feel constantly an obligation to talk, and an inability to talk naturally. To all her remarks Lo would reply appropriately, even amiably, yet whatever she said seemed to make matters worse. Whenever Lo was present, Pax would seem ill at ease. She would make silly little mistakes in her work, putting things into wrong drawers, sewing buttons on in the wrong place, breaking her needle, and so on. And everything took longer than it should.

I never discovered why Pax was so uncomfortable with Lo. The girl was, indeed, a disconcerting person, but I should have expected Pax to be more, not less, able to cope with her than others were. It was not only Lo's silence that was so disturbing, but also her almost complete lack of facial expression, or rather of changes of expression for her very absence of expression was itself expressive of a profound detachment from the world around her. In all ordinary social situations, when others would show amusement or pleasure or exasperation, and Ng-Gunko would register intense emotion, Lo's features remained unmoved.

At first I imagined that she was simply insensitive, perhaps dull-witted; but one curious fact about her soon proved that I was wrong. She discovered a passion for the novel, and most of all for Jane Austen. She read all the works of that incomparable authoress over and over again, indeed so often that John, whose interest ran in very different channels, began to chaff her. This roused her to deliver her one long speech. 'Where I come from,' she said, 'there is nothing like Jane Austen. But in me there is something like that, and these old books are helping me to know myself. Of course, they are only "sapient", I know; but that is half the fun. It's so interesting to transpose it all to suit *us*. For instance, if Jane could understand me, which she couldn't, what, I ask myself, would she say about me? I find the answer extraordinarily enlightening. Of course, our minds are quite outside her range, but her *attitude* can be applied to us. Her attitude to her little world is so intelligent and sprightly that it gives it a significance that it could never have discovered in itself. Well, I want to regard even us, even our virtuous Colony, in a Jane-like manner. I want to give it a kind of significance that would have remained hidden even from its earnest and noble leader. You know, John, I fancy *Homo sapiens* has still quite a lot to teach you about personality. Or if you are too busy to learn, then I must, or the colony will be intolerable.'

To my surprise John replied by giving her a hearty kiss, and she remarked, demurely, '*Odd* John, you have indeed a lot to learn.'

This incident may suggest to the reader that Lo was lacking in humour. She was not. Indeed she had a gift of not unkindly wit. Though she seemed incapable of smiling, she often roused others to laughter. And yet, as I say, she was mysteriously disconcerting to most of us. Even John was sometimes uncomfortable in her presence. Once when he was giving me some instructions about finance he broke off to say, 'That girl's laughing at me, in spite of her solemn face. She never laughs at all, and yet she's always laughing. Now tell me, Lo, *what's* amusing you.' Lo replied, 'Dear and important John, it is you who are laughing, at your own reflection in me.'

Lo's chief occupation during her few weeks in England was to master the science and art of medicine, and to make herself acquainted with all the most advanced work on the subject of embryology. The reason for this I did not learn till later. Her vocational training she pursued partly by means of an intensive study under an embryologist of some distinction at the local university, partly by prolonged discussion with John.

As the time approached when the yacht was to be ready and the adventure to begin, Lo's studies became more and more exacting. She began to show signs of strain. We urged her to take a holiday for a few days. 'No,' she said, 'I *must* get to the end of this business before we sail. Then I will rest.' We asked if she was sleeping all right. She was evasive. John became suspicious. '*Do* you sleep, ever?' he asked. She hesitated, then replied, 'Not *ever*, if I can help it. In fact it is some years since I last slept. And then I slept for ages. But I will *never* sleep again if I can help it.' Her first answer to John's incredulous 'Why?' was a shudder, then she added as an afterthought. 'It is a waste of time. I do go to bed, but I read all night; or just think.'

I forget whether I mentioned that all the other supernormals were brief sleepers. John, for instance, was satisfied with four hours a night, and could comfortably do entirely without sleep for three nights at a stretch.

A few days after this incident I learned that Lo had not come down to breakfast, and that Pax had found her still in bed, and asleep. 'But it's all wrong,' said Pax, 'It's more like a fit. She's lying there with her eyes tight shut and awful expressions of horror and rage passing over her face; and she keeps muttering Russian or something, and her hands keep clawing at her chest.'

We tried to wake her, but could not. We sat her upright. We

put cold water on her. We shouted at her. We shook her and pricked her, but it was no good. That evening she began to scream. She kept it up, off and on, all that night. I stayed with the Wainwrights, though I could do nothing. But somehow I couldn't go. The whole street was kept awake. It was sometimes just an inarticulate screech like an animal beside itself with pain and fury, sometimes a torrent of Russian, shouted at the top of her voice, but so blurred that John could make nothing of it.

Next morning she quietened down, and for more than a week she slept without stirring. One morning she came down to breakfast as though nothing had happened, but looking, so John said, 'like a corpse animated by a soul out of Hell.' As she sat down she said to John, '*Now* do you understand why I like Jane Austen, better for instance than Dostoievski?'

It took her some time to regain her strength and her normal equanimity. One day, when she had settled down to work again, she told Pax a bit about herself. Away back in her infancy, before the Revolution, when her people lived in a small town beyond the Urals, she used to sleep every night; but she often had bad dreams, which she said were extremely terrifying, and completely indescribable in terms of any normal experience. All she could say of them was that she felt herself turn into a mad beast or a devil, yet that inwardly she always remained her sane little self, an impotent spectator of her own madness. As she grew older, these infantile terrors left her. During the Revolution and the years immediately following it her family experienced terrible sufferings from civil war and famine. She was still in appearance an infant but mentally well able to appreciate the significance of events going on around her. She had, for instance, already reached a conviction that, though both sides in the civil war were equally capable of brutality and generosity, the spirit of the one was on the whole right, the other wrong. Even at that early age she felt, vaguely but with conviction, that the horror of her life, the bombardments, the fires, the mass executions, the cold, the hunger, must somehow be embraced, not shunned. Triumphantly she did embrace them. But there came a time when her town was sacked by the Whites. Her father was killed. Her mother fled with her in a refugee train crowded with wounded men and women. The journey was, of course, desperately fatiguing. Lo fell asleep, and was plunged once more into her nightmare, with the difference that it was now peopled with all the horrors of the civil war, and she herself was forced to watch impotently while her other self perpetrated the most hideous atrocities.

Ever since those days any great strain was liable to bring sleep upon her, with all its horrors. She reported, however, that the attacks were now much less frequent; but that on the other hand the content of her dreams was more terrible, because – she couldn't properly explain – because it was more universal, more metaphysical, more cosmically significant, and at the same time more definitely an expression of something Satanic (her own word) within her very self.

XVIII
The *Skid*'s First Voyage

Henceforth Pax was more at ease with Lo. She had nursed her, received her confidence, and found occasion to pity her. All the same it was clear that the continued presence of Lo was a strain on Pax. When the yacht was launched, John himself said to me, 'We must get away as soon as possible now. Lo is killing Pax, though she does her best not to. Poor Pax! She's being driven into old age at last.' It was true. Her hair was fading, and her mouth drawn.

It was with mixed feelings that I learned that I was not to take part in the coming voyage in search of additional members for the colony. I could live my own life. I could marry and settle down, holding myself in readiness to serve John when he should need me. But how could I live without John? I tried to persuade him that I was necessary to him. A saucer-like craft wandering the oceans with a crew of three children would attract less attention if she carried one adult. But my suggestion was dismissed. John claimed that he no longer looked a child, and further declared that he could touch up his face so as to appear at least twenty-five.

I need not describe in detail the preparations which these three young eccentrics undertook in order to fit themselves for their adventure. Both Ng-Gunko and Lo had to learn to fly; and all three had to become familiar with the mannerisms of their own queer aeroplane and their own queer yacht. The vessel was launched on the Clyde by Pax, and christened *Skid*, under which odd but appropriate name she was duly registered. I may mention that for the Board of Trade inspection she was fitted with a normal motor-engine, which was subsequently removed to make room for the psycho-physical power unit and motor.

When both yacht and plane were ready for use, a trial trip was made among the Western Isles. On this trip I was tolerated as a guest. The experience was enough to cure me of any desire for a longer voyage in such a diabolical vessel. The three-foot model had somehow failed to make me imagine the discomforts of the actual boat. Her great beam made her fairly steady, but she was so shallow, and therefore low in the water, that every considerable wave splashed over her, and in rough weather she was always awash. This did not greatly matter, as her navigating controls were all under cover in a sort of streamlined deck-house reminiscent of a sporting saloon motorcar. In fine weather one could stretch one's legs on deck, but below deck there was scarcely room to move, as she was a mass of machinery, bunks, stores. And there was the plane. This strange instrument, minute by ordinary standards, and folded up like a fan, occupied a large amount of her space.

After emerging from Greenock we skidded comfortably down the Clyde, past Arran, and round the Mull of Kintyre. Then we struck heavy weather, and I was violently sick. So also, much to my satisfaction, was Ng-Gunko. Indeed, he was so ill that John decided to make for shelter, lest he should die. But quite suddenly Ng-Gunko learned to control his vomiting reflexes. He stopped being sick, lay still for ten minutes, then leapt from his bunk with a shout of triumph, only to be hurled into the galley by a lurch of the ship.

The trials were said to be entirely successful. When she was going full speed the *Skid* lifted the whole fore part of herself right out of the water and set up a mountain-range of water and foam on either side of her. Though the weather was rather wild, the plane also was tested. It was heaved out aft on a derrick and unfolded while afloat. All three members of the crew took a turn at flying it. The most surprising thing about it was that, owing to its cunning design and its immense reserve of power, it rose straight from the water without taxiing.

A week later the *Skid* set out on her first long voyage. Our farewells were made at the dock. The Wainright parents reacted very differently to the departure of their youngest son. Doc was genuinely anxious about the dangers of the voyage in such a vessel, and mistrustful of the abilities of the juvenile crew. Pax showed no anxiety, so complete was her confidence in John. But clearly she found it difficult to face his departure without showing distress. Hugging her, he said, 'Dear Pax,' then sprang on board. Lo, who had already made her farewells, came back to Pax, took both her hands, and said, actually smiling, 'Dear mother of important John!' To this odd remark Pax replied simply with a kiss.

My slender knowledge of the voyage is derived partly from John's laconic letters, partly from conversation after his return. The programme was determined by his telepathic researches. Distance, apparently, made no difference to the case with which he could pick up the psychic processes of other supernormals. Success depended entirely on his ability to 'tune in' to their mental 'setting' or mode of experience, and this depended on the degree of similarity of their mode to his own. Thus he was already in clear communication with a supernormal in Tibet, and two others in China, but for the rest he could only make the vaguest guesses as to the existence and location of possible members of the colony.

Letters told us that the *Skid* had spent an unprofitable three weeks on the West Coast of Africa. John had flown into the hinterland, pursuing traces of a supernormal in some oasis in the Sahara. He struck a sand storm of peculiar violence, and made a forced landing in the desert, with his engine choked with sand. 'When the wind had dropped I cleaned her guts,' said John, 'and then flew back to the *Skid*, still chewing sand.' What epic struggles were involved in this adventure I can only guess.

At Cape Town the *Skid* was docked, and the three young people set off to comb South Africa, following up certain meagre traces of the supernormal mentality. Both John and Lo soon returned empty-handed. In his letter John remarked, 'Delicious to watch the Whites treating the Blacks as an inferior species. Lo says it reminds her of her mother's stories of Tsarist Russia.'

John and Lo waited impatiently for some weeks while Ng-Gunko, doubtless revelling in his return to native conditions, nosed about in the remote woodlands and saltpans of Ngami-land. He was in telepathic communication with John, but there seemed to be some mystery about his activities. John grew anxious, for the lad was dangerously juvenile, and possibly of a less balanced type than himself. At last he was driven to tell Ng-Gunko that if he did not 'chuck his antics' the *Skid* would sail without him. The reply was merely a cheerful assurance that he would be starting back in a day or two. A week later came a message that combined a cry of triumph and an S.O.S. He had secured his prey, and was making his way through the wilds to civilization, but had no money for the return railway journey. John therefore set out to fly to the spot indicated, while Lo, single handed, took the *Skid* round to Durban.

John had already been waiting some days at the primitive settlement when Ng-Gunko appeared, dead beat, but radiant. He removed a bundle from his back, uncovered the end of it, and displayed to the indignant John a minute black infant, immature, twitching and gasping.

Ng-Gunko, it seems, had traced the telepathic intimations to a certain tribe and a certain woman. His African experiences had enabled him to detect in this woman's attitude to the life of the forest something akin to his own. Further investigation led him to believe that though she herself was in some slight degree supernormal, the main source of those obscure hints which he had been pursuing was not the mother but her unborn child in whose prenatal experiences Ng-Gunko recognized the rudiments of supernormal intensity. It was indeed remarkable that before birth a mind should have any telepathic influence at all. The mother had already carried her baby for eleven months. Now Ng-Gunko knew that he himself had been born late, and that his mother had not been delivered of him till certain incentives had been used upon her by the wise women of the tribe. This treatment he persuaded the black matron to undergo, for she was weary to death. As best he could, Ng-Gunko applied what he knew of the technique. The baby was born, but the mother died. Ng-Gunko fled with his prize. When John asked how he had fed the baby on the long journey, Ng-Gunko explained that in his Abyssinian days he and other youngsters used to milk wild antelopes. They stalked them, and by means of a process that reminded me of 'tickling' trout, they persuaded the mothers to let themselves be milked. This trick had served on the journey. The infant, of course, had not thrived, but it was alive.

The kidnapper was pained to find that his exploit, far from being applauded, was condemned and ridiculed. What on earth, John demanded, could they possibly do with the creature? And anyhow, was he really at all worth bothering about? Ng-Gunko was convinced that he had secured an infant superman who would outclass them all; and in time John himself was impressed by his telepathic explorations of the newcomer.

The plane set out for Durban with the baby in Ng-Gunko's arms. One would have expected the care and maintenance of it to fall on Lo, but her attitude toward it was aloof. Moreover, Ng-Gunko himself made it clear that he would bear all responsibility for the newcomer, who somehow acquired the name Sambo. Ng-Gunko became as devoted to Sambo as a mother to her firstborn or a schoolboy to his white mice.

The *Skid* now headed for Bombay. Somewhere north of the Equator she ran into very heavy weather. This was a matter of small importance to a craft of her seaworthiness, though it must have greatly increased the discomfort of her crew. At a much later date I learned of a sinister incident that occurred in those wild days, an incident to which John made no reference in his letters. The *Skid* sighted a small British steamer, the *Frome*, in distress. Her steering engine was out of action, and she was labouring broadside-on to the storm. The *Skid* stood by, till, when the *Frome*'s plight was obviously hopeless, the crew took to the two remaining boats. The *Skid* attempted to take them both in tow. This operation was evidently very dangerous, for a sea flung one of the boats bodily on to the afterdeck of the yacht, thrusting her stern under water, and threatening to sink her. Ng-Gunko, who was dealing with the tow rope, had a foot rather badly crushed. The boat then floated off, and capsized. Of her crew only two were rescued, both by the *Skid*. The other boat was successfully taken in tow. A few days later the weather improved, and the *Skid* and her charge made good progress toward Bombay. But now the two strangers on board the *Skid* began to show great curiosity. Here were three eccentric children and a black baby cruising the ocean in a most eccentric craft driven by some unintelligible source of power. The two seamen were loud in praise of their rescuers. They assured John that they would speak up for him in the public inquiry which would be held over the loss of the *Frome*.

This was all very inconvenient. The three supernormals discussed the situation telepathically, and agreed that drastic action was demanded. John produced an automatic pistol and shot the two guests. The noise caused great excitement in the boat. Ng-Gunko slipped the tow rope, and John cruised round while Ng-Gunko and Lo, lying on the deck with rifles, disposed of all the *Frome*'s survivors. When this grim task was finished, the corpses were thrown to the sharks. The boat was scrubbed of blood stains, and then scuttled. The *Skid* proceeded to Bombay.

Long afterwards, when John told me about this shocking incident, I was as much perplexed as revolted. Why, I asked, if he dared not risk a little publicity, had he been willing to risk destruction in the work of rescuing the ship's boats? And how did he fail to realize, during that operation, that publicity was inevitable? And was there, I demanded, any enterprise whatever, even the founding of a new species, that could justify such cold butchery of human beings? If this was the way of *Homo superior*, I said, thank God I was another species. We might be weak and stupid, but at least we were able sometimes to feel the sanctity of human life. Was not this piece of brutality on exactly the same footing as the innumerable judicial murders, political murders, religious murders, that had sullied the record of *Homo sapiens*? These, I declared had always seemed to their perpetrators righteous acts, but were regarded by the more human of our kind as barbarous.

John answered with that mildness and thoughtfulness with which he treated me only on those rare occasions when I gave him matter for serious consideration. He first pointed out that the *Skid* had still to spend much time in contact with the world of *Homo sapiens*. Her crew had work to do in India, Tibet and China. It was certain, therefore, that if their part in the *Frome* incident became public, they would be forced to give evidence at the inquiry. He insisted, further, that if they were discovered, their whole venture would be ruined. Had they at that early stage known all that they knew later about hypnotically controlling the humbler species, they might indeed have abolished from the minds of the *Frome*'s survivors all memory of the rescue. 'But you see,' he said, 'we could not do it. We had deliberately risked publicity, as we had risked destruction by the storm, *hoping* to avoid it. We *tried* to set up a process of "oblivifaction" in our guests, but we failed. As for the wickedness of the act, Fido, it naturally revolts you, but you are leaving something out of account. Had we been members of your species, concerned only with the dreamlike purpose of the normal mind, what we did would have been a crime. For today the chief lesson which your species has to learn is that it is far better to die, far better to sacrifice even the loftiest of all "sapient" purposes, than to kill beings of one's own mental order. But just as you kill wolves and tigers so that the far brighter spirits of men may flourish, so we killed those unfortunate creatures that we had rescued. Innocent as they were, they were dangerous. Unwittingly they threatened the noblest practical venture that has yet occurred on this planet. Think! If *you*, and Bertha, had found yourselves in a world of great apes, clever in their own way, lovable too, but blind, brutish, and violent, would you have refused to kill? Would you have sacrificed the founding of a human world? To refuse would be cowardly, not physically, but spiritually. Well, if we could wipe out your whole species, frankly, we would. For if your species discovers us, and realizes at all what we are, it will certainly destroy us. And we know, you must remember, that *Homo sapiens* has little more to contribute to the music of this planet, nothing in fact but vain repetition. It is time for finer instruments to take up the theme.'

When he had done, John looked at me almost pleadingly. He seemed to long for my approval, the approval of a half-human thing, his faithful hound. Did he, after all, feel guilty? I think not. I think this strong desire to persuade me sprang simply from affection. For my part, such is my faith in John, that though I cannot approve, I cannot condemn. There must surely be some aspect that I am too stupid or insensitive to grasp. John, I feel, *must* be right. Though he did what would have been utterly wrong if it had been done by any of us, I have an almost passionate faith that, done by John, and in John's circumstances, the terrible deed was right.

But to return to the story. At Bombay John and Lo spent some time studying Indian and Tibetan languages, and otherwise preparing themselves for contact with Eastern races. When at length they left the *Skid*, and Bombay, Ng-Gunko remained behind to nurse Sambo and his damaged foot. The two explorers set out together in the plane; but Lo, disguised as a Nepalese boy, was put down at an Indian hill station. There, it was hoped, she might develop a telepathic contact which was thought to indicate a supernormal in some such environment. John himself continued his flight over the great mountains to Tibet to meet the young Buddhist monk with whom he had often been in communication.

In his brief letter describing his expedition to Tibet John scarcely mentioned the actual journey, though the flight over the Himalayas must have been an exacting task even for a superman in a superplane. He said only, 'She took the jump splendidly, and then was blown right back again into India, head over heels, too. She dropped my thermos flask. Coming back I saw it on the ridge, but let it lie.'

As the Tibetan monk was able to guide him telepathically, he found the monastery quite easily. John described Langatse as a supernormal of forty years, physically but little advanced beyond the threshold of manhood. He had been born without eyes. Blindness had forced him to concentrate on his telepathic powers, which he had developed far beyond John's own attainment. He could always see telepathically what other people were seeing; consequently, for reading he had simply to use someone else's eyes. The other would cast his eye over the page while Langatse followed telepathically. He had trained several young men to perform this task for him so well that he could read almost as quickly as John. One curious effect of his blindness was that, since he could use many pairs of eyes at a time, and could see all round an object at once, his mental imagery was of a kind quite inconceivable to ordinary persons. As John put it, he *grasped* things visually, instead of merely having a single aspect of them. He saw things mentally from every point of view at once.

John had originally hoped to persuade Langatse to join his great adventure, but he soon found that this was out of the question. The Tibetan regarded the whole matter much as Adlan had done. He was interested, encouraging, but aloof. To him the founding of a new world, though it must indeed someday be accomplished by someone, was not a matter of urgency, and must not tempt him from his own more lofty spiritual services. Nevertheless he consented gladly to be the spiritual adviser of the colony, and meanwhile he would impart to John all that he knew of the telepathic technique and other supernormal activities. At one time Langatse suggested that John should give up his enterprise and settle in Tibet to share the more exacting and more exalted spiritual adventures on which he himself was engaged. But, finding that John was not to be easily persuaded, he soon desisted. John stayed at the monastery a week. During his return flight he received a message from Langatse to the effect that, after grave spiritual exercise, he had decided to help John by seeking out and preparing any young supernormals that were in Asia and suited to the adventure.

John received a communication also from Lo. She had discovered two remarkable sisters, both younger than herself. They would join the expedition; but as the elder was just now in a very poor state of health, and the younger a little child, they must stay where they were for the present.

The *Skid* now set her course for the China Seas. In Canton John met Shên Kuo, the Chinese supernormal boy with whom he had already had some communication. Shên Kuo readily agreed to make his way inland to join the two other boys and two girls whom Langatse had discovered in the remote Eastern Province of Sze Chwan. Thence the five would journey to Tibet to Langatse's monastery, to undergo a course of spiritual discipline in preparation for their new life. Langatse reported that he had also secured three Tibetan boys and a girl for the colony, and that these also would be prepared at the monastery.

One other convert was made. This was a half-caste Chinese American girl resident in San Francisco. This child, who went by the name of Washingtonia Jong, was also discovered by Langatse telepathically. The *Skid* crossed the Pacific to pick her up, and she straightway became a member of the crew. I did not meet her till a much later date; but I may as well say at once that 'Washy', as she was called, appeared to me at first a quite normal young person, a keen little American flapper with rather Chinese eyes and black cropped hair. But I was to find that there was more in her than that.

John's next task was to discover a suitable island for the colony. It must have a temperate or subtropical climate. It must have a fertile soil, and be well situated for fishing. It must be remote from any frequented steamer route. This last requirement was extremely important, for complete secrecy was essential. Even the most remote and unconsidered island would certainly be visited sooner or later; so John had thought out certain steps to prevent ships from reaching his island, and certain others to ensure that any visitors who should make a landing should not spread news of the colony among the normal species. Of these devices I shall speak in due season.

The *Skid* crossed the Equator and began a systematic exploration of the South Seas. After many weeks of cruising a suitable though minute island was discovered somewhere in the angle between the routes from New Zealand to Panama and New Zealand to Cape Horn, and well away from both courses. This discovery was an incredible stroke of luck, indeed it might well have been an act of Providence. For the island was one which was not marked on any charts, and there were clear signs that it had only within the last twenty years or so been thrown up by sub-oceanic disturbance. There were no non-human mammals on it, and no reptiles. Vegetation was still scanty and undiversified. Yet the island was inhabited. A small native group had taken possession of it, and were living by fishing around its coasts. Many varieties of plants and trees they themselves had brought over from their original home and established on the island.

I did not hear about these original inhabitants till much later, when I visited the island. 'They were simple and attractive creatures,' said John, 'but, of course, we could not allow them to interfere with our plans. It might have been possible to obliterate from their minds every recollection of the island and of ourselves, and then to transport them. But though I had learned much from Langatse, our technique of oblivifaction was still unreliable. Moreover, where could we have deposited the natives without rousing protests, and curiosity? We might have kept them alive on the island, as domestic animals, but this would have wrecked our plans. It would also have undermined the natives spiritually. So we decided to destroy them. One bit of hypnotic technique (or magic, if you like) I felt sure I could now perform successfully on normal minds in which there were strong religious convictions. This we decided to use. The natives had welcomed us to their island and arranged a feast for us. After the feast there were ritual dances and religious rites. When the excitement was at a climax I made Lo dance for them. And when she had done, I said to them, in their own language, that we were gods, that we needed their island, that they must therefore make a great funeral pyre for themselves, mount it together, lie down together, and gladly die. This they did, most gladly, men, women and children. When they had all died we set fire to the faggots and their bodies were burnt.'

I cannot defend this act. But I may point out that, had the invaders been members of the normal species, they would probably have baptised the natives, given them prayer books and European clothes, rum and all the diseases of the White Man. They would also have enslaved them economically, and in time they would have crushed their spirits by confronting them at every turn with the White Man's trivial superiority. Finally, when all had died of drink or bitterness, they would have mourned for them.

Perhaps the only defence of the psychological murders which the supernormals committed when they took possession of the island would run as follows. Having made up their minds that at all costs the island must be theirs, and unencumbered, they did not shirk the consequences of their decision. With open eyes they went about their task, and fulfilled it in the cleanest possible way. Whether the end which they so ruthlessly pursued did in fact justify the means, I simply do not feel competent to decide. All my sympathies lie with the view that murder can never be justified, however lofty the end at stake. Certainly, had the killing been perpetrated by members of my own kind, such a deed would have deserved the sternest condemnation. But who am I that I should judge beings who in daily contact with me constantly proved themselves my superiors not only in intelligence but in moral insight?

When the five superior beings, John and Lo, Ng-Gunko and Washingtonia and the infant Sambo, had taken possession of the island, they spent some weeks resting from their travels, preparing the site for future settlement, and conferring with Langatse and those who were under his guidance. It was arranged that as soon as the Asiatics were spiritually equipped they should find their way as best they could to one of the French Polynesian islands, whence the *Skid* would fetch them. Meanwhile, however,

the *Skid* would make a hurried trip to England *via* the Straits of
Magellan to secure materials for the founding of the colony, and
to fetch the remaining European supernormals.

XIX
The Colony is Founded

The *Skid* reached England three weeks before the date on which
I was to be married. As she had no radio, and her voyage had
been speedy, she arrived unannounced. Bertha and I had been
shopping. We called at my flat to deposit some parcels before
going out for the evening. Arm in arm, we entered my sitting-
room, and found the *Skid*'s crew snugly installed, eating my
apples and some chocolates which I kept for Bertha's entertainment. We stood for a moment in silence. I felt Bertha's arm
tighten on mine. John was enjoying his apple in an easy chair by
the fire. Lo, squatting on the hearthrug, was turning over the
pages of the *New Statesman*. Ng-Gunko was in the other easy
chair, chewing sweets and bending over Sambo. I think he was
helping the infant to readjust the thick and unfamiliar clothes
without which he could not have faced the English climate.
Sambo, all head and stomach, with limbs that were mere buds,
cocked an inquisitive eye at me. Washingtonia, whom I had
not seen before, struck me at that moment as reassuringly
commonplace among those freaks.

John had risen, and was saying with his mouth full, 'Hullo, old
Fido, hullo, Bertha! You'll hate me, Bertha, but I *must* have Fido
to help me for a few weeks, buying stores and things.' 'But we're
just going to get married,' I protested. 'Damn!' said John. Then
to my surprise I assured John that of course we would put it off
for a couple of months. Bertha wilted on to a chair with a
voiceless 'Of course.' 'Good,' cried John cheerfully. 'After this
affair I may not bother you anymore.' Unexpectedly my heart
sank.

The following weeks were spent in a whirl of practical activities. The *Skid* had to be reconditioned, the plane repaired. Tools and machinery, electric fittings and plumbing materials must be bought and shipped to Valparaiso to await transhipment. Timber must be sent from the South American forests to the same port. General stores must be purchased in England. My task was to negotiate all these transactions under John's direction. John himself prepared a list of books which I must somehow procure and dispatch. There were to be scores of technical works on various biological subjects, tropical agriculture, medicine and so on. There were to be books on theoretical physics, astronomy, philosophy, and a rather intriguing selection of purely literary works in many languages. Most difficult to procure were many scores of Asiatic writings with titles suggestive of the occult.

Shortly before the *Skid*'s next sailing-date the additional European members of the party began to arrive. John himself went to Hungary to fetch Jelli, a mite said to be seventeen years old. She was no beauty. The frontal and the occipital regions of her head were repulsively over-developed, so that the back of her head stretched away behind her, and her brow protruded beyond her nose, which was rudimentary. In profile her head suggested a croquet mallet. She had a harelip and short bandy legs. Her general appearance was that of a cretin; yet she had supernormal intelligence and temperament, and also hypersensitive vision. Not only did she distinguish two primary colours within the spectrum-band that we call blue, but also she could see well down into the infra-red. In addition to this colour-discrimination, she had a sense of form that was, so to speak, much finer-grained than ours. Probably there were more nerve-endings in her retinae than in normal eyes, for she could read a newspaper at twenty yards' distance, and she could see at a glance that a penny was not accurately circular. So sensitive was she to form that, if the parts of a puzzle picture were flung down before her, she took in their significant relations at a glance, and could construct the picture without a pause. This amazing percipience often caused her distress, for no man-made article appeared to her to achieve the shape that its maker intended. And in the sphere of art she was excruciated, not merely by inaccuracy of execution but also by crudity of conception.

Besides Jelli, there was the French girl, Marianne Laffon, quite normal in contrast with Jelli, and rather pretty with her dark eyes and olive skin. She was seemingly a repository of the whole of French culture, and could quote any passage of any classic, and, by some magic of her own, so amplify it that one seemed to plumb the author's mind.

There was also a Swedish girl, Sigrid, whom John called the Comb-Wielder, 'because she had such a gift for combing out tangled minds till they're all sleek and sane.' She had been a consumptive, but had apparently cured herself by some sort of mental 'immunizing' of her tissues. Even after her cure she retained the phthisic's cheerfulness. A great-eyed, fragile thing, she combined her wonderful gift of sympathy and insight with a maternal tenderness toward brute strength. When she found it being brutal, she censured but still loved it. She was moved to send it away howling with its tail between its legs, but at the same time she 'felt all sloppy about it, as though it were just a delicious little naughty boy.'

Several young male supernormals turned up, one by one, to join the *Skid*. (The Wainwrights' house became at this time a shocking slum.) There was Kemi, the Finn, a younger John; Shahîn, the Turk, a few years older than John, but well content to be his subordinate; and Kargis from the Caucasus.

Of these, Shahîn was from the normal point of view the most attractive, for he had the build of a Russian dancer and in social intercourse a lightness of touch which one took according to one's mood, either as charming frivolity or as sublime detachment.

Kargis, who was not much younger than John, arrived in a state bordering on mania. He had had a very trying journey in a tramp steamer, and his unstable mind had failed to stand the strain. In appearance he was of John's type, but darker and less hardy. I found it very difficult to form a consistent idea of this strange being. He oscillated between excitement and lethargy, between passion and detachment. The cause of these fluctuations was not, I was assured, anything in his body's physiological rhythm, but external events which were hidden from me. When I inquired what kind of events, Lo, who was trying to help me, said, 'He's like Sigrid in having a great sense of personality. But he regards persons rather differently from her way. She just loves them, and laughs at them too, and helps them, and cures them. But for him each person is like a work of art, having a particular quality or style, or ideal form which he embodies well or ill. And when a person is jarringly untrue to his peculiar style or ideal form, Kargis is excruciated.'

The ten young people and one helpless infant set sail in the *Skid* in August of 1928.

John kept in communication with us by the ordinary mail. As I shall shall explain later, the *Skid*, and sometimes the plane, had occasion to make frequent voyages among the Islands or to Valparaiso. Thus it was possible to post John's brief and guarded letters. From these documents we learned first that the voyage out had been uneventful; that they had called at Valparaiso to load as much of the stores as possible; that they had reached the island; that the *Skid*, manned by Ng-Gunko, Kemi and Marianne, was plying to and from Valparaiso to transport the rest of the stores; that the building of the settlement was now well under way; that the Asiatic members had arrived, and were 'settling in nicely'; that a hurricane had struck the island, destroying all the temporary buildings, depositing the damaged *Skid* on a little hill beside the harbour, and hurting one of the Tibetan boys; that they had sowed large tracts of fruit and vegetables; that they had built six canoes for fishing; that Kargis had fallen seriously ill of some digestive disease and was expected to die; that he had recovered; that the remains of a Galapagos lizard had been washed up on the shore after God knows how long a journey; that Sigrid had tamed an albatross, and that it stole the breakfast; that the Colony had suffered its first tragedy, for Yang Chung had been caught by a shark, and Kemi had been seriously mauled in the vain attempt to rescue him; that Sambo was spending all his time reading, but could not yet sit upright;

that they had made for themselves pipes on the James Jones model, but with special attachments so that they could be played by normal five-fingered hands; that Tsomotre (one of the Tibetans) and Shahîn were composing wonderful music; that Jelli had developed acute appendicitis and Lo had operated successfully; that Lo herself had been working too hard on some embryological experiments and had fallen into one of her terrible nightmares; that she was awake again; that Marianne and Shên Kuo had gone to live on the far side of the Island 'because they wanted to be alone for a bit'; that 'Washy' was going mad, for she complained of feeling hate for Lankor (a Tibetan girl) who had won the heart of Shahîn; that 'Washy' had tried to kill Lankor and herself; that Sigrid, in spite of prolonged and patient efforts, had failed to cure 'Washy', and was now herself showing signs of strain; that both girls were not being cured from afar by Langatse's telepathic influence; that the Colonists had completed their stone library and meetinghouse, and the observatory was being started; that Tsomotre and Lankor, who were evidently the most expert telepathists, were now able to provide the colony with the news of the world in daily bulletins; that the more advanced members of the party, under the direction of Langatse, were undergoing severe exercises in spiritual discipline, which in time should raise them to a new plane of experience; that a severe earthquake had caused the whole island to sink nearly two feet, so that they had to lay several new courses of stone on the quays, and would henceforth need to keep the *Skid* in readiness for a sudden exodus, in case the island should disappear.

As the months protracted themselves into years, John's letters became less frequent and more brief. He was evidently entirely absorbed in the affairs of the colony; and as the party became more and more concerned with supernormal activities, he found it increasingly difficult to give us an intelligible account of their life.

In the spring of 1932, however, I was greatly surprised to receive a long letter from John, the main purport of which was to urge me to visit the island as soon as possible. I quote the essential passage. 'You will laugh when I tell you I want you to come and use your journalistic prowess upon us. In fact I want you to write that threatened biography after all, not for our sakes but for your own species. I must explain. We have made a wonderful start. Sometimes it was a bit grim, but now we have worked out a very satisfactory life and society. Our practical activities run smoothly, delightfully, and we are able at last to join in a great effort to reach the higher planes of experience. Already we are very different mentally from what we were when we landed. Some of us have seen far and deep into reality, and we have at least gained a clear view of the work we have undertaken. But a number of signs suggest that before very many months have passed the colony will be destroyed. If your species discovers us, it will certainly try to smash us; and we are not yet in a position to defeat it. Langatse has urged us (and he is right) to push on with the spiritual part of our work, so as to complete as much as possible of it before the end. But also we may as well leave records of our little adventure as an example for any future supernormals who may attempt to found the new world, and for the benefit of the more sensitive members of *Homo sapiens*. Langatse will take charge of the record for supernormals; the record for your species entails only normal powers and can be done satisfactorily by yourself.'

I was now a tolerably successful freelance journalist, and I had a full programme before me. I was married, and Bertha was expecting a child. Yet I eagerly accepted the invitation. That afternoon I made inquiries about steamers for Valparaiso, and replied to John (*post restante* at that city), telling him when to expect me.

Guiltily, I broke my news to Bertha. She was hard hit by it, but she said, 'Yes, if John wants you, of course you must go.' Then I went round to the Wainwrights'. Pax greatly surprised me, for no sooner had I begun to tell her about the letter than she interrupted me. 'I know,' she said, 'for some weeks he has been giving me little stray visions of the island, and even talking to me. He *said* he would be asking for you.'

XX
The Colony in Being

When I arrived at Valparaiso the *Skid* was waiting for me, manned by Ng-Gunko and Kemi. Both lads had appreciably matured since I had last seen them, nearly four years earlier. Those crowded years seemed to have speeded up the slow growth natural to their kind. Ng-Gunko, in particular, who was actually sixteen and might have been taken for twelve, had acquired a grace and a seriousness which I never expected of him. Both seemed in a great hurry to put to sea. I asked if there was any special engagement to keep on the island. 'No,' said Ng-Gunko, 'but we may have less than a year to live, and we love the island, and all our friends. We want to go home.'

As soon as my baggage and some cases of books and stores had been transhipped in the *Skid*'s dinghy, we got under way. Ng-Gunko and Kemi promptly divested themselves of their clothes, for it was a hot day. Kemi's fair skin had been burnt to the colour of the teak woodwork of the *Skid*.

When we had come within about forty miles of the island, Kemi, who was at the helm, said, glancing from the magnetic to the gyroscopic compass, 'They must be using the deflector. That means some ship has come too close, and they're heading her off.' He went on to explain that on the island they had an instrument for deflecting a magnetic compass at any range up to about fifty miles. This was the fourth occasion for its use.

At last we sighted the island, a minute grey hump on the horizon. As we approached, it rose and displayed itself as a double mountain. Even when we were quite close to land I failed to detect any sign of habitation. Ng-Gunko explained that the buildings had all been placed in such a manner as to escape detection. Not till the island opened out its little harbour to embrace us did I see the corner of one wooden building protruding from behind some trees. Not till we had entered the inner harbour did the whole settlement appear. It consisted of a score or more of small wooden buildings, with a larger stone building behind them and slightly higher up the slope. Most of the little wooden buildings, I was told, were the private houses of the residents. The stone building was the library and meetinghouse. There were also buildings on the quayside, including a stone power-station. Somewhat remote from the rest of the settlement was a collection of wooden sheds which were said to be temporary labs.

The *Skid* was moored alongside the lowest of three stone quays, for the tide was out. The colonists were waiting to receive us and unload. They were a bunch of naked, sunburnt youngsters of both sexes and very diverse appearance. John sprang on board to greet me, and I found myself tongue-tied. He had become a dazzling figure, at least to my faithful eyes. There was a new firmness and a new dignity about him. His face was brown and smooth and hard like a hazel nut. His whole body was like shaped and beeswaxed oak. His hair was bleached to a dazzling whiteness. I noted among the party several unfamiliar faces, the Asiatics, of course, from China, Tibet and India. Seeing all these super-normals together, I was struck by a pervading Chinese or Mongolian expression about them. They had come from many lands, but they had a family likeness. John might well be right in guessing that all had sprung from a single 'sporting point' centuries ago, probably in Central Asia. From that original mutation, or perhaps from a number of similar mutations, successive generations of offspring had spread over Asia, Europe, Africa, interbreeding with the normal kind, but producing occasionally a true supernormal individual.

Subsequently I learned that Shên Kuo's direct researches in the past had confirmed this theory.

I had been dreading life in this colony of superior persons. I expected to feel unwanted, to be as useless and distracting as a dog at a highbrow concert. But my reception reassured me. The younger members accepted me gaily and carelessly, treating me much as nieces and nephews might treat an uncle whose special office it was to make a fool of himself. The elders of the party were more restrained, but genial.

I was assigned one of the wooden cottages or shacks as my private residence. It was surrounded by a verandah. 'You may prefer to have your bed out here,' said John. 'There are no mosquitoes.' I noticed at once that the cottage had been made with the care and accuracy of fine cabinet-making. It was sparsely furnished with solid and simple articles of waxed wood. On one wall of the sitting-room was a carved panel representing in an abstract manner a boy and a girl (of the supernormal type) apparently at sea in a canoe, and hunting a shark. In the bedroom was another carving, much more abstract, but vaguely suggestive of sleep. On the bed were sheets and blankets, woven of rough yarns unknown to me. I was surprised to see electric light, an electric stove, and beyond the bedroom a minute bathroom with hot and cold taps. The water was heated by an electric contrivance in the bathroom itself. Fresh water was plentiful, I was told, for it was distilled from the sea as a sort of by-product of the psycho-physical power-station.

Glancing at the small electric clock, let in to the wall, John said, 'There'll be a meal in a few minutes. That long building is the feeding-house, with the kitchen alongside of it.' He pointed to a low wooden building among the trees. In front of it was a terrace, and on the terrace, tables.

I shall not forget my first meal on the island. I was seated between John and Lo. The table was crowded with unfamiliar eatables, especially tropical and sub-tropical fruits, fish, and a queer sort of bread, all served in vessels made of wood or of shell. Marianne and the two Chinese girls seemed responsible for the meal, for they kept disappearing into the kitchen to produce new dishes.

Looking at the slight naked figures of various shades from Ng-Gunko's nigger-brown to Sigrid's rich cream, all seated round the table and munching with the heartiness of a school treat, I felt that I had strayed into an island of goblins. This was in the main an effect of the two rows of large heads and eyes like field-glass lenses, but was accentuated by the disproportionately large hands which were busy with the food. The islanders were certainly a collection of young freaks, but one or two of them were freakish even in relation to the standards of the group itself. There was Jelli with her hammer-head and harelip, Ng-Gunko with his red wool and discrepant eyes, Tsomotre, a Tibetan boy, whose head seemed to grow straight out of his shoulders without the intervention of a neck, Hwan Tê, a Chinese youngster, whose hands outclassed all the others in size, and bore, in addition to the normal set of fingers, an extra and very useful thumb.

Since the death of Yang Chung the party comprised eleven youths and boys (including Sambo) and ten girls, of whom the youngest was a little Indian child. Of these twenty-one individuals, three lads and a girl were Tibetan, two youths and two girls were Chinese, two girls were Indian. All the others were of European origin, except Washingtonia Jong. I was to discover that of the Asiatics the outstanding personalities were Tsomotre, the neckless expert in telepathy, and Shên Kuo, a Chinese youth of John's age who specialized in direct research into the past. This gentle and rather frail young man, who I noticed, was given specially prepared food, was said to be in some ways the most 'awakened' member of the colony. John once said half seriously, 'Shên Kuo is a reincarnation of Adlan.'

On my first afternoon John took me for a tour of inspection round the island. We went first to the power-house, a stone building on the quay. Outside the door the infant Sambo lay upon a mat, kicking with his crooked black legs. Curiously, he seemed to have changed less than the other supernormals. His legs were still too weak to support him. As we passed, he piped to John, 'Hi! What about a bit of a talk? I've got a problem.' John replied without checking his progress, 'Sorry, too busy just now.' Within we found Ng-Gunko, his back shining with sweat, shovelling sand, or rather dried ooze, into a sort of furnace. 'Convenient,' I said, laughing, 'to be able to burn mud.' Ng-Gunko paused, grinning, and wiping his brow with the back of his hand.

John explained. 'The element that we use now is particularly easy to disintegrate by the psychical technique, but also it occurs only in very small quantities. Of course, if we disintegrated *all* this mass of stuff and let it go off with a bang, the whole island would be blown up. But only about a millionth part of the raw material is the element we want. The furnace merely frees the desired atoms as a sort of ash, which has to be refined out of the other ash, and stored in that hermetically sealed container.'

He now led the way into another room, and pointed to a much smaller and very solid-looking bit of mechanism. 'That,' he said, 'is where the real business is done. Every now and then Ng-Gunko puts a pinch of the stuff on a sticky wafer, pops it in there, and "hypnotizes" it. That makes it go invisible and intangible and *materially* non-existent, at least for ordinary purposes; because, you see, it has gone to sleep and can't take *any* effect on anything. Well, either Ng-Gunko wakes it up again at once, and it sends the hell of a blast of power into that engine, to drive the dynamos; or it is taken away for use on the *Skid*, or elsewhere.'

We passed into a room full of machinery, a mass of cylinders, rods, wheels, tubes, dials. Beyond that were three dynamos, and beyond them the plant for distilling sea-water.

We then moved over to the laboratory, a rambling collection of wooden buildings rather apart from the settlement. There we found Lo and Hwan Tê working with microscopes. Lo explained that they were 'trying to spot a bug that's got at the maize plantation.' The place was much like any ordinary lab., crowded with jars, test-tubes, retorts and so on. It evidently served for work on both the physical and the biological sciences, but the biological was preponderant. On one side of the room was an immense cupboard, or rather series of small cupboards. These, I learned, were incubators for use in embryological work. I was to hear more of this later.

The library and meeting-room was a stone erection which had evidently been built to last, and to delight the eye. It was quite a small building of one storey, and I was not surprised to learn that most of the books were still housed in wooden sheds. But the shelves of the library itself were already filled with all the most prized volumes. When we entered the room, we found Jelli, Shên Kuo and Shahîn surrounded by piles of books. The smaller half of the building was occupied by the meeting-room, which was panelled with strange woods and decorated with much-stylized carvings. Of these works, some repelled and intrigued me, others moved me not at all. The former, John said, had been done by Kargis, the latter by Jelli. It was plain that Jelli's creations had a significance unperceived by me, for John was evidently held by them, and to my surprise we found Lankor, the Tibetan girl, standing motionless before one of them, her lips moving. When he saw her, John said, lowering his voice, 'She's far away, but we mustn't risk disturbing her.'

After leaving the library we walked through a big kitchen garden, where several of the young people were at work, and thence up the valley between the island's two mountains. Here we passed through fields of maize and groves of baby orange-trees and shaddock, which, it was hoped, would some day bear a rich crop. The vegetation of the island ranged from tropical to subtropical and even temperate. The extinct native pioneers had introduced much valuable tropical vegetation, such as the ubiquitous and invaluable coco-palm, and also breadfruit, mango, and guava. Owing to the saltness of the air none but the coco-palm had really prospered until the supernormals had invented a spray to counteract the salt. When we had climbed out of the valley by a little track amongst a tangle of aromatic bushes, we presently emerged upon a tract of bare hillside consisting of rock, covered in places with dried sub-oceanic ooze. Here and there a wind-borne seed had alighted and prospered, and founded a little colony of vegetation. On a shoulder of the mountain John pointed out 'the island's main attraction for sightseers.' It was the keel and broken ribs of a wooden vessel evidently wrecked and sunk before the island rose from the bottom of the Pacific. Within it were bits of crockery and a human skull.

On the top of the little mountain we came upon the unfinished observatory. Its walls had risen only a foot from the ground, yet the whole place had a deserted look. To my question John replied, 'When we found out how short a time lay before us, we abandoned all work of that kind, and concentrated on undertakings that we could bring to some sort of conclusion. I'll tell you more about them, some day.'

I have reached the part of my narrative that I intended to present with most detail and greatest effect, but several attempts to tackle it have finally convinced me that the task is beyond my powers. Again and again I have tried to plan an anthropological and psychological report on the colony. Always I have failed, I can give only a few incoherent observations. I can say, for instance, that there was something incomprehensible, something 'inhuman', about the emotional life of the islanders. In all normal situations, though of course their behaviour varied from the exuberance of Ng-Gunko and the fastidiousness of Kargis to the perfect composure of Lo, their emotions seemed on the whole normal. Doubtless, even in the most hearty expression of normal emotion in everyday situations, there was a curious self-observation and a detached relish, which seemed to me not quite 'human'. But it was in grave and exceptional situations and particularly in disaster that the islanders revealed themselves as definitely of a different texture from that of *Homo sapiens*. One incident must serve as an example.

Shortly after my arrival Hsi Mei, the Chinese girl, commonly called May, was seized with a terrible fit, and in disastrous circumstances. In her, apparently, the supernormal nature, though highly developed, was very precariously established. Her fit was evidently caused by a sudden reversion to the normal, but to the normal in a distorted and savage form. One day she was out fishing with Shahîn, who had recently become her mate. She had been strange all the morning. Suddenly she flew at him and began tearing him with nails and teeth. In the scuffle the boat capsized, and the inevitable shark seized May by the leg. Fortunately Shahîn wore a sheath-knife, for use in cleaning fish. With this he attacked the shark, which by good luck was a young one. There was a desperate struggle. Finally the brute released its prey and fled. Shahîn, mauled and exhausted, succeeded with great difficulty in bringing May back to land. During the following three weeks he nursed her constantly, refusing to allow anyone to relieve him. What with her almost severed leg and her mental disorder, she was in a desperate plight. Sometimes her true self seemed to reappear, but more often she was either unconscious or maniacal. Shahîn was hard put to it to restrain her from doing serious hurt to herself or to him. When at last she seemed to be recovering, Shahîn was ecstatically delighted. Presently, however, she grew much worse. One morning, when I took his breakfast over to their cottage, he greeted me with a gaunt but placid face, and said, 'Her soul is torn too deeply now. She will never mend. This morning she knows me, and has reached out her hand for me. But she is not herself, she is frightened. And very soon she will not know me ever again. I will sit with my dear this morning as usual, but when she is asleep I must kill her.' Horrified, I rushed to fetch John. But when I had told him, he merely sighed and said, 'Shahîn knows best.'

That afternoon, in the presence of the whole colony, Shahîn carried the dead Hsi Mei to a great rock beside the harbour. Gently he laid her down, gazed at her for a moment with longing, then stepped back among his companions. Thereupon John, using the psycho-physical technique, caused a sufficient number of the atoms of her flesh to disintegrate, so that there was a violent outpouring of their pent-up energies, and her whole body was speedily consumed in a dazzling conflagration. When this was done, Shahîn passed his hand over his brow, and then went down with Kemi and Sigrid to the canoes. The rest of the day they spent repairing the nets. Shahîn talked easily, even gaily, about May; and laughed, even, over the desperate battle of her spirit with the powers of darkness. And sometimes while he worked, he sang. I said to myself, 'Surely this is an island of monsters.'

I must now try to convey something of my vivid impression that strange and lofty activities were all the while going on around me on the island although I could not detect them. I felt as though I were playing blind man's buff with invisible spirits. The bodily eye watched unhindered the bright perceived world and the blithe physical activities of these young people;

but the mind's eye was blindfold, and the mind's ear could gather only vague hints of incomprehensible happenings.

One of the most disconcerting features of life on the island was that much of the conversation of the colonists was carried on telepathically. So far as I could judge, vocal speech was in process of atrophy. The younger members still used it as the normal means of communication, and even among the elders it was often indulged in for its own sake, much as we may prefer to walk rather than take a bus. The spoken language was prized chiefly for its aesthetic value. Not only did the islanders make formal poems for one another as frequently as the cultured Japanese; they also delighted sometimes to converse with one another in subtle metre, assonance and rhyme. Vocal speech was used also for sheer emotional expression, both deliberately and inadvertently. Our civilization had left its mark on the island in such ejaculations as 'damn' and 'blast' and several which we do not yet tolerate in print. In all reactions to the personality of others, too, speech played an important part. It was often a vehicle for the expression of rivalry, friendship and love. But even in this field all finer intercourse, I was told, depended on telepathy. Speech was but an obbligato to the real theme. Serious discussion was always carried on telepathically and in silence. Sometimes, however, emotional stress would give rise to speech as a spontaneous but unconsidered accompaniment of telepathic discourse. In these circumstances vocal activity tended to be blurred and fragmentary like the speech of a sleeper. Such mutterings were rather frightening to one who could not enter into the telepathic conversation. At first, by the way, I had been irrationally disturbed whenever a group of the islanders, working in silence in the garden or elsewhere, suddenly began to laugh for no apparent reason though actually in response to some telepathic jest. In time I came to accept these oddities without the 'nervy' creepiness which they used to arouse in me.

There were happenings on the island far more strange than the normal flow of telepathic conversation. On my third evening, for instance, all the colonists gathered in the meeting-room. John explained that this was one of the regular twelfth-day meetings, 'to review our position in relation to the universe'. I was advised to come, but to go away when I was bored. The whole party sat in the carved wooden chairs round the walls of the room. There was silence. Having had some experience of Quaker meetings, I was not at first ill at ease. But presently a rather terrifying absolute stillness came upon the company. Not only gross fidgetings, but even those almost imperceptible movements which characterize all normal living, ceased, and became noticeable through their absence. I might have been in a roomful of stone images. On every face was an expression of intent but calm concentration which was not solemn, was even perhaps faintly amused. Suddenly and with keen scrutiny, all eyes turned upon me. I was seized with a sudden panic; but immediately there came over all the intent faces a reassuring smile. Then followed an experience which I can only describe by saying that I felt directly the presence of those super-normal minds, felt telepathically a vague but compelling sense of their immature majesty, felt myself straining desperately to rise to their level, felt myself breaking under the strain, so that I had finally to flee back into my little isolated and half-human self, with the thankfulness of one who falls asleep after great toil, but with the loneliness of an exile.

The many eyes were now turned from me. The young winged minds had soared beyond my reach.

Presently Tsomotre, the neckless Tibetan, moved to a sort of harpsichord, tuned to the strange intervals which the islanders enjoyed. He played. To me his music was indescribably unpleasant. I could have screamed, or howled like a dog. When he had done, a faint involuntary murmur from several throats seemed to indicate deep approval. Shahîn rose from his seat, looking with keen inquiry at Lo, who hesitated, then also rose. Tsomotre began playing once more, tentatively. Lo, meanwhile, had opened a huge chest, and after a brief search she took from it a folded cloth, which when she had shaken it out was revealed as an ample and undulatory length of silk, striped in many colours. This she wrapped around her. The music once more took definite form. Lo and Shahîn glided into a solemn dance, which quickened presently to a storm of wild movement. The silk whirled and floated, revealing the tawny limbs of Lo; or was gathered about her with pride and disdain. Shahîn leapt hither and thither around her, pressing toward her, was rejected, half accepted, spurned again. Now and then came moments of frank sexual contact, stylized and knit into the movement-pattern of the dance. The end suggested to me that the two lovers, now clinging together, were being engulfed in some huge catastrophe. They glanced hither and thither, above, below, with expressions of horror and exaltation, and at one another with gleams of triumph. They seemed to thrust some invisible assailant from them, but less and less effectively, till gradually they sank together to the ground. Suddenly they sprang up and apart to perform slow marionette-like antics which meant nothing to me. The music stopped, and the dance. As she returned to her seat, Lo flashed a questioning, taunting look at John.

Later, when I had described this incident in my notes, I showed my account of it to Lo. When she had glanced at it, she said, 'But you have missed the point, you old stupid. You've made it into a love story. Of course, what you say is all right – but it's all wrong too, you poor dear.'

After the dance the company relapsed into silence and immobility. Ten minutes later I slipped away to refresh myself with a walk. When I returned, the atmosphere seemed to have changed. No one noticed my entrance. There was something indescribably eerie in the spectacle of those young faces staring with adult gravity at nothing. Most disturbing of all was Sambo, sitting like a little black doll in his ample chair. Tears were trickling down his cheeks, but his soft little mouth seemed to have grown hard and proud and old. After a few minutes I fled.

Next morning, though the meeting had not ended till dawn, the normal life of the colony was afoot once more. I asked John to explain what had been happening at the meeting. He said they had at first merely been looking into their motives. The young especially had still a lot to learn in this respect. Both young and old had also done a good deal of work upon their deeper mutual relations, relations which in the normal species would have been far below the threshold of consciousness.

All the colonists, John said, had been engaged in making themselves known to one another as fully as possible. They had also, all of them, been disciplining themselves, making their minds more seemly and more effective. This they had performed in the presence of Langatse, their spiritual adviser, and of course under his guidance. With him they had also meditated deeply about metaphysics. In addition to all this, said John, they had been learning to expand their 'now' to embrace hours, days; and narrowing it also to distinguish the present and the past strokes of a gnat's wing. 'And we explored the remote past,' he said, 'helped greatly by Shên Kuo, whose genius moves in that sphere. We attained also a kind of astronomical consciousness. Some of us at least glimpsed the myriads of peopled worlds, and even the minds of stars and of nebulae. We saw also very clearly that we must soon die. And there were other things which I must not tell you.'

Life on the island did not consist entirely of this exalted corporate activity. The islanders had to do a good deal of hard work of a much more practical kind. Every day two or three canoes would go out fishing. Nets and boats and harpoons had to be repaired. There was constant work in the garden and fruit-groves, and the maize-fields. Hitherto there had been endless building operations in wood and stone, but when the islanders had discovered their impending fate, such work was abandoned. A good deal of minor woodwork was still afoot. Much of the 'crockery' was made of wood, and the rest of shell or gourd. The machinery needed constant attention, and so did the *Skid*. I was surprised to learn that the *Skid* had made many voyages among the Polynesian Islands, actually bartering some of the handicrafts of the colony for native produce. Later I found that these voyages had another purpose.

All this manual work was entered into rather as sport than as toil, for it had never been a tyranny. The most serious attention of every member was given to very different matters. The younger islanders spent much time in the library and the lab., absorbing the culture of the inferior species. The elders were concerned with a prolonged research into the physical and mental attributes of their own kind. In particular they were grappling with the problem of breeding. At what age might their young women safely conceive? Or should reproduction be ectogenetic? And how could they ensure that the offspring should be both viable and supernormal? This research was evidently the chief work of the laboratory. Originally its aim had been mainly practical, but even after the discovery of their impending doom the islanders continued these biological experiments for their theoretical interest.

When we entered the labs we found several persons at work. Lo, Kargis and the two Chinese boys were apparently in charge of the research. Delicate experiments were being carried out on the germ cells of molluscs, fishes and specially imported mammals. Still more difficult work was in progress upon human ova and spermatozoa, both normal and supernormal. I was shown a series of thirty-eight living human embryos, each in its own incubator. These startled me considerably, but the story of their conception and capture startled me even more. Indeed, it filled me with horror, and with violent though short-lived moral indignation. The eldest of these embryos was three months old. Its father, I was told, was Shahîn, its mother a native of the Tuamotu Archipelago. The unfortunate girl had been seduced, brought to the island, operated upon, and killed while still under the anaesthetic. The more recent specimens, however, had been secured by milder methods, for Lo had invented a technique by which the fertilized ovum could be secured without violence to the mother. In all the more recent cases the mother had yielded up their treasure unwittingly, and without leaving their native islands. They were merely persuaded to agree to comply with certain instructions given by the supernormal father. The technique apparently combined physical and psychical methods, and was imposed upon the girls as a sublime religious ritual.

There was also a series of five much younger and ectogenetically fertilized ova. In these cases both father and mother were members of the colony. Lo herself had contributed one specimen. The father was Tsomotre. 'You see,' she said, 'I am rather young for gestation, but my ova are all right for experimental purposes.' I was puzzled. I knew well that sexual intercourse was practised on the island. Why then had the *fertilization* of this ovum been carried out artificially? As tactfully as I could, I stated my difficulty. Lo answered with some asperity, 'Why, of course, because I was not in love with Tsomotre.'

Since I am on this subject of sex I had better pursue it. The younger members of the colony, such as Ng-Gunko and Jelli, were only on the threshold of adolescence. Nevertheless, they were very sensitive to one another, both physically and mentally. Moreover, though physically backward, they were (so to speak) imaginatively precocious, as John had been. Consequently the mental side of sexual love was surprisingly developed among them.

Among the elder members there were, of course, more serious attachments. As they had discovered how to bring conception under direct voluntary control, their unions were followed by no practical difficulties. They had, however, produced a crop of emotional stresses.

From what I was told, I had gathered that there must have been a subtle difference between the love experiences of the islanders and those of normal persons. So far as I can tell, the difference was caused by two characteristics of the supernormal, namely, more discriminate awareness of self and of others, and greater detachment. The greater accuracy of self- and other-consciousness was of course responsible for a high degree of mutual understanding, tolerance and sympathy in ordinary relations. It seems to have rendered the loves of these strange beings at once exceptionally vivid and in most cases exceptionally harmonious. Occasionally some surge of crude and juvenile emotion would threaten to blot out this insight, but then detachment would normally supervene to prevent disaster. Thus between the very different spirits of Shahîn and Lankor there arose a passionate relationship in which there were frequent conflicts of desire. With beings like us this would have produced endless strife. But in them mutual insight and self-detachment seems to have kindled in each the spirit of the other, so that the result was not strife but the mental aggrandizement of both. On the other hand, when the unhappy Washingtonia found herself forsaken by Shahîn, primitive impulses had triumphed in her to such an extent that, as I have reported, she hated her rival. Such an irrational emotion was from the supernormal point of view sheer insanity. The girl herself was terrified at her own derangement. A similar incident occurred when Marianne favoured Kargis rather than Huan Tê. But the Chinese youth apparently cured himself without help. Yet not strictly without help, for all the islanders had formed a habit of recounting their amatory experiences to Jacqueline, far away in France; and she had often played the part of the wise woman, comforting them, helping these complicated and inexperienced young creatures to make effective spiritual contact with one another.

When the young people had enjoyed one another promiscuously for a period of many months, they seem to have passed into a new phase. They gradually sorted out into more or less constant couples. In some cases a couple would actually build for themselves a single cottage, but as a rule they were content to make free of each other's private homes. In spite of these permanent 'marriages' there were many fleeting unions, which did not seem to break up the more serious relationship. Thus at one time or other nearly every lad was mated with nearly every lass. This statement may suggest that the islanders lived in a ceaseless round of promiscuous sexual activity. They did nothing of the sort. The sexual impulse was not violent in them. But though coitus was on the whole a rare event on the island, it was always permitted when both parties desired it. Moreover, though the culminating sexual act was rare, much of the normal social life of the island was flushed, so to speak, with a light-hearted and elegant sexuality.

I believe that there were only one male and one female who had never spent a night in one another's arms, and indeed had never embraced at all. These, suprisingly, and in spite of their long connection and deep mutual intimacy and respect, were John and Lo. Neither of them had a permanent mate. Each had played a part in the light-hearted promiscuity of the colony. Their seeming detachment from one another I attributed at first to sheer sexual indifference. But I was mistaken. When I remarked to John in my blundering way that I was surprised that he never seemed to be in love with Lo, he said simply, 'But I am in love with Lo, always.' I concluded that she was not attracted by him, but John read my thoughts, and said, 'No, it's mutual all right.' 'Then *why*?' I demanded. John said nothing until I had pressed him again. He looked away, like any bashful adolescent. Just as I was about to apologize for prying, he said, 'I just don't know. At least, I half know. Have you noticed that she never lets me so much as touch her? And I'm frightened of touching her. And sometimes she shuts me right out of her mind. That hurts. I'm frightened even of trying to make telepathic contact with her, unless she begins it; in case she doesn't want it. And yet I know her so well. Of course, we are very young, and though we have both had many loves and have learnt a lot, I think we mean so much to one another that we are afraid of spoiling it all by some false step. We are frightened to begin until we have learned much more about the art of living. Probably if we were to live another twenty years – but we shall *not*.' That 'not' sounded with an undercurrent of grief which shocked me. I did not believe John would ever be shaken by purely personal emotion.

I decided to make an opportunity for asking Lo about her relations with John. One day, while I was meditating a tactful approach, she discovered my intention telepathically, and said, 'About me and John – I keep him away because I know, and he knows too, that we are not in a position yet to give our best to one another. Jacqueline advised me to be careful, and she's right. You see, John is amazingly backward in some ways. He's cleverer than most of us, but quite simple about some things. That's why he's – *Odd* John. Though I'm the younger, I feel much older. It would never do to go all the way with him before he's really grown up. These years on the island with him have been very beautiful, in their kind. In another five we might be ready. But of course, since we have to die soon, I shall not wait too long. If the tree is to be destroyed, we must pluck the fruit before it is ripe.'

When I had written and revised the foregoing account of life on the island, I realized that it failed almost completely to convey even so much of the spirit of the little community as I myself had been able to appreciate. But, try as I may, I cannot give concrete embodiment to that strange combination of lightness and earnestness, of madness and superhuman sanity, of sublime common sense and fantastic extravagance, which characterized so much on the island.

I must now give up the attempt, and pass on to describe the sequence of events which led to the destruction of the colony, and the death of all its members.

XXI
The Beginning of the End

When I had been on the island nearly four months a British surveying vessel discovered us. We knew beforehand from telepathic sources that she was likely to come our way, for she had orders to study the oceanic conditions of the South-east Pacific. We knew also that she had a gyroscopic compass. It would be difficult to lead her astray.

This vessel, the *Viking*, strayed about the ocean for some weeks, following the dictates of research. With innumerable zigzags she approached the island. When she came within range of our deflector her officers were perplexed by the discrepancy between the magnetic and gyroscopic compasses, but the ship maintained her true course. On one of her laps she passed within twenty miles of the island, but at night. Would she on the next lap miss us entirely? No! Approaching from the south-west, she sighted us far away on the port bow. The effect was unexpected. Since no island had any business to be in that spot, the officers concluded that the gyro was wrong after all, although their observation of the sun had seemed to confirm it. This island, then, must be one of the Tuamotu Group. The *Viking*, therefore veered away from us. Tsomotre, our chief telepathist, reported that the officers of the *Viking* were feeling very much like people lost in the dark.

A month later the *Viking* sighted us again. This time she changed her course and headed for the island. We saw her approaching, a minute toy vessel, white, with buff funnel. She plunged and swayed, and grew larger. When she was within a few miles of the island, she cruised round it, inspecting. She came a mile or two nearer and described another circle, at half speed, using the lead. She anchored. A motor-launch was lowered. It left the *Viking* and nosed along the coast till it found the entrance to our harbour. In the outer harbour it came to shore and landed an officer and three men. They advanced inland among the brushwood.

We still hoped that they might make a perfunctory examination and then return. Between the inner and the outer harbours, and along the slopes of the outer harbour itself, there was a dense wilderness of scrub, which would give pause to any explorer. The actual channel to the inner harbour had been concealed with a curtain of vegetation hung from a rope which stretched from shore to shore.

The invaders wandered about in the comparatively open space for a while, then turned back to the launch. Presently one of them stooped and picked up something. John, who was in hiding beside me, watching both the bodies and the minds of the four men, exclaimed, 'God! He's found one of your bloody cigarette-ends – a fresh one, too.' In horror I sprang to my feet, crying, 'Then he must find me.' I plunged down the hillside, shouting. The men turned and waited for me. As I approached, naked, dirty and considerably scratched by the scrub, they gaped at me in astonishment. Panting, I poured out an impromptu story. I was the sole survivor of a schooner, wrecked on the island. I had smoked my last cigarette today. At first they believed me. While we made our way toward the launch, they fired questions at me. I played my part tolerably well, but by the time we reached the *Viking*, they were growing suspicious. Though superficially dirty after my stampede, I was quite decently groomed. My hair was short, I was beardless, my nails were cut and clean. Under cross-examination by the Commander of the vessel I became confused; and finally, in despair, I told them the whole truth. Naturally they concluded that I was mad. All the same, the Commander determined to make further investigations on the island. He himself came with the party. I was taken, too, in case I should prove useful.

I now feigned complete idiocy, hoping they might still find nothing. But they discovered the camouflage curtain, and forced the launch through it into the inner harbour. The settlement was now in full view. John and the others had decided that it was useless to hide, and were standing about on the quay, waiting for us. As we came alongside, John advanced to greet us. He was an uncouth but imposing figure, with his dazzling white hair, his eyes of a nocturnal beast, and his lean body. Behind him the others waited, a group of unclad boys and girls with formidable heads. One of the *Viking*'s officers was heard to exclaim, 'Jesus Christ! What a troupe!'

The invaders were fluttered by the sight of naked young women, several of whom were of the white race.

We took the officers to the feeding-house terrace, and gave them light refreshments, including our best Chablis. John explained to them rather fully about the colony; and though, of course, they could not appreciate the more subtle aspect of the great adventure, and were frankly though politely incredulous of the 'new species' idea, they were sympathetic. They appreciated the sporting aspect of the matter. They were also impressed by the fact that I, the only adult and the only normal human figure among these juvenile freaks, was obviously a quite unimportant person on the island.

Presently John took them to see the power-station, which they just wouldn't believe, and the *Skid*, which impressed them more than anything else. To them she was a subtle blend of the crazy and the shipshape. There followed a tour of the other buildings and the estate. I was surprised that John was so anxious to show everything, more surprised that he made no attempt to persuade the Commander not to report on the island and its inhabitants. But John's policy was more subtle. After the tour of inspection he persuaded the Commander to allow all his men to leave the launch and come to the terrace for refreshments. There the party spent another half-hour. John and Lo and Marianne talked to the officers. Other islanders talked to the men. When at last the party made its farewells on the quay, the Commander assured John that he would make a full report on the island, and give high praise to its inhabitants.

As we watched the launch retreating, several of the islanders showed signs of mirth. John explained that throughout the interview the visitors had been subjected to an appropriate psychological treatment, and that by the time they reached the *Viking* their memory of recent events on the island would be so obscure that they would be quite unable to produce a plausible report, or even to give their shipmates an account of their adventure. 'But,' said John, 'this is the beginning of the end. If only we could have treated the whole ship's company thoroughly, all might have been well. As it is, some distorted information is sure to get through and rouse the curiosity of your species.'

For three months the life of the island proceeded undisturbed. But it was a changed life. Knowledge that the end could not be far off produced a fresh intensity of consciousness in all personal relations and social activities. The islanders evidently discovered a new and passionate love of their little society, a kind of poignant and exalted patriotism, such as must have been felt in Greek city-states when the enemy was at the gates. But it was a patriotism curiously free from hate. The impending disaster was regarded less as an attack by human enemies than as a natural catastrophe, like destruction by an avalanche.

The programme of activities on the island was now altered considerably. All work that could not bear fruit within the next few months was abandoned. The islanders told me that they had certain supreme tasks on hand which must if possible be finished before the end. The true purpose of the awakened spirit, they reminded me, is twofold, namely to help in the practical task of world-building, and to employ itself to the best of its capacity in intelligent worship. Under the first head they had at least created something glorious though ephemeral, a microcosm, a world in little. But the more ambitious part of their practical purpose, the founding of the new species, they were destined never to fulfil. Therefore they were concentrating all their strength upon the second aim. They must apprehend existence as precisely and zestfully as they could, and salute That in the universe which was of supreme excellence. This purpose, with the aid of Langatse, they might yet advance to a definite plane of achievement which at present still lay beyond them, though their most mature minds had already glimpsed it. With their unique practical experience and their consciousness of approaching doom they might, they said, within a few months offer to the universal Spirit such a bright and peculiar jewel of worship as even the great Langatse himself, alone and thwarted, could not create.

This most exalting and most exacting of all tasks made it necessary for them to give up all but the necessary daily toil in the fields and in the canoes. Not that very much of their time could be devoted to their spiritual exercises, for there was danger of overstraining their powers. It was necessary therefore to secure plentiful relaxation. Much of the life of the colony during this period seemed to consist of recreation. There was much bathing in the shark-free harbour, much love-making, much dancing and music and poetry, and much aesthetic juggling with colour and form. It was difficult for me to enter into the aesthetic appreciation of the islanders, but from their reactions to their own art in this period I judged that the pervading sense of finality had sharpened their sensibility. Certainly in the sphere of personal relations the knowledge that the group would soon be destroyed produced a passion of sociality. Solitariness lost its charm.

One night Chargut, who was on duty as telepathic lookout, reported that a British light cruiser was under orders to make a search for the mysterious island which had somehow temporarily undermined the sanity of so many of the *Viking*'s crew.

Some weeks later the vessel entered the zone of our deflector, but had little difficulty in keeping her course. She had expected some sort of craziness on the part of the magnetic needle, and trusted only to her gyroscopic compass. After some groping, she reached the island. This time the islanders made no attempt at concealment. From a convenient shoulder of the mountain we watched the grey ship drop anchor and heave slowly in the swell, displaying her red bottom-colour. A launch left her. When it was near enough, we signalled it round to the harbour entrance. John received the visitors on the quay. The lieutenant (in white duck and stiff collar) was inclined to stand on his dignity as the representative of the British Navy. The presence of naked white girls obviously increased his hauteur by upsetting his equilibrium. But refreshments on the terrace, combined with secret psychological treatment, soon produced a more friendly atmosphere. Once more I was impressed by John's wisdom in keeping a store of good wine and cigars.

I have not space to give details of this second encounter with *Homo sapiens*. There was unfortunately much coming and going between the cruiser and the shore, and it was impossible to administer a thorough hypnotic inoculation to every man who saw the settlement. A good deal was achieved, however, and the visit of the Commander himself, a grizzled and a kindly gentleman of the sea, was particularly satisfactory. John soon discovered telepathically that he was a man of imagination and courage, and that he regarded his calling with unusual detachment. Therefore, seeing that a number of the naval men had escaped with only slight psychological treatment, it seemed best not to administer 'oblivi-faction' to the Commander, but instead to attempt the more difficult enterprise of rousing in him an overmastering interest in the colony, and loyalty to its purpose. The Commander was one of those exceptional seamen who spent a good deal of their time in reading. His mind had a background of ideas which rendered him susceptible to the technique. His was not, indeed, a brilliant intellect, but he had dabbled in popular science and popular philosophy, and his sense of values was intuitively discriminate, though uncultivated.

The cruiser remained for some days off the island, and during this time the Commander spent much of his time ashore. His first official act was to annex the island to the British Empire. I was reminded of the way in which robins and other birds annex gardens and orchards, regardless of human purposes. But alas in this case the robin represented a Great Power – the power, indeed, of the jungle over this minute garden of true humanity.

Though the Commander alone was to be allowed clear memory of his experiences on the island, all the visitors were treated in such a way as to help them to appreciate the colony as well as it was in them to do. Some were of course impervious, but many were affected to some extent. All were forced to use every ounce of their imagination to envisage the colony at least as a gay and romantic experiment. In most cases, doubtless, the notion that they conceived of it was extremely crude and false; but in one or two, besides the Commander, all sorts of rudimentary and inhibited spiritual capacities were roused into unfamiliar and disturbing activity.

When at last the time came for the visitors to leave the island, I noticed that their demeanour was different from what it had been on their arrival. There was less formality, less of a gulf between officers and men, less strict discipline. I noticed, too, that some who had formerly looked at the young women with disapproval or lust or both, now bade them farewell with friendly courtesy, and with some appreciation of their uncouth beauty. I noticed also on the faces of the more sensitive a look of anxiety, as though they did not feel altogether 'at home' in their own minds. The Commander himself was pale. As he shook hands with John, he muttered, 'I'll do my best, but I'm not hopeful.'

The cruiser departed. Events on board her were followed by our telepathists with intense interest. Tsomotre and Chargut and Lankor reported that amnesia for all events on the island was rapidly spreading; that some of those who still had clear recollection were so tortured by their spiritual upheaval, and the contrast between the island and the ship, that they were losing all sense of discipline and patriotism; that two had committed suicide; that a vague panic was spreading, a sense that madness was afoot among them; that, apart from the Commander, none who had been in close contact with the islanders could now recall more than the most confused and incredible memories of the island; that those who escaped severe psychological treatment were also very confused, but that they remembered enough to make them a source of grave danger; that the Commander had addressed the whole ship's company, ordering them, imploring them, to keep strict silence ashore on the subject of their recent experiences. He himself must of course report to the Admiralty, but the crew must regard the whole matter as an official secret. To spread incredible stories would only cause trouble, and get the ship into disgrace. Privately, of course, he intended to make a perfectly colourless and harmless report.

Some weeks later the telepathists announced that fantastic stories of the island were current in the Navy; that a reference had been made in a foreign paper to 'an immoral and communistic colony of children on a British island in the Pacific'; that foreign secret services were nosing out the truth, in case it should prove diplomatically useful; that the British Admiralty was holding a secret inquiry; that the Commander of the cruiser had been dismissed from the Service for making a false report; that the Soviet Government had collected a good deal of information about the island, and intended to embarrass Britain by organizing a secret expedition to make contact with the colony; that the British Government had learnt of this intention, and was determined to evacuate the island at once. We were told also that the world at large knew practically nothing of the matter. The British Press had been warned against making any reference to it. The Foreign Press had not given serious attention to the vague rumour which one paper had published.

The visit of the second cruiser ended much as the previous incident, but at one stage it entailed desperate measures. The second Commander had perhaps been chosen for his uncompromising character. He was in fact a bit of a bully. Moreover, his instructions were emphatic, and he had no thought but to carry them out promptly. He sent a launch to give the islanders five hours to pack up and come aboard. The lieutenant returned 'in a state of nerves' and reported that the instructions were not being carried out. The Commander himself came ashore with a party of armed men. He was determined to stand no nonsense. Refusing offers of hospitality, he announced that all the islanders must come aboard at once.

John asked for an explanation, trying to lead the man into normal conversation. He also pointed out that most of the islanders were not British subjects, and that the colony was doing no harm to anyone. It was no use. The Commander was something of a sadist, and the sight of unclad female flesh had put him in a mood of ruthlessness. He merely ordered the arrest of every member of the colony.

John intervened in a changed and solemn voice. 'We will not leave the island alive. Anyone that you seize will drop down dead.'

The Commander laughed. Two tars approached Chargut, who happened to be the nearest. The Tibetan looked around at John, and, at the first touch of the sailors' hands, he dropped. The sailors examined him. There was no sign of life.

The Commander was flustered; but, pulling himself together, he repeated his order. John said, 'Be careful! Don't you see yet that you're up against something you can't understand? Not one of us will be taken alive.' The sailors hesitated. The Commander snapped out, 'Obey orders. Better begin on a girl, for safety.' They approached Sigrid, who turned with her bright smile to John, and extended a hand behind her to feel for Kargis, her mate. One of the sailors laid a gentle and hesitating paw on her shoulder. She collapsed backwards into the arms of Kargis, dead.

The Commander was now thoroughly upset, and the sailors were showing signs of insubordination. He tried to reason with John, assuring him that the islanders would be well treated on the ship; but John merely shook his head. Kargis was sitting on the ground with the dead Sigrid in his arms. His own face looked dead. After a moment's contemplation of Kargis the Commander said, 'I shall consult with the Admiralty about you. Meanwhile you may stay here.' He and his men returned to their boat. The cruiser departed.

On the island the two bodies were laid upon the great rock by the harbour. For some time we all stood round in silence, while the seagulls cried. One of the Indian girls, who had been attached to Chargut, fainted. But Kargis showed now no sign of grief. The desolate expression that had come over his face when Sigrid fell dead in his arms had soon cleared. The super-normal mind would never for long succumb to emotion that must perforce be barren. For a few moments he stood gazing on the face of Sigrid. Suddenly he laughed. It was a John-like laugh. Then Kargis stooped and kissed the cold lips of his mate, gently but with a smile. He stepped aside. Once more John availed himself of the psycho-physical technique. There was a fierce blaze. The bodies were consumed.

Some days later I ventured to ask John why he had sacrificed these two lives, and indeed why the islanders could not come to terms with Britain. No doubt the colony would have to be disbanded, but its members would be allowed to return to their respective countries, and each of them might expect a long life of intense experience and action. John shook his head and replied, 'I cannot explain. I can only say that we are one together now, and there is no life for us apart. Even if we were to do as you suggest and go back into the world of your species, we should be watched, controlled, persecuted. The things that we live for beckon us to die. But we are not ready yet. We must stave off the end for a while so that we may finish our work.'

Shortly after the departure of the second cruiser an incident occurred which gave me fresh understanding of the mentality of the islanders. Ng-Gunko had for some time been absorbed in private researches. With the self-importance and mysteriousness of a child he announced that he would rather not explain until he had finished his experiments. Then one day, grinning with pride and excitement, he summoned the whole company to the laboratory and gave a full account of his work. His speech was telepathic; so also were the subsequent discussions. My report is based on information given me by John, and also by Shên Kuo and others.

Ng-Gunko had invented a weapon which, he said, would make it impossible for *Homo sapiens* ever again to interfere with the island. It would project a destructive ray, derived from atomic disintegration, with such effect that a battleship could be annihilated at forty miles' distance, or an aeroplane at any height within the same radius. A projector placed on the higher of the two mountain-tops could sweep the whole horizon. The designs were complete in every detail, but their execution would involve huge co-operative work, and certain castings and wrought-steel parts would have to be ordered secretly in America or Japan. Smaller weapons, however, could be laboriously made at once on the island, and fitted to the *Skid* and the plane to equip them for dealing with any attack that might be expected within the next few months.

Careful scrutiny proved that the invention was capable of doing all that was claimed for it. The discussion passed on to the detailed problems of constructing the weapon. But at this point, apparently, Shên Kuo interposed, and urged that the project should be abandoned. He pointed out that it would absorb the whole energy of the colony, and that the great spiritual task would have to be shelved, at any rate for a very long time. 'Any resistance on our part,' he said, 'would bring the whole force of the inferior species against us, and there would be no peace till we had conquered the world. That would take a long time. We are young, and we should have to spend the most critical years of our lives in warfare. When we had finished the great slaughter, should we be any longer fit mentally for our real work, for the founding of a finer species, and for worship? No! We should be ruined, hopelessly distorted in spirit. Violent practical undertakings would have blotted out for ever such insight as we have now gained into the true purpose of life. Perhaps if we were all thirty years older we should be sufficiently mature to pass through a decade of warfare without becoming too impoverished, spiritually, for our real work. But as things are, surely the wise course is to forego the weapon, and make up our minds to fulfil as much as possible of our accepted spiritual task of worship before we are destroyed.'

I could tell by merely watching the faces of the islanders that they were now in the throes of a conflict of wills such as they had never before experienced. The issue was not merely one of life and death; it was one of fundamental principle. When Shên Kuo had done, there was a clamour of protest and argument, much of which was actually vocal; for the islanders were deeply moved. It was soon agreed that the decision should be postponed for a day. Meanwhile there must be a solemn meeting in the meeting-room, and all hearts must be deeply searched in a most earnest effort to reach mental accord and the right decision. The meeting was silent. It lasted for many hours. When it was over I learned that all, including Ng-Gunko and John himself, had accepted with conviction and with gladness the views of Shên Kuo.

The weeks passed. Telepathic observation informed us that, when the second cruiser had left us, considerable amnesia and other mental derangements had occurred among those of the crew who had landed on the island. The Commander's report was incoherent and incredible. Like the first Commander, he was disgraced. The Foreign Offices of the world, through their secret services, ferreted out as much as possible of this latest incident. They did not form anything like an accurate idea of events, but they procured shreds of truth embroidered with fantastic exaggeration. There was a general feeling that something more was at stake than a diplomatic coup, and the discomfiture of the British Government. Something weird, something quite beyond reckoning was going on on that remote island. Three ships had been sent away with their crews in mental confusion. The islanders, besides being physically eccentric and morally per-verse, seemed to have powers which in an earlier age would have been called diabolic. In a vague subconscious way *Homo sapiens* began to realize that his supremacy was challenged.

The Commander of the second cruiser had informed his Government that the islanders were of many nationalities. The Government, feeling itself to be in an extremely delicate position in which a false step might expose it as guilty of murdering children, yet feeling that the situation must be dealt with firmly and speedily before the Communists could make capital out of it, decided to ask other Powers to co-operate and share responsibility.

Meanwhile the Soviet vessel had left Vladivostok and was already in the South Seas. Late one afternoon we sighted her, a small trading-vessel of unobtrusive appearance. She dropped anchor and displayed the Red Flag, with its golden device.

The Captain, a grey-haired man in a peasant blouse, who seemed to me to be still inwardly watching the agony of the Civil War, brought us a flattering message from Moscow. We were invited to migrate to Russian territory, where, we were assured, we should be left free to manage our colony as we wished. We should be immune from persecution by the Capitalist Powers on account of our Communism and our sexual customs. While he was delivering himself of this speech, slowly, but in excellent English, a woman who was apparently one of his officers was making friendly advances to Sambo, who had crawled towards her to examine her boots. She smiled, and whispered a few endearments. When the Captain had finished, Sambo looked up at the woman and remarked. 'Comrade, you have the wrong approach.' The Russians were taken aback, for Sambo was still in appearance an infant. 'Yes,' said John, laughing, 'Comrades, you have the wrong approach. Like you, we are Communists, but we are other things also. For you, Communism is the goal, but for us it is the beginning. For you the group is sacred, but for us it is only the pattern made up of individuals. Though we are Communists, we have reached beyond Communism to a new individualism. Our Communism is individualistic. In many ways we admire the achievements of the New Russia; but if we were to accept this offer we should very soon come into conflict with your Government. From our point of view it is better for our colony to be destroyed than to be enslaved by any alien Power.' At this point he began to speak in Russian, with great rapidity, sometimes turning to one or other of his companions for confirmation of his assertions. Once more the visitors were taken aback. They interjected remarks, they began arguing with each other. The discussion seemed to become heated.

Presently the whole company moved to the feeding terrace, where the visitors were given refreshments, and their psychological treatment was continued. As I cannot understand Russian I do not know what was said to them; but from their expressions I judged that they were greatly excited, and that, while some were roused to bewildered enthusiasm, others kept their heads so far as to recognize in these strange beings a real danger to their species and more particularly to the Revolution.

When the Russians departed, they were all thoroughly confused in mind. Subsequently, we learned from our telepathists that the Captain's report to his Government had been so brief, so self-contradictory and incredible, that be was relieved of his command on the score of insanity.

News that the Russian expedition had occurred, and that it had left the islanders in possession, confirmed the worst fears of the Powers. Obviously, the island was an outpost of Communism. Probably it was now a highly fortified base for naval and aerial attack upon Australia and New Zealand. The British Foreign Office redoubled its efforts to persuade the Pacific Powers to take prompt action together.

Meanwhile the incoherent stories of the crew of the Russian vessel had caused a flutter in the Kremlin. It had been intended that when the islanders had been transported to Russian territory the story of their persecution by Britain should be published in the Soviet Press. But such was the mystery of the whole matter that the authorities were at a loss, and decided to prevent all reference to the island.

At this point they received a diplomatic note protesting against their interference in an affair which concerned Britain alone. The party in the Soviet Government which was anxious to prove to the world that Russia was a respectable Power now gained the upper hand. The Russian reply to Britain was a request for permission to take part in the proposed international expedition. With grim satisfaction Britain granted the request.

Telepathically the islanders watched the little fleet converging on it from Asia and America. Near Pitcairn Island the vessels assembled. A few days later we saw a tuft of smoke on the horizon, then another, and others. Six vessels came into view, all heading toward us. They displayed the ensigns of Britain, France, the United States, Holland, Japan, and Russia; in fact, 'the Pacific Powers'. When the vessels had come to anchor, each dispatched a motor-launch, bearing its national flag in the stern.

The fleet of launches crowded into the harbour. John received the visitors on the quay. *Homo superior* faced the little mob of *Homo sapiens*, and it was immediately evident that *Homo superior* was indeed the better man. It had been intended to effect a prompt arrest of all the islanders, but an odd little hitch occurred. The Englishman, who was to be spokesman, appeared to have forgotten his part. He stammered a few incoherent words, then turned for help to his neighbour the Frenchman. There followed an anxious whispered discussion, the rest of the party crowding round the central couple. The islanders watched in silence. Presently the Englishman came to the fore again, and began to speak, rather breathlessly. 'In the name of the Government of the Pacif—' He stopped, frowning distractedly and staring at John. The Frenchman stepped forward, but John now intervened. 'Gentlemen,' be said, pointing, 'let us move over to the shady end of that terrace. Some of you have evidently been affected by the sun.' He turned and strode away, the little flock following him obediently.

On the terrace, wine and cigars appeared. The Frenchman was about to accept, when the Japanese cried, 'Do not take. It is perhaps drugged.' The Frenchman paused, withdrew his hand and smiled deprecatingly at Marianne, who was offering the refreshments. She set the tray on the table.

The Englishman now found his tongue, and blurted out in a most unofficial manner, 'We've come to arrest you all. You'll be treated decently, of course. Better start packing at once.'

John regarded him in silence for a moment, then said affably, 'But please tell us, what is our offence, and your authority?'

Once more the unfortunate man found that the power of coherent speech had left him. He stammered something about

'The Pacific Powers' and 'boys and girls on the loose', then turned plaintively to his colleagues for help. Babel ensued, for every one attempted to explain, and no one could express himself. John waited. Presently he began speaking. 'While you find your speech,' he said, 'I will tell you about our colony.' He went on to give an account of the whole venture. I noticed that he said almost nothing about the biological uniqueness of the islanders. He affirmed only that they were sensitive and freakish creatures who wanted to live their own life. Then he drew a contrast between the tragic state of the world and the idyllic life of the islanders. It was a consummate piece of pleading, but I knew that it was really of much less importance than the telepathic influence to which the visitors were all the while being subjected. Some of them were obviously deeply moved. They had been raised to an unaccustomed clarity and poignancy of experience. All sorts of latent and long-inhibited impulses came to life in them. They looked at John and his companions with new eyes, and at one another also.

When John had finished, the Frenchman poured himself out some wine. Begging the others to fill their glasses and drink to the colony, he made a short but eloquent speech, declaring that he recognized in the spirit of these young people something truly noble, something, indeed, almost French. If his Government had known the facts, it would not have participated in this attempt to suppress the little society. He submitted to his colleagues that the right course was for them all to leave the island and communicate with their Governments.

The wine was circulated and accepted by all, save one. Throughout John's speech the Japanese representative had remained unmoved. Probably he had not understood well enough to feel the full force of John's eloquence. Possibly, also, his Asiatic mind was not to be mastered telepathically by the same technique as that which applied to his colleagues. But the main source of his successful resistance, so John told me later, was almost certainly the influence of the terrible Hebridean infant, who, ever desiring to destroy John, had contrived to be telepathically present at this scene. I had seen John watching the Jap with an expression in which were blended amusement, anxiety and admiration. This dapper but rather formidable little man now rose to his feet, and said, 'Gentlemen, you have been tricked. This lad and his companions have strange powers which Europe does not understand. But we understand. I have felt them. I have fought against them. I have not been tricked. I can see that these are not boys and girls; they are devils. If they are left, some day they will destroy us. The world will be for them, not for us. Gentlemen, we must obey our orders. In the name of the Pacific Powers I – I—' Confusion seized him.

John intervened and said, almost threateningly, 'Remember, any one of us that you try to arrest, dies.'

The Japanese, whose face was now a ghastly colour, completed his sentence, 'I arrest you all.' He shouted a command in Japanese. A party of armed Japanese sailors stepped on to the terrace. The lieutenant in command of them approached John, who faced him with a stare of contempt and amusement. The man came to a stand a few yards from him. Nothing happened.

The Japanese Commander himself stepped forward to effect the arrest. Shahîn barred his way, saying, 'You shall take me first.' The Jap seized him. Shahîn collapsed. The Jap looked down at him with horror, then stepped over him and moved toward John. But the other officers intervened. All began talking at once. After a while it was agreed that the islanders should be left in peace until the representatives of *Homo sapiens* had communicated with their Governments.

Our visitors left us. Next morning the Russian ship weighed anchor and sailed. One by one the others followed suit.

XXII
The End

John was under no illusion that the colony had been saved; but if we could gain another three months' respite, he said, the immediate task which the islanders had undertaken would be finished. A minor part of this work consisted in completing certain scientific records, which were to be entrusted to me for the benefit of the normal species. There was also an amazing document, written by John himself, and purporting to give an account of the whole story of the Cosmos. Whether it should be taken as a plain statement of fact or a poetic fantasy I do not know. These various documents were now being typed, filed and packed in wooden cases; for the time had come for my departure. 'If you stay much longer,' John said, 'you will die along with the rest of us, and our records will be lost. To us it matters not at all whether they are saved or not, but they may prove of interest to the more enlightened members of your own species. You had better not attempt to publish them till a good many years have passed, and the Governments have ceased to feel sore about us. Meanwhile, if you like, you can perpetuate the biography – as fiction, of course, since no one would believe it.'

One day Tsomotre reported that a party of toughs was being secretly equipped for our destruction by agents of certain governments which I will not name.

The wooden chests were loaded on to the *Skid* along with my baggage. The whole colony assembled on the quay to bid me farewell. I shook hands with them all in turn; and Lo, to my surprise, kissed me. 'We do love you, Fido,' she said. 'If they were all like you, domestic, there'd have been no trouble. Remember, when you write about us, that we loved you.' Sambo, when his turn came, clambered from Ng-Gunko's arms to mine, then hurriedly back again. 'I'd go with you if I wasn't so tied up with these snobs that I couldn't live without them.'

John's parting words were these. 'Yes, say in the biography that I loved you very much.' I could not reply.

Kemi and Marianne, who were in charge of the *Skid*, were already hauling in the mooring lines. We crept out of the little harbour and gathered speed as we passed between the outer headlands. The double pyramid of the island shrank, faded, and was soon a mere cloud on the horizon.

I was taken to one of the least important of the French islands, one on which there were no Europeans. By night we unloaded the baggage in the dinghy and set it on a lonely beach. Then we made our farewells, and very soon the *Skid* with her crew vanished into the darkness. When morning came I went in search of natives and arranged for the transport of my goods and myself to civilization. Civilization? No, that I had left behind for ever.

Of the end of the colony I know very little. For some weeks I hung about in the South Seas trying to pick up information. At last I came upon one of the hooligans who had taken part in the final scene. He was very reluctant to speak, not only because he knew that to blab was to risk death, but also because the whole affair had evidently got on his nerves. Bribery and alcohol, however, loosened his tongue.

The assassins had been warned to take no risks. The enemy, though in appearance juvenile, was said to be diabolically cunning and treacherous. Machineguns might be useful, and it would be advisable not to parley.

A large and well-armed party of the invaders landed outside the harbour, and advanced upon the settlement. The islanders must have known telepathically that these ruffians were too base to be dealt with by the technique which had been used on former invaders. Probably it would have been easy to destroy them by atomic disintegration as soon as they landed; though I remember being told that it was much more difficult to disintegrate the atoms of living bodies than of corpses. Apparently no attempt was made to put this method in action. Instead, John seems to have devised a new and subtler method of defence; for according to my informant the landing-party very soon 'began to feel there were devils in the place'. They were apparently seized with a nameless horror. Their flesh began to creep, their limbs to tremble. This was all the more terrifying because it was broad daylight, and the sun was beating heavily down on them. No doubt the supernormals were making their presence felt telepathically in some grim and formidable manner unintelligible to us. As the invaders advanced hesitatingly through the brushwood, this terrifying sense of some overmastering presence became more and more intense. In addition they began to experience a crazy fear of one another. Every man cast sidelong glances of fright and hate at his neighbour. Suddenly they all fell upon one another, using knives, firearms, teeth and fingers. The brawl lasted only a few minutes, but several were killed, many wounded. The survivors took to their heels, and to the boats.

For two days the ship lay off the island, while her crew debated violently among themselves. Some were for abandoning the venture; but others pointed out that to return empty-handed was to go to certain destruction; for the great ones who had sent them had made it clear that, though success would be generously rewarded, failure would be punished ruthlessly. There was nothing for it but to try again. Another landing-party was organized, and fortified with large quantities of rum. The result was much the same as on the former occasion; but it was noticed that those who were most drunk were least affected by the sinister influence.

The assassins took three more days to screw up their courage for another landing. The bodies of their dead comrades were visible upon the hill-side. How many of the living were destined to join that ghastly company? The party made itself so drunk that it could hardly row the boats. It braced itself with uproarious song. Also it carried the brave liquor with it in a keg. After the landing the gruesome influence was again felt, but this time the invaders answered it with reinforcements of rum and revelry. Reeling, clinging together, dropping their weapons, tripping over roots and one another's feet, but defiantly singing, they advanced over the spur of hill, and saw the harbour and the settlement beneath them. They floundered down the slope. One of them accidentally discharged a pistol into his own thigh. He collapsed, yelling, but the others rushed on.

They stumbled into the presence of the supernormals, who were gathering near the power-station. There the reeling assailants sheepishly came to a stand. By now the effects of the rum were somewhat abated; and the sight of those strange beings, motionless, with their great calm eyes, seems to have dismayed the assassins. Suddenly they fled.

For some days they wrangled among themselves, and kept to their ship. They dared not land again; they dared not sail.

One afternoon, however, they were amazed to see a prodigious and dazzling spread of flame rise from behind the hill, and light up land and sea. There followed a muffled roar which echoed from the clouds like thunder. The blaze died down, but it was followed by an even more alarming phenomenon. The whole island began to sink. Waves appeared to be clambering up the hills. Presently the ship's anchor released itself from the sinking bottom, and she was cast adrift. The island continued to descend, and the sea swept in upon it, bearing the gyrating vessel over the tops of the sunken trees. The twin peaks were submerged. Converging currents met above their heads and reared a great spout of ocean. This liquid horn, descending, drove hills of water outwards in all directions. The ship was overwhelmed. Her top-hamper, boats, and most of her deck-houses were torn away. Half the crew were lost overboard.

This cataclysm apparently occurred on the 15th December 1933. It may, of course, have been an effect of purely physical causes. Even when I first heard of it, however, I was inclined to think that it was not. I suspected that the islanders had been holding their assailants at bay in order to gain a few days for the completion of their high spiritual task, or in order to bring it at least to a point beyond which there was no hope of further advancement. I liked to believe that during the few days after the repulse of the third landing-party they accomplished this aim. They then decided, I thought, not to await the destruction which was bound sooner or later to overtake them at the hands of the less human species, either through these brutish instruments or through the official forces of the Great Powers. The super-normals might have chosen to end their career by simply falling dead, but seemingly they desired to destroy their handiwork along with themselves. They would not allow their home, and all the objects of beauty with which they had adorned it, to fall into subhuman clutches. Therefore they deliberately blew up their power-station, thereby destroying not only themselves but their whole settlement. I surmised further that this mighty convulsion must have spread downwards into the precarious foundations of the island, disturbing, them so violently that the whole island collapsed.

As soon as I had gleaned as much information as possible, I hurried home with my documentary treasures, wondering how I should give the news to Pax. It did not seem to me likely that she would have learnt it already from John. When I landed in England, she and Doc met me. Her face showed me that she was prepared. At once she said, 'You need not break the news gently, because we know the main part of it. John gave me visions of it. I saw those tipsy brutes routed by his power. And in a few days afterwards I saw many happy things on the island. I saw John and Lo, walking together on the shore, like lovers at last. One day I saw all the young people sitting in a panelled room, evidently their meeting-room. I heard John say that it was time to die. They all rose and went away, in couples and little groups; and presently they gathered round the door of a stone building that must have been their power-station. Ng-Gunko went through the door, carrying Sambo. Suddenly there was blinding light and noise and pain, then nothing.'

Olaf Stapledon was born in 1886 near Liverpool. After going to Balliol College, Oxford, he started work in the family shipping office in Port Said. This experience, along with his time spent during the First World War as a member of the Friends' Ambulance Unit, was to influence his ideas on 'true community' and pacifism. In 1914 he had a small book of verse published called *Latter Day Psalms*. In 1925 he took a doctorate in Philosophy at Liverpool University and in 1929 his first non-fiction work, *A Modern Theory of Ethics*, was published. This was followed in 1930 by his first novel, *Last and First Men*, which was a critical success, praised by such contemporaries as Arnold Bennett and J. B. Priestley. He had never heard of 'science fiction' and was quite surprised to find that both *Last and First Men* and *Star Maker* (1937) were held in such regard by SF writers and fans. He continued to write and lecture until his death in 1950.

SF MASTERWORKS

* no longer available

* no longer available